HUSHED

Gina Robinson

Gina Robinson
SEATTLE, WASHINGTON

Book Layout ©2014 BookDesignTemplates.com
Photography: Kelsey Keeton of K Keeton Designs
Models: Anna Marie and Eric Madden

Hushed/ Gina Robinson. — 1st ed.
ISBN 978-0692372289

For Jeff

Also by
GINA ROBINSON
NEW ADULT ROMANCE
RUSHED
CRUSHED
RECKLESS LONGING
RECKLESS SECRETS
RECKLESS TOGETHER

THE AGENT EX SERIES
"Full of laughter, intrigue, and, of course, steamy
spies." —*RT Book Reviews*

LICENSE TO LOVE
THE SPY WHO LEFT ME
DIAMONDS ARE TRULY FOREVER
LIVE AND LET LOVE
LOVE ANOTHER DAY

HISTORICAL ROMANCE
THE LAST HONEST SEAMSTRESS
THE UNION
THE ESCORT

WOMEN'S FICTION
PINK SLIPPER

CONTEMPORARY ROMANCE
ECHO BAY CHRISTMAS

May 18, 1980

Laura

I was determined to get a golden glow to set off my white halter dress. And make it impossible for Rick to keep his eyes, and hands, off me when he got back tonight.

Sandy was lying next to me on the sun porch on her stomach. With her hair pulled up and the strings to her bikini top untied and sprawled out beside her to avoid tan lines.

"Squirt my back, will you?" Sandy turned her head to face me. "What are you and Rick doing tonight? *If* he makes it back."

I frowned at her. It was none of her business what
we had planned. This might be *the* night. "Shut up.
He'll make it back."

I hoped. I was still a little peeved with him for going
home to Seattle for the weekend when summer vaca-
tion was looming dangerously close. Just another couple weeks until dead week and finals. Our relationship
was barely older than that. Too new. Summer and sep-
aration had been known to kill *much* more established
couples. I wouldn't lose Rick. I *wouldn't.* I was going to
give him what he wanted. What I wanted, too.

But now, after months of geologists' empty promises, that stupid volcano had *finally* erupted. The news
was full of dire predictions and stories of death on
Mount St. Helens. Some old guy named Harry Truman
had refused to leave and was presumed dead. Which
was sad, of course. But right now I was worried about
Rick driving back and the reports of roads closing between here and Seattle.

As I sprayed Sandy's back, the portable radio next
to me crackled. I reached over to adjust the dial on the
university-run station. Mostly it was DJ-free and
played a tape of music in an endless loop. After a while
I felt almost psychic as I began humming the next song
in the rotation without thinking. "Dream Police" was
on the tip of my brain as an announcer broke in with
another volcano update.

"We interrupt this broadcast for a special report.
The ash cloud that has been blowing east on the jet
stream and heading toward the university since the
eruption of Mount St. Helens this morning has arrived!

"University staff and geologists have gotten the first glimpse of the ash cloud from the top of the physics building. Because health risks from breathing ash are unknown, students are advised to head inside and close all windows—"

I snapped the dial and turned the radio off.

Sandy shook her head, pretending to be bored with it all. But she was worried. Her body language gave her away.

A girl leaned out her dorm window above us and yelled down to those of us on the sun porch, "We can see the cloud from up here!"

A couple of girls next to us jumped up and headed inside.

Sandy sighed and reached behind to tie her top on. "How many times will a volcano erupt in our lifetime?"

I pulled on my bright yellow terry cloth jumper over my bikini, stood, and slid on my platform flip-flops. Sandy got to her feet.

On the top floor, half a dozen girls had gathered at the end of the hall by the only west-facing window. They silently stepped aside for us. I didn't understand their mood until I went to the window and saw for myself.

My heart stopped. The sky looked bruised, as if it had taken a beating at the hands of nature. Purple, green, and black, a cloud of sorts, though I'd never seen anything like it, rolled over the hills, taking all light with it. Blocking out the sun with complete darkness as it descended on the town and university like hell itself had come calling.

"Rick," I whispered, suddenly understanding the panic spreading across the state. No one could see to drive in that blackness.

"Oh my God!" someone whispered. It was more a prayer than anything else. A plea to the Almighty to do something. *Anything.*

"So that's an ash cloud," the girl behind me said, as if she was finally getting it. We were all getting it.

More girls gathered behind me in an awed hush. The edges of the cloud moved toward us like an angry thunderstorm. But unlike an approaching storm, there was no smell of rain in the air. No wind blowing it in. No bursts of lightning. No claps of thunder. The air didn't cool like before a storm. Or when evening fell.

The cloud was not only in the sky, but on the ground. Denser than any fog. Powerful enough to laugh at the inability of the sun to penetrate it. Quiet. Calm. Frightening.

As the first gray flecks of ash began to fall, I grabbed Sandy's arm. "Come on! Let's get our stuff."

By the time we reached the sun porch, the birds were roosting, even though it was only three in the afternoon and the days were long in May. Twilight had already fallen, and with it, bits of ash. The lighting was eerie. Scary. It was like all sense of well-being in the world had disappeared.

Sandy held her hand out to catch some of the falling ash. "It's so weird. It looks like snow. I almost expect it to be cold, but it feels gritty, like sand."

"It is." I coughed on the thick air. "It's pulverized mountain."

The few diehards who'd stayed on the sun porch were grabbing their stuff and scrambling to get inside. My towel was already covered in a fine coating of light gray dust. I grabbed it and shook it out. Someone's radio was blaring the number of people missing and presumed dead in the eruption. Shaking, and trying to hide it, I picked up my radio and my tanning lotion and headed back into the dorm.

By the time I reached my room on the second floor, it was almost completely dark outside. I wanted to call the Tau Psi house and see if Rick had made it back. I needed to hear his voice. Hear him laugh and tell me I worried too much.

But the line in the hall outside the two phone carrels on my floor ran the length of the hall with girls waiting to call home. Some girls were crying. Others prayed.

I fought the urge to push them out of the way. *Rick, where are you?*

Becky, from 210, came out of one of the carrels and shook her head. "It's no good. The phone lines are overloaded. All circuits are busy. You can't get through. All you get is a fast busy."

I swallowed hard and flipped on my portable radio. We sat in the hall and listened in silence. *Get inside. Stay off the phones. Leave them open for emergency situations.*

Everything was stalled, including the news crews. No one knew anything new.

"Is the ash poisonous? Will we die, like the people in Pompeii?" one of the girls who was a notorious worrier asked.

"Shut up!" Sandy's eyes snapped. "We're still here. Still breathing. No one on the news said anything about dying."

I switched stations, looking for music, something cheery. Nothing but news was on. Even that stupid taped music on the university station had been replaced with constant volcano updates and repeated warnings to stay inside.

Two girls came up from the living room downstairs, where they'd been watching TV. They paused and listened to the radio. "They're saying the same thing on TV. It's all over the national news."

Our resident assistant Carla came through. "Close the windows! Make sure all the windows are closed! Every one. Don't run the bathroom fans! They bring in the outside air." She ducked into a bathroom to check on it.

The dorm wasn't air-conditioned. All closed up, it quickly grew hot and stuffy and tense inside.

I cracked. I couldn't take it anymore. "This is ridiculous." I sounded braver than I felt. "I'm not sitting around waiting for the worst to happen. Let's put some music on. Any requests?"

As I stood to go to my room to put a record on, the fire door at the end of the hall opened. Rick Butler strode through the door as casually as if it were an ordinary Sunday afternoon.

My heart stopped. My legs went weak.

Rick was Rick, heart-poundingly gorgeous. A total fox. Looking perfectly normal and relaxed. The same as usual, except for the white dust covering the hems of his faded, ass-hugging jeans. *Ash.* A battered Tau Psi spring fling T-shirt skimmed his broad shoulders and showed off his perfectly formed biceps. His hair and those toned shoulders were covered in a film of light gray ash.

He had never looked so good. *No one* had ever looked so good. A ripple of giggles, whispers, and awe erupted among my dorm mates in the hall. I almost collapsed with relief at the sight of him.

When he spotted me, his face lit up, emphasizing the dimple in one cheek. Having only one dimple should have made his face lopsided. Instead it added character and made him all the more attractive.

My heart fluttered wildly. Standing there, staring at me as if we were the only two in the hall, he was as sexy and confident as a rescuing white knight. God knew I needed a hero just then, someone reckless and unafraid of anything. How was it that he was always coming to my rescue?

Damn him. He had a way of stealing my breath just by being. His dark blue eyes danced with excitement, like being in the middle of a volcanic eruption was an epic adventure.

"You're back!" I ran to him and threw myself into his arms. "You're safe." I lifted my face to his. "You scared me. I was worried you'd be stranded in the ash. The news says it's clogging air filters and stalling cars all across the state."

"You shouldn't have worried. In my Camaro, I can outrun Satan." He grinned, but his eyes were apologetic as he stroked my cheek. "That damn cloud must have been going at least seventy. I had the pedal to the metal the whole way back. I beat the storm to town by minutes."

He tucked a lock of hair behind my ear. "I've been trying to call. The trunk lines have been busy since I arrived." He tipped my chin up and pressed his lips to mine.

I opened my mouth to him, like I'd opened my heart. So glad, so completely happy he wasn't stranded somewhere in the ash. Reassured. With Rick beside me, I was unafraid. The taste of beer on his tongue was as intoxicating as the heat of his body next to mine.

Rick is back! My heart danced at the thought.

I wanted to kiss and kiss and kiss him. To cuddle into his arms and never let go. To hell with the ash. The world could completely crumble and it didn't matter now. Rick was back!

Eventually, I pulled away and pressed my head against Rick's chest, listening to the strong, steady beat of his heart.

"How long have you been back?" I let suspicion fill my voice. "Long enough to pound one down? You taste like beer."

He laughed, not looking even a tiny bit sorry or ashamed. "There's a party going on at the frat."

"Then what are you doing here?" I lifted my head and stared at him wide-eyed with admiration as I clucked my tongue. "It's not like you to miss a good party. And no one is supposed to go outside. You broke university rules."

He laughed. "Yeah? So what else is new." He leaned in and whispered, "I came to get you. You promised to come to the frat tonight and hang out. I'm not letting you back out because of a little thing like a volcanic eruption and stupid university scare tactics. Not when I drove like hell to get back to you."

My heart skipped a beat. I couldn't keep a ridiculous grin off my face. Being this in love with him was dangerous business. "Anyone ever tell you you're crazy?"

"Every day." His eyes danced.

"According to the authorities, that stuff outside poses possible serious health risks, even death, eventually. They're saying it could cause cancer. We're not even supposed to open a window. The consequences could be deadly." I lowered my voice, mimicking the newscasters and their doom and gloom solemnity.

Rick laughed again and shook his head. "Do I look like I have the black lung?" His breath was hot in my ear. "They're just trying to control us by scaring us."

I put my hands on his shoulders. "I can't believe you risked your life to come see me."

I was teasing, of course, flirting, playing up to him. Inordinately pleased, almost euphoric. And relieved by his careless, fearless attitude.

"Risked my life?" The whole situation seemed to amuse him. "Baby, I *would* risk my life for you. But this is nothing. I'm just here to rescue you from certain boredom."

He looked down the quiet hall. "Talk about dead. *We* have a keg and more half racks than you can count.

"The Tau Psis are having a volcano party!" he yelled over my shoulder to the girls loitering in the hall. "You're all invited."

He lowered his voice and focused his attention on me again. "Get your purse and let's go."

"But—"

He raised an eyebrow. "Afraid of a little ash?"

"No way!" I paused. Maybe I was a little afraid of going out in the stuff.

Rick made a sigh of exaggerated exasperation. "The university has more to worry about right now than you disobeying their martial-law-imposed curfew." He squeezed my hands. "Don't worry. I'll protect you from any big, bad enforcers on the way. Besides, it's dark as hell out there. We'll be hard to spot from more than a couple feet away."

I bit my lip and hesitated. "You can find your way back?"

He grinned. "I'm like a bat. I can find my way back to the frat from anywhere by feel. I've done it dead drunk before."

I opened my mouth again to protest, but the sexy look he gave me stopped me cold. If this *was* my last day on earth, I wanted to spend it with him. I nodded and pulled him by the hand to my room.

My roommate was out, leaving us alone in my room. He pulled me into a kiss as soon as I closed the door. I opened my mouth to him and kissed him back as he grabbed my ass and rocked my crotch into his, showing me how hard he was for me.

"We could stay here," I whispered, trying to sound enticing.

"My roommate's spending the night at his girl-friend's." His eyes were round with desire and his voice was filled with innuendo.

My heart raced at the implication.

I nodded and pulled away to grab my purse and a sweater, even though it was still hot and stuffy inside.

He leaned in and whispered, "Grab a toothbrush. The ash cloud, and the party, could last all night."

I hesitated and swallowed hard.

His eyes sparkled with desire. "You promised you'd spend the night sometime soon. This could be our last chance." He grinned as he brushed a lock of hair out of my face, knowing full well he was taking advantage of the situation. "Who knows how dangerous that ash cloud could get?" His voice held a hint of tease and enough promise to make me feel tight and tingly all over.

I *had* promised. I never went back on my promises. I wanted to be with him so badly.

I nodded and grabbed my toiletries, threw them in my backpack, and took his hand. "Let's go."

He took the backpack from me and tossed it over one shoulder. At the front door of the dorm, he hesitated with one hand on the doorknob and one clutching mine, his eyes searching mine. "You're sure about this?"

I nodded. "I've never been *more* certain."

He brushed my lips with a light kiss and threw open the door, pulling me, laughing, into the darkness of the falling ash.

The air was oppressive with heat and heavy with ash. Foolishly, I inhaled too deeply and didn't cover my mouth. It was like breathing in the air behind a car driving down a dusty road. Only worse. The thick air burned on the way down. I choked on it and coughed.

Ricked had pulled the hem of his T-shirt up and held it to his mouth to screen out the ash. He stopped when I started coughing like a spaz. "You okay?"

I nodded, still sputtering. "I'm fine."

"Try this."

I shook my head, still coughing. "You just want me to lift my shirt so you can see my boobs."

"I always want to see your boobs." He stripped his shirt off and held it out to me. "Hold this over your nose. Just avoid the armholes." He grinned. "I might have pitted them out."

When I wouldn't take it, he thrust it into my hands.

"I just wanted to see your abs," I teased as I covered my nose and mouth with his shirt. I didn't care if it was pitted out. It smelled deliciously like him.

He laughed, coughed, squeezed my hand, and pulled me forward through a strange, unfamiliar world.

The streets were dark. The streetlights were on, but couldn't penetrate the darkness. Lights from dorm porch lights and windows and sororities and frats along the way were just as ineffective.

The sounds of rock music and the smell of beer on the ash guided us along Greek Row toward the frats.

The dorms bordering Greek Row were all girls' dorms. They were quiet with worry. The sororities were the same. But the frats were partying. Hard. As if the world was ending. Strains of Pink Floyd's "Comfortably Numb" and The Cars' "Just What I Needed" filled the air.

By the time we reached the Tau Psi house, we were both covered in ash.

Joel, a frat buddy of Rick's, met us at the door, smoking a joint and in a mellow, happy high. "Rick, buddy, you're covered in powder. You got that cement dust statue thing going. Cool, man. Dust yourself off and come in out of the ash." His eyes were glazed. "What happened to your shirt?"

I held it up. "I used it as a dust mask."

"Cool," Joel said.

"Dust myself off? When did you become Mr. Clean?" Rick brushed my shoulder a couple of times and gave up. "It's a lost cause." He whispered seductively in my ear, "We are *so* dirty."

Joel stepped aside to let us in, and grinned at me. "You brought more girls."

"*A* girl. And she's *mine*." Rick squeezed my hand. "Keep a lookout for more. I invited her whole floor."

"Excellent." Joel blew a burst of sweet smoke at us. "Beer's in the kitchen. On tap or in the can. We were lucky to get the keg. Last one the pub had. We pretty much cleaned out the beer aisle at the grocery store, too." He laughed. "Had to fight off the Zeta Nus."

The living room was packed with guys and girls drinking, dancing, and partying. The windows were closed, making it stifling and hot.

Rick looked around and headed for a window. "It's stuffy in here." His hand was on the latch when Joel tapped him on the shoulder.

Joel shook his head. "Tried that already. Campus security came by and ordered us to close them. We get caught again, they'll shut this party down." He yelled at the top of his lungs, "Volcano party!"

Several guys whooped and cheered.

Rick backed away from the window and whispered in my ear, "I have a fan in my room."

"Do you really?" I stroked his arm.

He grinned and nodded.

"I don't even get a beer first?"

"Do you want a beer? I'll grab you one on the way."

He threaded his way through the crowd and into the kitchen, where he ignored the keg and pulled two cans from a cooler full of ice. He carried them in one hand, holding on to mine with the other, stroking my palm with his thumb.

He let us into his room and locked the door behind us. A necessary precaution. His frat brothers thought it was funny to barge in on couples.

He tossed my backpack into a chair while I dusted myself off. "That was an adventure. I'm making a dust cloud and getting ash all over your floor."

"Keep patting yourself." His eyes were wide and round. "You're gorgeous when you're dirty."

"Really?" I laughed. "And the floors?"

"I'll make a pledge vacuum up later."

As he set the beers on his desk, his muscles rippled. I thought, *Joel's right. Rick looks like a finely sculpted statue, like the David.*

Rick turned a fan on near the bed. He stepped up next to me as I was running my hands over my hips, trying to get the sticky ash off.

"Let me do that," he said.

He started at my hips, gently brushing and caressing as he leaned in and kissed my neck. I let his hands wander to my butt.

"This is very dirty." His voice was low and sweet as he gently swatted my butt.

"Is it?" I grabbed his ass, pulling his crotch against mine, and gently slapped him back on the butt.

He laughed. "You have ash everywhere." He ran his hands over my hips again. "Here." He dusted my shoulders and kissed them. "And here."

I was melting in his arms, breathless and getting tighter by the minute. I untied the straps of my romper and let them dangle loose.

"So do you." I ran my hands through his thick hair, shaking the dust out. "It's in your hair. And on your shoulders." I kissed the top of them as his hands skimmed my breasts.

"How did these get so dusty?" He cupped them and rubbed my nipples through the terry cloth fabric of my romper and my bikini top beneath.

I reached behind my neck and untied my bikini top. "This is filthy, too." I arched my neck and let him kiss it the way he liked, one hot kiss trailing after another to the hollow where my pulse beat for him.

His hands were hot as he slid the elastic holding the top half of my romper down. Untied the bottom string of my bikini top and tossed the top aside. He looked at my now naked breasts as if they were objects of awe.

He kissed them. Ran his tongue around the nipples. One and then the other. While I sighed and ran my hands through his hair, pressing his head against me.

"I could do this all day." He grinned up at me and kissed his way back up my neck, finally cupping my face between his hands. "You are so damned beautiful." He backed me up to the lower bunk of his bed.

I knew how to neck with him, knew what he liked. I nibbled on his lips. Teased him with my tongue. Stroked his backside and ran my long nails gently up his spine until he shuddered with pleasure.

I knew how to pet him, but I didn't know how to make love to him. As he laid me on the bed, my heart beat wildly with both fear and anticipation.

He lay down beside me, stroking my arm. I kicked my flip-flops off and ran my bare feet up his calves, catching the hems of his jeans with my toes and riding them up.

He slid his hand beneath the back of my neck and kissed me until I was breathless and eager. His kisses slid down my neck and to the tops of my breasts.

"I missed you so damned much. As I was driving ahead of the cloud, I kept thinking, *If the world is ending tonight, I have to get back and spend it with you.* That would be my dying wish."

His voice was hoarse with desire, seductive, and at the same time amused and mock serious. Like he never thought he'd been in any real danger.

"That is some line." I traced his chest. "Do you say that to all the girls?"

He grinned. "Only to the one I risked my life through an ash storm to get back to." He paused and wiped all teasing from his face. "I'm completely serious."

He rolled on top of me, holding his full weight off me with his elbows and staring down at me with solemn eyes. He pressed the hard bulge in his jeans between my legs.

I tightened again, wanting him.

"If this is it"—his voice was low and sultry—"I only have one regret—that I didn't get to make love to you."

I studied him, willing my heart not to melt. "You're full of it, frat boy."

"I mean it, Laur." His Adam's apple bobbed. "I know we haven't been seeing each other long, but being away from you just for a weekend made me realize..."

He hesitated. "I'm falling in love with you. I think I have been since...you know, we first met." He was suddenly modest.

Maybe it was a calculated play, but it made me go soft and mushy inside all the same.

I held his gaze and blinked back tears of happiness. "Since you rescued me from certain death?"

He'd saved me in so many ways.

"Yeah, that, too."

"I'm falling in love with you, too." There, I'd said what had been on my mind. There was no taking it back. I reached for the zipper of his fly.

"Damn, Laura. I've been dreaming of this." His voice was ragged. "The whole drive back this is all I could think of."

I slid his zipper down, wanting him more than anything.

But my mind kept racing with the thought *Rick Butler is falling in love with me.*

CHAPTER ONE

Present Day
Maddie
As January and the new semester began, I had a good feeling. One of those intuitive gut instincts that defy logic and reason. That you simply can't explain. And you wouldn't want to. You just *know*. This semester was going to *the one*. The one where life changed and great things happened.

I leaned into the mirror over my sink in the bathroom of my apartment and carefully applied a second coat of mascara.

Next to me, my roommate Olivia stood over her sink and made a face at herself in the mirror. "Ugh. Dark circles. Can I borrow your concealer? I'm out. I need to make a run to the store."

"Help yourself."

She slid open the mirrored door of the cabinet below the mirror over the sink and found what she wanted.

Our university-owned townhouse apartment only had one bathroom. And still had the same crappy, cracking countertops and vinyl in the awful goldenrod and avocado colors of the seventies when it was built. And brown carpet so worn it was barely recognizable as carpeting. But at least the apartment had two sinks and we each had our own room. Short of a major disaster, our damage deposit was safe. Hang as many posters as we wanted. Ding the walls. Spill on the carpet. As if anyone *could* notice. And the apartment was cheap, even if we were always calling maintenance because one thing or another was broken.

"HBM 225—the fundamentals of cooking and dining service." I slid the brush back into the mascara tube. "Process of elimination. If my gut feeling is about a guy, he has to be there. All my other classes will have the usual food science suspects. This one will have a slew of fresh hotel and business management majors. Why are all the hot guys in my major taken?"

"I told you freshman year you should have gone after Zach," she said.

I shrugged. "I had a crush on him for, like, two seconds. Until I realized, yeah, he's hot. But there's no chemistry between us. Except, back then, our actual chemistry class. I like him as he is—my best study buddy." I picked up my curling iron to touch up my hair.

After two years of a science-heavy curriculum that included microbiology, physics, organic chem, and bio chem, I was looking forward to one of the fun classes. HBM 225 was an elective for me, but highly recommended by my advisor. All the big food companies that courted our grads wanted cooking experience. The class was taught by an award-winning chef who'd run numerous five-star restaurants, and the new kitchen was state-of-the-art.

"I still don't see why you think this class is going to be your life-changing moment." She put some lip gloss on and puckered her lips to make sure it was even.

"Gut instinct." I finished my hair and turned off the curling iron.

"I think your gut instinct is more about your brother teaching here this semester. It's freaked you out."

I didn't argue with her. She was partly right. Ian taking a job here had freaked me a little. We walked out of the bathroom and downstairs together, grabbed our coats and backpacks, and stepped out into the bracingly cold air of January.

Our apartment sat on a hill next to campus. We had to walk down a long set of concrete stairs to get the edge of the main part of campus. Going down was fine. Coming back up at the end of the day with a heavy backpack was tortuous. It was the joke on campus that to get anywhere you had to walk down a hill then up a hill. Or up a hill then down a hill. This was exactly true. We came down the hill, then had to head up one to the buildings where our classes were.

Olivia and I parted company at the main part of the mall. "Good luck." She gave me a hug. "See you this evening."

"I might be late. I'm having dinner with Ian."

"Tell your brother hi from me." She blew a breath of frosty air out. "If I get to the store, I'll pick up some chocolate. Just in case your intuition fails you and 'the life-changing event or guy' is not in HBM 225." She winked. "Chocolate is better than guys, anyway. It never acts like a douche and makes you cry. I'll get dark. It's healthier."

I shook my head, annoyed and amused by her at the same time. "Later."

The lecture part of HBM 225 was in a medium-sized lecture hall in the College of Business building. Tuesday was lecture. I had a Thursday cooking lab in the new state-of-the-art kitchen the university had just completed last academic year. The lecture hall seated about a hundred and was nearly half full when I arrived.

I stood at the bottom of the tiered lecture room and expectantly looked up over the sea of faces. Heart pounding. What was I expecting? To get hit over the head with magical lightning like some sort of princess? For some guy to jump out of his seat and start throwing rose petals at me and go down on one knee? To extend his long-fingered hand and help me up to a happily ever after?

I scanned the crowd. Too many girls. Too many guys who were not my type. Too many familiar faces. Too little chance for anything new and adventurous.

I found a seat in an empty row, holding out faint hope for the rest of the class that had yet to arrive.

My study buddy Zach Harris walked in. I frowned as a tall, sexy, familiar-looking blond guy strolled in next to Zach with his arm looped around a blond Double Deltsie sorority girl. His head was bent over hers like he was *so* into her. I was practically predestined to dislike the Double Deltsies on account of my mom. Who'd threatened to disown me if I so much as thought about going through rush and pledging them. What she had against them, I didn't know. Just that they were bitches by birth. My hackles immediately went up.

"Ian," I whispered beneath my breath like a curse. It was just like my big brother to prank me by coming to my class with a Double Deltsie on his arm. Although Ian was thirty-four, he looked much younger and could easily pass for a student—a grad student, anyway.

He'd been teasing and threatening to spy on me and "ruin my life," which is what I'd repeatedly accused him of during my emotional adolescent years, since he'd taken the professorship in the chemistry department.

Zach spotted me and waved. He said something to the girl and came toward me while I pondered ways to kill my only brother. If Ian had also infiltrated my other friends and the rest of my study partners...

Olivia had to be in on this, too! I cursed them both. Including Olivia's laughter at my gut feeling about this class. And her stupid offer to buy dark chocolate.

Ian paused at the end of the aisle and looked up as he waited for the girl to go in first. Our eyes met. Mine snapping with sisterly indignation. His a startling hazel that were almost green in the light and held absolutely no spark of recognition. Only a healthy appreciation of what he saw. A real player.

Crap, crap, crap, crap, crap, crap, crap!

Now that he was closer I realized he was *not* my brother. *Definitely* not my brother. And not just because Ian's eyes were blue.

I couldn't help staring at this guy, really gawking. If I hadn't forced myself to maintain some composure, my jaw would have been on the floor. This guy's eyes and face were the same shape as Ian's. His hair the same color. He smiled the same charismatic, confident smile my brother used on all the girls. He even had the same characteristic dimple in just his right cheek. But he was sexy as hell. And worse, I was reacting to him!

I had a hot brother—like, a really hot brother. When he walked down the street, girls looked. Even though he was way older than me, my friends thought he was smokin'. You know what a disability having a brother like that is? Your friends always asking if he'll be around and drooling all over him when he is?

I thought it was worse for Mom. I mean, it had to be worse having your friends tell you how sexy your *son* was. And that he could turn them into cougars. Mom seemed mellow about it, taking it in good humor. Her pride evident as she threatened to lock up her baby boy. Ha! But there had always been something wistful about her, too. Something I couldn't understand.

They say everyone has a twin out there somewhere. I'd just run into my brother's younger, hotter double. I couldn't stop staring at him. Which was probably totally giving him the wrong impression.

Zach set his backpack down and looked at me, confused, like, *What the hell are you staring at?* Or maybe it was more like, *Oh crap, not again.*

"Maddie, this is my roommate, Seth." Zach's brow furrowed, as if he was expecting trouble. He sounded almost tentative as his gaze bounced between Seth and me. As if he sensed my immediate lust for his roommate, like someone had sprayed pheromones in the air. And Zach just wanted them put back in the bottle.

Hey, hanging around Ian, I knew the feeling and sympathized completely. I'd had it many times myself.

"And Kayla," Zach said. "Seth, Kayla, Maddie."

Oh, crap, I thought as recognition dawned. *His roommate? The charmer of the Double Deltsie house.* I wanted to laugh at myself and the total ridiculousness of the whole situation. So much for intuition and my life-changing HBM 225 class. Not only did Seth obviously have a girlfriend—boo, not much chance for me—Zach, always acting like a protective brother, had warned me off him. Since, I dunno, the first time he'd mentioned Seth.

"Hey, Maddie." Seth's voice was deep and sexy, too. Like he could be on the radio. How unfair was that?

He gave me a definite up-and-down. With Kayla right next to him. Douche. Like Ian, he was used to girls liking his attention. That much was pretty clear.

"Nice to meet you, Kayla." I smiled at her.

She flashed me a smile as her gaze, too, bounced between Seth and me with a knowing look in her eye. Which I didn't understand at all.

Finally, I gave Seth my undivided attention. "So you're the infamous Seth." I smiled like I wasn't interested in him. Like his charm had no effect on me. Even though I was lying and my pulse was racing as if I'd just sprinted a mile. "The other guy on campus who lives in a sorority."

I don't know why I said it that way, like I was putting him down. Maybe I was just subliminally trying to fight feeling attracted to a guy who reminded me of my brother. To the ultimate hookup king.

"Lived." Seth seemed intent on correcting me. "I moved in with Zach at his apartment at semester. And to be clear, your math is off. There were four of us houseboys." His smile deepened. "And you must be Zach's study partner, the infamous Maddie."

"Infamous?" What had Zach said about me? I shot him an inquiring look.

The bell rang before either guy could answer. The instructor, Chef Steven, took the podium.

I pulled my laptop out to take notes. *No, my intuition is wrong this time.* But my gaze kept drifting back to Seth. *No, not him. Definitely not him. He can't be the good thing I've had a feeling about.*

Seth

Maddie. Maddie. Maddie. She was hot. Simply gorgeous. I couldn't get her out of my mind. I barely heard Chef Steven's lecture. Something about kitchen safety and the set of knives we were supposed to order for lab. She'd messed with my mind so badly I couldn't concentrate. If I accidentally sliced my finger off in the kitchen, it was good to know it would all be because of a girl. Then again, what wasn't?

I hadn't been looking for a girl. Certainly not in this class, among the usual HBM suspects and Zach's food science buddies. Then I spotted Maddie all alone in a row of seats and was mesmerized. Partly by her indifference to me. Give me a challenge and I will take it.

When class ended, she grabbed her backpack and dashed into the far aisle like she was in a big hurry to escape. Like we had BO or something.

I pushed Zach and Kayla to keep up with her, almost running over them to get next to her. I couldn't let her escape without making an impression.

"Maddie?" I grabbed her arm, stopping her from disappearing into the crowded hall. As I did, I caught a whiff of her perfume. "Where's the fire? Come get some coffee with us."

She looked into my eyes and away again just as quickly. "Thanks. I can't. My next class is across campus."

"Maybe another time?"

She nodded.

"When's your lab?"

Her eyes were wide as she answered, "Thursday at one."

"Good." I grinned down at her. "So's mine. I'll see you there." I released her arm.

She nodded and raced off.

Zach and Kayla came up beside me.

"So's yours?" Kayla laughed at me. "*You* have lab tomorrow at nine."

"Not anymore." I watched Maddie until she disappeared around a corner. "I think she likes me."

Kayla shook her head. "Yeah. Sure looks that way." She shoved me playfully and pointed between us. "I think she thinks you and me..."

"No." I shook my head. Kayla had a douchebag boyfriend named Eric. She and I were just pals. Had been since I started working at the house.

Zach lifted one eyebrow, like he agreed with her.

"Shit," I said. "Zach, buddy, wingman, you're going to have to talk me up and make it clear I'm single."

"If she's interested, she'll check out your status online," he said.

I shook my head. "Not all of us update that shit."

"Guys!" Kayla sighed. "I have a class across campus, too. I have to run." She rolled her eyes and grinned before turning to walk off.

I watched her go and turned to Zach. "You've been holding out on me. How come you never mentioned how hot Maddie is? One look at her and you *know* she's my type."

Zach rolled his eyes. "Dude, I told you about Maddie. Dozens of times. I even tried to set you up. Before I realized she's totally sweet and deserves better than a commitment-phobe like you."

I looked at him blankly. I didn't remember him mentioning Maddie as anything but a smart chick.

He laughed. "You were after some other girl at the time. You blew me off. Why would I push it? I gave up."

Zach started walking. "You missed your opp, dude. Did you see the way she ran off like she couldn't stand the sight of your ugly face? Maddie's not into your type."

"My type? What's that supposed to mean?" I fell into step with him.

He punched me playfully in the arm. "Guys who rely on their looks and charisma to get by."

"You're saying I have no substance? Bullshit."

"Not me, bro." Zach kept walking. "You said it." He pushed the door to the outside open. "But if the shoe fits..."

"You're full of crap." I took a deep breath of the bracing air.

"Make it easy on yourself—don't change your lab to get into hers. Leave her alone. You're setting yourself up for failure."

Like hell, I thought. Maddie was the first girl I'd met in a long time who intrigued me.

CHAPTER TWO

Maddie

My brother lived in a rented house on a hill across town from campus in the professional, and new, part of town. The house had a spectacular view of campus and the signature clock tower, and rolling wheat fields. He picked me up after my last class of the day. I studied Ian while he drove.

He frowned. "What's wrong? Do I have something on my face?"

I scrunched my mouth to one side and looked at him like he was under my microscope, trying not to laugh at my own inside joke. And make him uncomfortable at the same time. How had I confused Seth for him? "No. You're fine."

"Then what's wrong with you? Why are you looking at me like that?"

"I'm trying to decide what the girls see in you." I was really trying to analyze my instant attraction to Seth.

When Ian grinned, his smile was eerily like Seth's. Or maybe Seth's was eerily like his. Ian was older and I'd known him all my life, so he should be the standard.

"Isn't it obvious?" he said.

I shook my head. "Oh, brother! And I mean that literally." I sighed with mock exasperation.

He pulled into a spot in front of my favorite Chinese restaurant and shut off the car. "I'll run in and pick up our carryout. I'll be just a minute. Are you coming in or waiting in the car?"

"Coming in, of course." I slid out of the car and met him at the door.

He held the restaurant door open for me. When he stepped inside next to me, I slid my arm through his and laughed as I leaned my head on his shoulder. And batted my eyes at him like he was just the most adorable thing on the planet. Like I was madly in love with him and totally flirting with him.

He shook his head. "Not that again! I thought you'd outgrown pretending I'm your boyfriend to impress your friends." He grinned and glanced pointedly around the near-empty place. "Who are you trying to impress?"

"No one. I'll never outgrow teasing you, big bro."

As a kid, I used to use him for a fake boyfriend to make all the other girls green with envy. We were both blond, but we didn't look alike. Which helped with the deception. "Besides, dating a prof is hot!"

He sighed like he was resigned. And let me hang on his arm as if he barely tolerated it as we walked to the counter. He'd called in an order. It was waiting for us. He put up with me making a show of pretending we were a couple.

"First meal together in our new house," I said to the girl at the counter in a giddy, gooey voice. That sickening   we're-so-in-love-and-want-everyone-to-know-it voice.

"Ah!" she said, like that was so sweet! "Congratulations."

Man, this place really should hire someone who wasn't quite so naïve.

I was shaking with laughter when we reached the car.

"That was cruel," Ian said.

"But fun!"

He rolled his eyes and shook his head.

The drive to his house took less than ten minutes. I carried the food in and set it on the counter of his gleaming kitchen, with its totally unused stainless steel appliances. He'd moved in less than a week ago and clearly hadn't made use of the kitchen yet. There were boxes everywhere.

"We could have eaten at the restaurant," I said, looking around, hoping he'd unpacked some dishes.

"And put up with you making eyes at me like it was a great joke? And playing footsie under the table? No thanks."

I laughed and looked around for dishes. "Um, plates?"

"No idea. Eating out of the cartons is part of the fun." He opened the bag. "Chopsticks! Excellent. I haven't unpacked the flatware yet, either."

"You're becoming an absentminded professor." I opened his fridge and grabbed two cans of beer and put them on the table. "Like I said, we could have eaten at the restaurant."

He shook his head. "I wanted to use the kitchen."

"You call this using the kitchen?" I carried the cartons of takeout to the table and opened them up.

He handed me a pair of chopsticks. "I wanted to talk to you in private, okay? Sib to sib. No prying eyes."

I dug into my food. "That sounds ominous." Bad news ran counter to my gut good feeling about the semester. "And here I thought you just wanted to hear about my first couple days of class. And tell me about yours."

I shot him a worried look, trying to sound teasing to cover my fears. "Are the girls in your classes already falling all over themselves to get to know the dreamy Dr. Foster? Office hours packed full of helpless coeds desperate for your, ahem, knowledge?" I laughed again.

"Can it, kid sis."

"I worry about you, Ian. Personally, I don't see your appeal." I grinned to cover my apprehension. "But girls tell me you're hot. Way too hot to be a chemistry prof."

An image of Seth flashed through my mind. Why couldn't I get him out of it?

Even though I was teasing Ian, this was serious business. Ian had left his last position over some baseless accusations made by a grad student TA of his. She'd been in love with him and jealous when he "spurned her" for a fellow professor. Even though he'd never encouraged her affections in any way. In retaliation, she accused him of falsifying his research and making unwanted advances toward her. One look at her and anyone could tell she wasn't Ian's type.

The university had investigated and proved to their satisfaction that her accusations were false. But Ian left anyway, feeling his reputation had been irreparably damaged and it was better for everyone if he moved on.

Now he'd walked into a chemistry department rocked by a sexual scandal from last semester. A female professor was accused of raping several male students over the years. She was awaiting trial. The student newspaper was full of the story. I would have liked a smoother start for him. Walking into a department in turmoil wasn't what Ian needed.

He laughed my concerns off. "Nothing to worry about. No one's written their phone number on their eyelids yet."

"Yeah, well, chem profs don't really have that Indiana Jones thing going for them anyway." I stared at him, wondering what my brother was up to. And why, now at semester, he'd decided to invade my university when he'd had other offers.

My major required a lot of chemistry classes. Fortunately, I'd finished the last of them—biochemistry— last semester, neatly avoiding having to take any classes from my older brother. I wondered if that had played into his consideration at all. He was now free to invade my territory without having me underfoot in class and getting into the questionable ethics of having to grade his sister's work.

He claimed the university had offered him the most money and opportunity. It certainly presented the greatest challenges.

I shook my head. "Of all the universities in the world, you had to walk into mine, big bro."

"Still miffed about that?" He dug into his takeout carton.

"Not upset. Suspicious." I leaned toward him. "What are you up to? Besides spying on me for Mom."

"I'm not spying." He winked at me. "Why would I do that?"

I rolled my eyes. More likely he was here to protect and big brother me to death.

He laughed, becoming serious in the very next breath. "Come on, Mads. You're the only sibling I have. You can't blame me for wanting to protect you and get close to you. When I left for college, you were barely four. Do you even remember what it was like when I was at home?" He held my gaze steadily.

I tried not to look guilty. But the truth was, I had only sketchy memories, just snatches of life with him before he left for college. Of him playing with me. Of going to his games. Of his pretty girlfriend, who looked like a princess in her prom dress. I wasn't good with a poker face. Too late I realized he could read my thoughts.

He nodded. "That's what I thought. It's just you, me, and Mom now. You can't blame me for trying to bond with you, baby sis. Before you're out in the big, bad work world and get too busy for me."

I swallowed hard, feeling guilty for not keeping up as much since I'd come to college. "I'll never be too busy for you!"

I hadn't known my brother was the sentimental type.

I wished he would find someone and get married. In elementary school, I'd dreamed of being an aunt by the time I was twelve and got my babysitting card. Watching a little niece or nephew like my friend Carly did had sounded so cool. Those childish hopes had been pretty much dashed. I remained the baby of the family.

He continued studying me. "Have you ever wondered why there's such a large gap between you and me? Fourteen years. I'm *almost* old enough to be your dad."

"A very young dad," I pointed out.

He smiled. "A scandalously young dad." He paused. "I was in high school when you were born. Mom and Dad were within a few years of being empty nesters. Why did they start over again?"

I laughed. "Because without me, there was a big hole in their lives."

He rolled his eyes. "Yeah, that must be it." He paused again. "I'm serious, Mads. If you'd been an accident, I could see it."

He frowned like he was thinking over a puzzle. "But that wasn't the case. I remember them trying to get

pregnant with you. All the medical procedures and
Mom crying when they failed. It's no secret they got
married because Mom was pregnant with me. Then
they have a fourteen-year dry spell?"

I took a deep breath and shrugged. "Stop sounding
like there was something strange going on. A conspira-
cy. You know as well as I do that Dad had cancer right
after you were born. The treatment made him infertile.
They had to go through years of infertility procedures
to get me. And several miscarriages before I finally
stuck."

He got that teasing look on his face. "I can't believe
you bought that story. I've told you the truth a million
times—you were left on our doorstep. When we heard
you crying, I told Mom and Dad not to answer the door.
That it would only mean trouble. Would they listen?
No. They were too tender-hearted. Once they opened
the door, they couldn't leave you out in the cold."

"Shut up. I am not adopted. And I don't believe that
story anymore." I laughed. "But I *am* tenacious and
strong-willed. That's why I'm here." I paused. "I look
just like Mom and you know it."

"Yeah," he said, smiling at me. "But after all that
time, why didn't they give up? By then, having another
kid was like starting all over again with a second family."

I sighed. "You think too hard on things. If you're
that curious, ask Mom."

He frowned. "I've tried. Numerous times. She gives
me the same old vague answer. They wanted another
child."

I shrugged. "Maybe that's the simple truth. It sounds reasonable to me."

He still looked skeptical. I froze with my chopsticks halfway to my mouth. "What? What are you thinking?"

"Nothing." He paused. "Mom wasn't exactly thrilled when I decided to take the position here. She wasn't her usual excited self when you decided to go here, either. Have you ever wondered why? Why doesn't she ever talk about her college experience?"

"Maybe because there's not much to tell." I'd never really thought much about it. "She dropped out after just a year and got married." I paused. "You think there's more to the story?"

He grinned. "There's always more to the story."

Now he was being evasive.

He reached for an egg roll and got a faraway look in his eyes. "Mads, you're here. Mom and Dad met here. Our family history is here. I have a gut feeling this is where I need to be right now. Does that sound crazy?"

Yeah, Ian was really my brother. Us and our intuition. At least we understood each other.

"No, not at all." I meant it.

He stared into his carton of orange chicken and then back up at me. "I miss Dad, Mads. Every day." His Adam's apple bobbed. "I feel close to him here. Like even though he's gone, I feel like I'll get to know him better here. The young Dad, the healthy Dad. The one Mom fell in love with."

I reached across the table and squeezed my brother's hand, fighting back a sudden welling of tears. Dad died my junior year in high school. Over four years ago. But we never stopped missing him.

"I can't argue with that. I'm here, too, because of him. I knew it would make him happy if I went to his alma mater."

I hesitated, weighing whether I should say what was on my mind. Thinking about Dad brought up the uncomfortable subject of Mom's new fiancé. "Do you think Ken really makes Mom happy?"

Ian stared at me like he wasn't sure what I was asking. "Sure. I wouldn't have agreed to give her away if I had any doubts. Why?"

Ian was protective of Mom, too. If he wasn't concerned, maybe I was just imagining things.

"I don't know. I'm her maid of honor." I paused again, trying to phrase things so Ian wouldn't miss my point. "So I feel guilty for even saying it, but...it seems to me like she's settling."

Ian squeezed my hand and shook it a little. "Maddie, no one's going to replace Dad. You don't have to worry about that. Ken doesn't have to be like Dad for Mom to be happy. He's a good guy."

I couldn't help frowning. Ian kept misunderstanding. "Yes, but...he's steady and reliable, just like Mom has always told me I should look for. She's big into that. Like you can learn to love a reliable guy. But does she love him?"

Ian gave my hand one final squeeze and released it, frowning now, too. "I'm sure she does. They've been friends since she and Dad first married."

"Yes," I said. "I'm sure she loves him like a friend. But does she *love* him?"

"I'd rather not think about that." Ian did an exaggerated hate shiver and made a look of disgust.

I laughed at my brother's antics. I couldn't help myself. He always knew how to lighten the mood. But even though I was laughing, I still wondered. There was a part of me that wanted to see Mom fall in love, really in love. Like a giddy girl. She needed some sizzle in her life.

Ian was watching me. "Maddie? You're wearing your wishing look. What are you wishing for now?"

I shrugged. "Am I?"

Ian swore beneath his breath. "Come on, Mads. Don't make me guess."

"I just think Mom deserves to be swept off her feet once in her life. To be madly, passionately in love."

His face clouded. "I didn't know you were such a romantic. Be careful what you wish for." He got a faraway look on his face.

I didn't understand him. What was wrong with him?

"You're just like Olivia," I said. "Too pragmatic. Now pass the moo shu pork."

CHAPTER THREE

Maddie

I walked into cooking lab with a certain nervous anticipation. And though I hated to admit it, Seth was the main cause of it. So maybe I *was* one of those girls who wanted a guy just like dear old dad. Or in this case, just like dear old older brother.

I'd been thinking about Seth for two days, wondering how I could be the tiniest bit attracted to him. Telling myself I wasn't. And yet I Facebook stalked him. Just to find out whether Kayla was his girlfriend or not.

His profile said he was single. Could I trust that? Maybe. But, you know, people lie on social media. For all kinds of reasons. He had some selfies of him and Kayla. And a few more pictures of him with her and a bunch of girls at the sorority house. When I checked out Kayla's profile, it said she was in a relationship with a guy named Eric. There you have it. My first impression of the two of them being a couple was wrong. If he was in a secret relationship, it wasn't with Kayla.

For all my nonchalance, I was still excited about seeing Seth in lab. And way too disappointed when I walked in and he wasn't there.

Lab was in a commercial-grade kitchen just like you see on the cooking reality shows on TV, but with a teaching station in the center of the room. The teaching station was a large stainless steel prep island with a sink and a mirror over it. There were four student prep stations around the kitchen, smaller versions of the teaching station, minus the mirror.

I was one of the first to arrive.

Chef Steven greeted me. "Pick a station, any station. You have your choice. Four people per."

I chose one near the door. It was closest to the refrigerators, proofing ovens, and salamander.

Chef Steven winked at me like he approved. I'd heard stories about him. He was self-effacing, humble given his considerable talents, but a perfectionist and taskmaster. A tireless worker. People swore he never slept.

His kitchen catered most university events. As part of the class, we were required to work a minimum of thirty hours during the semester. Semester after semester his kitchen put out five-star-quality food with a staff of new students. He just got them trained and the semester ended and he started over. The myth of Sisyphus in action.

We'd had to buy a white chef coat embroidered with our names, and black chef caps. The black caps signified we were students learning the craft. The tall white hat had to be earned and was reserved for trained chefs.

I'd pulled my hair into a ponytail, as required for class. But I'd applied my makeup with special care again. Primping for a guy who was not the one. But would be delicious to flirt with anyway.

I stuffed my ponytail under my cap. I was sliding on my chef's coat when Seth walked in. He grinned when he saw me. I smiled back, my heart beating way too fast in response to a guy who shouldn't have held my interest at all. I knew too much about him from Zach. Had heard too many funny stories about Seth and the Double Deltsies and his exploits with the girls.

Seth was a love-them-and-leave-them guy, according to Zach. A player. And I did not need a player. Or a hookup. Or a heartbreaker. Even though it would be a lovely sort of rebellion and I was tempted. What was it about bad boys, or even slightly naughty boys, that turned our heads?

He came right toward me. I was flattered. Right. Who wouldn't be? He dumped his backpack on the floor by my feet at my lab station. I'd been half afraid he wouldn't show up. And half afraid he would.

He gave me a slow up-and-down that would have been totally sexist if his eyes hadn't been full of appreciation and it hadn't made my toes curl with the sensuality of it. "Nice outfit."

He grinned and showed off that single dimple as he pulled his chef jacket out of his backpack and slid it on. *Seth Butler*. I don't know why I found the name monogrammed on his chef jacket so appealing. If I got the urge to scribble it on my notebook over and over, I was going to have to punch myself.

As he reached for the buttons of his white jacket, he looked at me like he'd suddenly just realized something, gasped, and made a look of mock horror. "Oh, no! Fashion faux pas." He leaned in so close that I caught a whiff of his cologne. "We're wearing the same outfit. You're going to have to change."

I laughed and pointed to my name on my chest. "No. Mine's a different label."

His gaze lingered on my chest. I guess I'd asked for it.

"I see the difference now." He laughed as he covered his thick, wavy hair with his black chef's cap. "How did you get here so fast? I have an eight o'clock. I ran all the way and you still beat me." A lock of his hair stuck out and his hat was cocked at a rakish angle.

I reached over without thinking, straightened the cap, and tucked that errant lock beneath his floppy felt chef cap. Like I would have for Ian. "There. Better."

Was I flirting with him? I wasn't sure. I'd acted on impulse. I looked away and pulled my roll of knives out of my backpack and set them on the stainless steel table in front of me. "This is my first class of the day."

"Okay, then. You get seat-saving duty."

Before I could respond, two other people—a guy and a girl, fellow hotel and business management majors that Seth knew—completed our cozy station of four.

The bell rang. Chef Steven called the class to order and began our first lesson, ordering us to the fridge to get a selection of carrots and fresh vegetables.

"These will be your stations and your partners for the rest of the semester. A good kitchen staff learns to work together as a team. Your grades will reflect your team's efforts.

"First lesson—how to use the knives. How to chop and slice like a master chef." He pulled out a bunch of carrots and demonstrated while we watched him work in the mirror above.

I was clumsy with my chopping. Seth sliced and diced like a pro. I couldn't believe I was being out-sliced by a guy.

He kept glancing at me, looking like he was dying to help me. Like I was a chopping embarrassment.

Finally, he set his knife down and came up behind me. "Here. Let me show you how it's done." He put his arms around me, and his hot hands over mine. "Curl your fingers so you don't chop them off." There was a grin in his voice, and his breath tickled my ear in the most delightful way.

He positioned the knife properly in my hand and guided my slices until I got the hang and the flow of it. Which I made sure to do extremely slowly. I wasn't usually a slow learner. But in this case...

"Very nice." He let go and stepped back to his place beside me.

I immediately missed the heat of his body next to mine and the way he'd had his arms around me. "And here I thought you were a short-order cook, not a master chef. That's what Zach told me."

"You were listening to a guy whose best dish, whose only dish, is scrambled eggs with cheese." Seth picked up his knife and rinsed it in the sink. "You can't believe everything Zach says." He stared at me like he meant about much more than cooking.

I was beginning to think Seth was right.

"What's your best dish?" I asked on impulse.

"I'll have you over to the apartment and show you sometime."

Crap, I felt myself glow with the thought. Here he was practically commanding me, acting as if I'd jump at the chance, and I didn't mind at all.

"Okay, best dish at the sorority house." I concentrated on slicing the onion before me and trying not to cry. It was a strong one.

Seth was watching me as, embarrassingly, my mascara began to run, and I fought to avoid touching my eyes.

"Breathe through your mouth, not your nose. You'll cry less." He was slicing his onion tear-free.

I mumbled something about mouth-breathers, but deep down, I was impressed. He knew a ton more about cooking than I did.

After slicing the vegetables, we moved on to "fabricating" a chicken, a fancy term for butchering a chicken. Taking a chicken apart seemed pretty much counterintuitive to me to the usual meaning of fabricating, which was to make something. Seth, again, had no problem. He knew how to cut and what pieces to make. I, however, had always been more of a baker than a cook. I winced when I had to snap the bones apart.

"Don't tell me you had to fabricate chickens at the sorority house, too."

Seth shook his head. "No. I left that to our cook. Dad taught me."

"Your dad is the cook in your family?"

His expression became blank, like he was trying to hide the pain of something. "It was just the two of us. It was either him or me."

Okay. He had no siblings and his mom was out of the picture for one reason or another.

I glanced at the clock just as Chef Steven ordered us to clean up. "That's all for today. Store your fabricated chickens in the freezer. We'll be making stock out of them next week."

As we washed our knives, the four of us at our station joked around and exchanged phone numbers. At Seth's suggestion. So we could get together and study if we needed to. For a cooking class? If I had been vain, I would have thought Seth was looking for a way to get my number without singling me out. I wasn't vain. But I still hoped that was the case.

Seth walked out of class with me. "Have plans for the weekend?" He sounded too casual, almost prying.

For an instant I got my hopes up that he was going to ask me out.

"I'm going country swing dancing with a group of friends at Bourbon Beach." I could have just said I was going dancing. But I added the location in case he wanted to find me. That was stupid.

"You like to dance?" He made a face like dancing wasn't his thing.

"You don't like to?"

He shrugged. "I'm not a big country music fan."

I didn't know why I felt so let down. It's just, I'd given him an opening and he hadn't taken it. Which was fine by me. Really.

"What are *you* up to?" I tried to sound casual, too, but I was curious about him now.

"The usual." He gave no clue what the usual was as he held the door open for me and we broke outside onto the sidewalk. "I'm headed this way." He pointed in the opposite direction I was headed.

"That way," I said.

He smiled. "Have a good weekend. See you in class on Tuesday, Maddie." He headed off without a backward glance at me.

Leaving me disappointed in his wake. What was up with him? Was flirting just a sport with him? I'd hinted that I was going dancing and even told him where. And he walked off like he wasn't interested. After he'd looked for a way to put his arms around me in class. I was sure he had. An enigma. A player. A player wrapped in an enigma.

Seth

I had a change of plan. At the last second. I was about to ask Maddie out when it suddenly seemed smarter just to show up at Bourbon Beach and ask her to dance. Wow her with my swing skills. The girls at the house loved dancing. They dragged some combination of Zach, Dillon, Paul, and me along to Bourbon Beach at every opportunity. For protection. And to assure that they had enough dance partners. I'd managed to avoid country swing for about a year now. I was thinking it was time to lift my embargo on country music.

Bourbon Beach had a different theme every night. The girls liked country and East Coast swing best. I'd gotten pretty good at both. Thanks to the girls and their tutoring. They weren't going to be embarrassed by a houseboy. And they claimed that dancing with someone who didn't know what he was doing was no fun. So the four of us became pretty decent dancers out of necessity.

The trick was convincing a couple of guys to go with me. You didn't show up at Bourbon Beach alone. Everyone traveled in packs. I probably could have convinced Zach and Alexis. But Zach was proving to be the worst wingman in the history of wingmen. I got lucky. Paul called and begged me to go with him and a group of the Double Deltsie girls. He didn't have to twist my arm too hard, though I made him work for it.

"Come on, man," Paul said. "You bail on me at semester. Leave me to train two newbies. The least you can do is help me escort half a dozen hot girls to the bar on a Friday night. Like that's tough duty. Why am I begging? They're not off limits for you anymore, dude. Man, I envy you!"

On the surface, it seemed like he was right. I was in the enviable position. But after spending several years in the house, most of the girls were like sisters to me now. The pledges, the new ones, seemed too young. Like baby sisters.

"Buy me a beer," I said, negotiating.

Paul swore beneath his breath. "Dude! One, or all, of the girls will. You know that. They have plenty of cash to throw around. They always treat us well."

"Yeah, but *country* swing?" I had an image to maintain. Country music wasn't part of it.

Paul swore some more. "Come on, man."

"All right. What time?"

"The action never starts until ten." The relief was evident in his voice. "Meet us at the house at nine thirty. Wear your cowboy hat, dude."

CHAPTER FOUR

Maddie

Country swing night was only on a Friday once a month. The other three weeks it was on Thursday night. I was a good little studying girl, which cut me out of it most Thursdays. Plus almost every semester since freshman year I'd had a Thursday night lab that conflicted.

I was excited about going dancing. Olivia and I dressed with care in tight boot-cut jeans, sparkly tank tops that bared our midriffs—dancing was hot business—and cowboy boots. Hair loose, long, and straight. Skipped the hat. It wouldn't last past the first dance. I was hoping some of the guys who knew how to dance would show up. There were a couple partners we all coveted.

By the time we arrived, the dance floor was crowded. I scanned the crowd for our faves. Cowboy Jake, as we called him, hadn't shown up.

"Robbie's not here, either," Olivia yelled to me over the music.

Crap, the two best dancers around hadn't shown up.

"Let's get something to drink." I headed past the dance floor to the bar.

There was a trick to being asked to dance. First, you had to make your presence known. Make eye contact with the likely candidates.

Olivia and I found a table. She was immediately asked to dance. I couldn't get the attention of a waitress to save my life. And I really needed a drink.

A commotion at the door caught my attention. A group of six or eight Double Deltsies arrived, accompanied by two guys. My heart fell into my stomach when I recognized Seth. So he hated country music, did he? Except when a group of hot blondes invited him out with them. So this was the something usual—hanging out with the girls from the house.

My face flamed. My stomach burned. I felt toyed with and in no mood. He was dressed in boot-cut jeans, boots, and a black T-shirt. The boots made him a couple inches taller. And he was plenty tall to begin with. He was even wearing a cowboy hat. He looked cowboy enough to me. And too hot for his own good. He wore cowboy well for someone who professed it wasn't his thing.

At that moment, I hated him for playing me. Flirting with me in class and then blowing me off like I was nothing. Stuck-up Double Deltsie former houseboys, anyway. Zach had been right to warn me off him. Though I didn't know why I cared.

The girls were laughing. He led one of them to the dance floor. I watched them with morbid curiosity. I knew I shouldn't have been looking. I knew I could have been caught in the act. But I couldn't look away.

Crap. He was a *good* dancer. Correction. He was an outstanding dancer of the caliber of Robbie or Cowboy Jake. Why hadn't I noticed him before? How could he be that good without being a regular?

I watched as he and the girl did the pretzel like they'd been dance partners since birth. They anticipated each other's moves. I felt myself turning a sickly shade of envy. Seth was smooth. When he dipped her, she laughed and smiled, obviously and totally trusting of him. When he lifted her in an aerial over his head and she struck a pose, the dancers around them cleared space and watched in awe.

Crap, every good female dancer in the crowd was suddenly eyeing him. He wouldn't have to ask another girl to dance all night. They'd mob him.

When he pulled her down from overhead and swung her out, she threw her legs around his waist and rode him like a bucking bronco. I should have turned away. But, of course, I didn't. Because you can't look away from a train wreck.

As soon as the dance ended, one of the other girls he'd come with claimed him. She wasn't as good a dancer. But they were still fun to watch. I guess I liked tormenting myself.

Finally, I looked away. Olivia didn't return to the table. I saw her out on the floor. She looked like she was having fun.

I caught a glimpse of myself in the reflection of a mirror over the bar. I was glaring, looking like an angry bitch. No wonder no guys had approached me. I looked like I was ready to bite their heads off.

Fine. I didn't need Seth Butler, anyway. I was acting like a petulant child who wants something she doesn't really want, just because. I took a deep breath and reset my face, making myself smile.

I still hadn't gotten a waitress to take my order, but a beer arrived as if ordered out of thin air. The cocktail waitress set it in front of me and pointed to a big, ugly drunk guy at the bar. "Compliments of that gentleman."

She walked off before I could refuse it or send it back. And he walked over, uninvited. I really hate it when drunks invade your personal space and get right in your face with their stale breath. I also hate being sent random drinks, as if I should be flattered some douche has sent me a cheap beer.

The douche took Olivia's empty stool next to me.

"Hey, beautiful." He slurred the words. He had two words to say and he couldn't get them right. The crappy night just got crappier. "You're the prettiest girl I've seen here in a long time."

And alone and separated from the herd, I thought. An easy mark. So he thought.

He was older, maybe thirty, and already working on an epic beer gut. Probably not a student, like most of the guys in the bar. Probably a local. But not university staff, from the looks of him.

"Wanna dance?" He burped.

Just kill me now. Yeah, I wanted to dance. With Robbie or Jake. Or Seth. Mostly Seth. Not with this burping drunk next to me. I would have been surprised if he could even stay on his feet.

The thing is, you have to trust your dance partner when you swing. 'Cause it's not one of the dances when you just move in the space next to each other, no touching required. And there's danger involved.

Flips, dips, aerials, and spins were risky in the wrong hands. I once had a guy give me a concussion when he dropped me in the middle of a low spin. Since then, I'd been more cautious and discerning in my choice of dance partners. Because sure as anything, some guy who's never danced before in his life will ask you out on the floor, and before you know it, he's showing off for his buddies. Especially if a few beers have given him confidence. And you're literally banging your head against the floor.

I held back a tart reply and slid the beer in front of the guy, even though it was the last thing he needed. "No thanks. I believe this belongs to you."

He ignored it, scooted his chair closer to me, and fixed his gaze on my breasts, talking to them like they might answer him. "Next song, then. I'm a good dancer. Real good. I know all the moves."

Ick. I wasn't doing any moves with him.

"No thanks." I got up. But not quickly enough.

He grabbed my wrist. "Where you going in such a hurry?"

I glanced around for a bouncer. Bourbon Beach was usually pretty good about having plenty around to break up trouble. Do you think I could find one when I needed one?

Just as I glared back at the douche holding my wrist, I felt a warm hand on my shoulder. An arm slid around my waist from behind and pulled me against a hard chest. I caught a whiff of cologne I recognized.

"Thanks for keeping my girl company. I'll take it from here." Seth's tone was just the right blend of threat and letting the guy save face as he removed my wrist from the douche's grip.

"Come on, baby. Let's dance." He pulled me toward the dance floor.

I held my breath as we walked away, hoping the drunk didn't come after us and take a swing at Seth. A sucker punch to the kidneys from behind was not what we needed.

Seth seemed unconcerned. It wasn't until I saw the other guy who'd come with him step between us and the drunk that I understood why. The guy looked like he was itching for a fight and could take just about anyone.

"Don't worry about Paul," Seth said in my ear with amusement in his voice. "He can take care of himself. He'd like nothing better than for that shithead to come after me or him."

The drunk wasn't stupid. He left us alone.

I leaned into Seth, cupping my hand to speak directly into his ear over the blasting music. "That was
smooth. You're good at this 'rescuing a damsel in distress' business."

When he grinned down at me, all my irritation at
him vanished and I felt a little weak in the knees.

"Paul and I have had a lot of practice. Why do you
think the girls keep us around?" He nodded toward a
couple of Double Deltsies who were headed out onto
the floor with a pair of obvious frat guys.

"So this is your usual—protecting girls at bars from
drunk douchebags? Is that some kind of weird super-
power?" I looked him directly in the eye. That usually
pierced the truth out of people.

His grin deepened. "No. That's Paul's duty tonight.
He and the girls begged me to come along. The girls
still think I work for them and expect me to play personal bouncer, like before. Force of habit." He
shrugged. "What could I do? They're like sisters to me.
I couldn't let them down."

We reached the edge of the dance floor. He hesitated. "I was serious about asking you to dance—do you
want to?"

"I thought you didn't like country music?"

"I don't."

His frank admission made me respect him more. "I
assumed you didn't swing dance, either?"

He raised one eyebrow. "You've made a lot of faulty
assumptions about me."

"You like dancing?" I was confused now. He was the
most confusing, amazing guy I'd ever met.

"With the right partner."

My heart fluttered like I was sure it was supposed to. "Me too." I paused a beat. Two could play the flirtation game. "With the right partner."

He led me to the center of the floor. When he took my hands in his as the music started, I felt another unexpected zing of attraction.

"I'm better at East Coast swing." His eyes sparkled in the lights on the dance floor.

He looked pretty good to me. And for the moment, I didn't want him to let go. I liked the feeling of my hand, small and protected, in his.

In country swing, there are some standard steps that you can do infinite variations on. There's only one rule—the guy leads. If he's good at it, you both look good on the floor. If the guy can't lead, or you fight him, you've got a problem.

Having seen Seth's moves, I was confident he knew how to lead. I was excited to follow. He started off with the pretzel, which is a basic country swing move. Though not basic in execution. There's a lot to the hand movements and twirls involved. Get off and you're sunk. All pretzelled up in completely the wrong way.

This is where you appreciate the expertise of the guy. Basically, you hold hands and sort of eggbeater around. There's a point in the move where you end up in his arms. If the guy's into you, it's the perfect opportunity for him to gaze longingly into your eyes.

Yeah, that sounds corny. But believe me, if you're dancing with a guy you like, it's anything but. In real time, the move goes by in seconds. But I was hyperaware of Seth, like we were the only two people in the room. My heart beat wildly, pounding in my ears above the beat of the music as he pulled me next to him, paused, and stared into my eyes.

My heart skipped a beat. Looking into his eyes was like looking into the future. There was something deep and magnetic about him. In an instant, it was over, and we were twirling around each other, hanging on to each other. His hands were warm and strong in the small of my back. At my waist. Holding mine again. A tantalizing touch each time. A flirtation and a tease.

I had never experienced a dance partner like Seth. Not someone who made me breathless and whom I didn't want to let go of. Not someone who danced so easily he had time to flirt and make me laugh.

I loved to dance. Dancing was the ultimate fun. But it had never been the ultimate seduction before. Much as I fought it, I felt myself falling for all of Seth's moves. He didn't even have to speak. He simply had to twirl me and hold me in his arms.

He pointed toward the ceiling, silently signaling a lift. I met his eyes and saw the challenge there. I nodded, like, *Bring it on.*

In time to the music, I did the prelude to the jump, coiled, and sprang as he circled my waist with his large, steady hands and propelled me above his head as if I weighed less than a feather. As I was twirling above his head, the crowd around us parted, giving us room to perform.

He dropped me from my perch. When you drop a girl in swing dancing, you don't drop them straight down with a plunk. You bring them into your chest and perch them against your hips. If you're the girl, you stare into his eyes like you want to take him to bed right then and there. Like you love him above all reason. Because you have to sell the dance. Because, like my dance teacher used to say, dancing is a mating ritual, even if you're only performing it.

He pulled me down and swung me out. I jumped and wrapped my legs around him, leaning back, letting my hair spin out as he twirled me. Feeling him hard against my crotch. Arching back to the applause around us.

My breath caught again as I stared into his eyes. Desire burned there. And I wondered if it was really for me, or if he was caught up in the heat of the dance. Selling it like I was.

I could have stared at him forever. But I broke the gaze and reached my toes for the floor.

I had never danced like this with anyone. Not even Robbie or Cowboy Jake, who were both smooth, confident, skilled partners. Their skills paled in comparison to Seth's. And maybe I was only kidding myself, but it was way too easy to sell the dance to myself.

The music ended. Seth ran his hand through his hair, spiking it up. Even with messy hair, he looked hot as he breathed hard. "Again?"

CHAPTER FIVE

Seth

Maddie made me hot in a way no girl had before. And I'd been hot for a good many girls. Maddie was different. She made me happy and nervous. For reasons I couldn't explain. I felt, more than saw, Kelly staring at me from across the room, glaring possessively like she needed a partner and why the hell wasn't I asking her to dance? Like I had an obligation to her.

The little bitch. Not that she couldn't have had her choice of partners. Not with the way she looked. But she wasn't trolling for guys tonight. She just wanted to dance with someone who knew how. And was pissed that the other good dancers hadn't shown up.

It wasn't like she had any designs on me. Other than I could dance better than most. Sure, we'd casually flirted with each other over the years. But it didn't mean anything to either of us. It was just what we did. Kelly was like a sister to me, but her sense of entitlement pissed me off.

On the other hand, I was completely mesmerized by Maddie. Couldn't Kelly see that? Damn, it felt embarrassingly like anyone with eyes could. I'd lost my calm. I ignored Kelly, heart pounding, mouth dry, until Maddie smiled and nodded.

I wanted to show off for Maddie. I wanted to feel her legs clamped around me and see her breathless and flushed with exercise. Girls liked this dancing shit. Why do you think I did it?

I looked her directly in the eye. "Do you know how to do the candlestick?"

Her eyes sparkled and she grinned. "Yeah. Do you?"

I liked the challenge in her tone. "Is that a rhetorical question?"

She laughed. Damn, she made me happy.

"We'll see how good you are in a minute. If you drop me—"

"Wouldn't dare. Unless it's into a waterfall."

She arched an eyebrow, giving me a smile that sent my heart racing out of control. This girl was messing with my mind.

"Spinning my butt on the floor in the mop." She took my hand, and damn, it felt good in mine. "Extremely low dips and spins. I can meet any challenge you throw at me. Bring. Them. On."

I squeezed her hand. "You're on. You can trust me. I haven't dropped a girl yet. But I can't promise not to step on your toes."

Our gazes were locked.

"When you dip and spin me, just don't bang my brains out."

Crap, she did that on purpose. Now I had a sudden vision of banging her brains out. But not that way.

The music started. I pulled her to an open spot on the dance floor. If you're going to do fancy moves, you have to stake out your territory and get them in early. Before the floor gets crowded. If you're good enough, people will continue to give you space to perform.

Maddie eyes sparkled with challenge. As if she wanted me to push her to the limits.

Damn if I wouldn't.

She began by slithering and slinking. With my hands all over her. I wanted her in my arms. Away from the crowd. But I would have to settle for this. For now.

I grabbed both her hands and whipped her around in a pretzel, faster and faster. Daring her to keep up or be caught in my arms. I was fast. She was just as fast. I liked the way she followed my lead, wishing relationships with girls were this easy off the dance floor. That communicating didn't need words.

I signaled for a candlestick. She grinned and immediately began the steps that led up to the jump. The next instant she was in the air and in my arms. I caught a whiff of her perfume and a glimpse of her moist, kissable lips. I swung her legs to my right. Then to my left.

And then she swung up and straddled me. *Ride 'em, cowgirl.* She was right where I wanted her. To stay.

With her crotch pressed against mine, I went hard. Involuntarily. Like I could help myself with the thoughts going through my head and Maddie bracing her legs around me and rubbing up against me. Was she trying to kill me?

I was sure she felt my boner. I felt every inch of her. She released her grip on my waist as I swung her upward until she stood straight up above me, her legs bent to make a four, her head resting on my shoulder.

I'd warned her we were going to show off. I spun with her braced above me, her feet pointing toward the ceiling. The crowd around us had been growing thick. Now it parted to watch us.

I stopped spinning and let her down, flipping her right side up, sliding her down me like I was a stripper pole, until we were face to face, hers perched just above mine. Our eyes locked. She cupped my face like a lover. This was the natural pause in the candlestick move. The place where you sold the audience on the seduction that was the dance. Where, from the right angle, the casual bystander would swear you kissed. Or should have.

I wanted like hell to kiss her. Her lips were moist and shiny. She was breathing hard. Just as I went to toss her to her feet, her lips came down on mine. Her lips parted. Her tongue darted across my lips.

And then she released me and slid free until her feet touched the floor. I was stunned. Reeling with the impact of her lips on mine.

I grabbed her around the waist and dipped her until her neck was arched beneath my lips and all I wanted to do was kiss her. I fought the urge and pulled her back to a stand. Extended her to arm's length. I was supposed to be leading. But she was pulling all my strings. Holding on to her, I lowered my arm, leading her down as she slid into a sit on the floor. This move was called the mop. Basically, you spun the girl on her butt on the floor, wiped the floor with her.

Wherever I led, she followed. However hard I pushed her, she pushed back, egging me to the limits. I lifted her into another aerial and dropped her in a waterfall. It was a dangerous move where the girl cascaded down you from above your head until you caught her in your arms. I'd only done it a handful of times. But the way we moved together was like we belonged with each other.

I set her on the floor and took her hands. We spun into the pretzel again, which felt basic and elementary now. I spun her low at arm's length, so low that her head nearly grazed the floor. Carefully keeping her safe. Seeing how far she trusted me.

As the song ended, I pulled her into my arms. We were both breathing hard. Our lips were inches apart.

"Nice dance, cowboy." Her gaze held mine.

I moved to close the gap and kiss her.

Kelly tapped me on the shoulder from behind.

I froze. *Shit.*

"You look thirsty." Kelly came up beside me and shoved a beer my way, looking at Maddie like she was an unwelcome intruder. Her gaze bounced back to me.

"*You* owe me a dance. And I expect some flair from you like I just saw."

She slid a sideways glance at Maddie and back at me. "I thought you swore off fancy moves last year. You big liar. I want to candlestick."

I rarely did extreme moves with the girls from the house. With any girl. I had to know she could move with me. There had to be an unspoken connection. The girl had to anticipate my moves and follow my lead without question. Kelly wasn't that kind of dancer.

Maddie spun out of my arms before I could reply. "Looks like you're in high demand, cowboy." She walked off before I could stop her.

Maddie

My knees were literally weak when I came off the dance floor. I was trembling and trying not to show it. I had never danced like that with anyone before. Following Seth's lead had been as natural as if we'd been born two halves of the same person. I tried to rationalize away my reaction to him. Maybe we were just born to be dance partners.

But the way my body reacted to him, I knew I was lying to myself. I wanted to make out with him in the corner. Let him buy me a drink and get drunk with him. I was already drunk on him. Talk to him all night. Find out everything about him. Even the mundane stuff like his favorite color and whether he liked broccoli.

And then that sorority bitch had come along and saved me from myself. I should have thanked her, really. Did I really need a Seth the Charmer in my life? Was I anything more to him than the next casual flirtation? A hookup?

I looked around for Olivia and spotted her sitting in the corner with her leg propped up on a chair, a soggy napkin, with melting ice, I presumed, on her ankle. *Crap.*

I made my way through the crowd to her. "What happened to you? Some guy step on your toes?" I pulled up a chair next to her.

She sighed dramatically. "While you were out there getting it on on the dance floor, I rolled my ankle. Some guys don't know how to lead."

"And some guys show off." I glanced at the dance floor and spotted Seth twirling the sorority babe. "Where's the guy?"

Olivia held up a martini. "He bought me a little something to numb the pain, slapped a napkin of ice on my ankle, and disappeared. Story of my life. I kind of liked him, too.

"What's your story? Who's the guy you were dancing with and why oh why did you let him get away? He's hot and he can dance as well or better than Robbie and Cowboy Jake. If I'd been dancing with him, I would have hogtied him rather than lose him to some bitch. I can't believe you let a Double Deltsie steal him."

"That's Seth. Zach's roommate." I rolled my eyes to emphasize my point and show I wasn't crazy. She knew all about Seth.

"Seth?" Her brow furrowed, like she was trying to remember everything I'd told her about him.

I nodded. "Love them and leave them Seth. Yep. That's him."

She glanced at the dance floor. "If I were you, I'd let him love me." She whistled. "But damn, girl. When I first saw you out on the floor, I thought you'd dragged Ian here behind my back. That you were pulling that old high school gag of letting people think your brother was your boyfriend. I actually did a physical double take." She nodded. "Seriously. Which is when I realized your guy was younger, and hotter, than your brother the professor."

I grinned. "Wow. Hotter than Ian? That's something coming from you. You were in love with him forever." I nudged her playfully.

She rolled her eyes. "In fifth grade." She shook her head. "Everyone's older brother is hot when you're in elementary school."

"Shut up," I said. "You've told me *much* more recently what a hot guy Ian is."

She laughed. And winced. "Crap, don't make me laugh. Any movement and my ankle kills me."

"Is it emergency room bad?" I asked.

"No, just *I wanna go home and keep it up* bad. As soon as I finish this martini."

Olivia had driven. I held out my hand. "Give me the keys. I'll drive."

She pulled them from her pocket and dropped them in my hand. "Bottoms up!" She downed her martini in a single gulp.

I helped her to her feet and let her lean on me as we limped our way across the dance floor and out to the car.

I had her settled on the sofa at home with a pillow behind her back, one beneath her ankle, a bag of frozen peas on top when my phone buzzed.

Where are you? One dance is not enough. Is your dance card full or do I have a chance?

Seth! I grinned stupidly. I couldn't help it.

Olivia gave me a suspicious look and started laughing. "Ohmygosh! That must be the Ian lookalike. Is he looking for you? Pining for you?"

"Shut up," I said to Olivia as I typed a response to Seth. *My dance card is completely blank. And out of commission for the night. My klutzy roommate twisted her ankle dancing. I had to drive back to the apartment* ☹

"You're flirting back, aren't you? Flirtexting!"

"That's not a word and it's not even clever," I said.

A text pinged in. *Damn! My dancing's no good without you. I told you I don't like country music, right? The only thing that makes it palatable is a superior dance partner.*

"Flirxting, then." Olivia leaned up on her elbow. "What did he say?"

I ignored her. *Poor baby.*

"Mads, what did he say?"

"He can't dance without me."

"That would be sweet if we hadn't seen him doing it when we left."

"I'm paraphrasing," I said.

Guess I'll have to drown my sorrows. Text you to-morrow?

I replied, *Only if you mean it.*

I mean it.

Text you tomorrow, then.

"Whoa!" Olivia said. "The texts are flying back and forth. You could make him wait for, like, nine seconds or something before you reply. You know the rules—don't be too eager. Make him sweat it."

"I don't string guys along." I slipped my phone into my pocket.

"You have it bad." She rearranged the peas on her ankle. "I can't believe you. Remember Kylie and Kurt in high school? Everyone thought they were such an incredibly cute couple, looking so adorably like brother and sister. Everyone but you. You mocked them merci-lessly behind their backs. And now, here you are, com-pletely gaga over a guy who could be your brother."

"Besides both being blond, Ian and I don't look alike. And that is the key difference. I'm not going for a guy who's like the guy version of myself." I gave her a look that said, *There. I run rings around you logically.*

She ignored my rational argument. "Maybe you *re-ally* are twins by different moms. Have you compared birthdays?"

"Shut up!" I gave her the narrow-eyed stare of righteous anger.

She shook her head in that patronizing way and sighed heavily, like she was resigned to my denial and it was almost cute. "Really? Snap a selfie of you two next time. He looks a lot like Ian. What is Ian going to think when he sees you two together? Is he going to wonder if there's an *Oedipus* thing going on with you?"

"Ick! That was a mother and son thing, so no." I made an exaggerated shudder. "Besides, people are wrong. They think Ian and I look alike just because we have the same coloring. People don't pay attention.

"And Ian is not *going* to see us together. Why would he?" I put a definite note of finality in my voice, like, *end of story*. "Unless he stops by my cooking class."

Olivia's eyes went wide and her face lit up. Oh, crap. She had that light-bulb-moment look on her face. "Wait a minute. Seth is in your HBM 225 class? The one where you were certain a life-changing event would take place? Looks like you found your event—a totally hot guy to play with!" She clapped her hands like a delighted child. "You told me your intuition was wrong. What happened? Wasn't he there the first day? Did he just transfer in? You're holding out on me. Why haven't you told me about him?"

"Maybe because there's nothing to tell." Why was I so defensive? "We're partners in cooking lab—"

"Partners!" She clapped again. "That sounds serious. You really are holding out on me."

I talked over her. "I ran into him tonight. He asked me to dance. End of story."

"Then he texts you minutes after you leave, longing for you tragically. Unable to dance with anyone else because no one feels as good in his arms as you do. No one understands his moves. Or follows his lead as well. Or captures his heart." She clasped her hands in front of her like a sappy romantic making her point.

I rolled my eyes. "Very funny."

She grinned evilly. "Sounds like a promising start to me. It's about time you found true love."

I shook my head. "Before you go too much farther and make a fool of yourself, maybe you didn't hear me well enough in the bar—Seth is *Seth*." I looked at her like she should immediately understand. "*The* Seth. You know, my study buddy Zach's former fellow Double Deltsie houseboy?"

She nodded. "I know. I heard you the first time. The hit-on-every-girl-in-the-Double-Deltsie-house Seth. The stud of Delta Delta Psi."

"Exactly." I nodded. "Hook up with any girl he can Seth. Yep. That's the one. A houseboy." I wrinkled my nose. "Okay, former houseboy now. For the Double Deltsies, of all places. Like he couldn't have worked in a house that actually has girls who are nice."

I couldn't hide the note of disgust in my tone. Or distrust. Maybe I was coming to my senses. Those of us outside the Greek system didn't like the Double Deltsies. They were inarguably the most stuck-up house on campus, full of drama queens and rich bitches.

Zach's funny stories about life in a sorority aside, I had never known how he could stand living there. Yeah, it was just about his only option. But still. And then he had *fallen in love* with *one*. His current girlfriend, Alexis. He claimed she was different. Time would tell.

But what about Seth? Why had he lived there? Easy access to the hotties?

"He was at Bourbon Beach with a big group of them."

Olivia frowned. "Oh. That sucks." She was quiet a minute, like she was thinking. "Maybe it's not as bleak as it looks, you losing your heart to a charming player who lived in a sorority."

"I didn't say I'd lost my heart. I grant you that he can dance. And that is a little sexy." I held my thumb and forefinger less than an inch apart to show her how little.

"As your roommate and best friend," Olivia said, "I have to say this—first, a warning. Watch yourself. And second, maybe we've misjudged Seth. Maybe there's more to him."

"You mean, maybe Zach's been making fun at Seth's expense?"

Olivia shrugged. "Maybe." She moved her leg and the peas nearly slid off her ankle. She leaned forward to catch them.

"He did save me from a douche at the bar," I said. "Do you need fresh peas?"

She laughed. "No, these are still frozen enough." She readjusted them. "Stop changing the subject. I'm just saying, you're usually a good judge of people. If you like him, maybe there's something there."

CHAPTER SIX

Seth

There's an art to texting women. It's in the timing. Which, believe it or not, guys stress over just as much as girls. Maybe more. If you text too soon or too often, you come off as a desperate stalker. On the other hand, wait too long and you lose your opportunity. Or piss her off with the impression you're not into her and are just getting in touch because you have nothing better to do.

If you reply to her texts too quickly, or too slowly, same deal. I'd already blown it with Maddie by appearing too eager. And using her number when I'd obtained it under false "studying only" purposes. To hell with that. A girl should be flattered a guy was into her that much. But being flattered was purely a matter of how much she was into you. And there was the rub. How could a guy know for sure?

Add to that the parsing. What does "text you to-morrow" really mean? Is it a throwaway flirt like "talk to you tomorrow"? See ya later? Have a nice day? When tomorrow would the timing be just right? What tone to take? Witty? Funny? Sarcastic? Ask her out? Suggest we study together? For cooking class? Shit, I wasn't usually this insecure.

I was spotting for Zach in the weight room at the rec center. I should have been paying attention rather than daydreaming and stressing about texting Maddie. But I couldn't get her smile out of my mind. Or stop thinking about the way she felt in my arms.

Zach was bench-pressing two-fifty with the help of my pointer fingers positioned at the center of the bar to help him balance. Funny how a finger or two lifting, at most, a few pounds by the spotter made all the dif-ference. However small my help was, he would have failed without it. Which was exactly like life. The smallest things made the difference. Right now, I had him at my mercy. He had to listen to my girl problems.

"So?" I said to Zach. "What do you think? When do I text her?"

His arms were shaking as he locked his elbows and let out a deep breath. Sweat beaded on his forehead.

"What the hell happened to your confidence, bro?" His face was red with exertion as he lowered the bar.

I guided the bar down with the tips of my fingers until he set it in its guide.

He wiped his hands. "That's it for me." He slid out from beneath the bar and sat up on the bench. "In answer to your question—never."

"Never? What the shit do you mean by that?" I glared at him. I should have made him answer when I had some power over him.

"Just what I said. Look, sorry, dude. I didn't think you two would ever get together. I've told her stories about you. About what a player you are."

I stared at him, stunned. "What? You talked about me? When? Why would you do that?"

He shook his head. "Since I first met her. You have to admit, some of the things you've done are pretty funny." He laughed like he was teasing. "Like chasing the girls in the house when you knew they were off limits and out of your league. Remember that time you went after Kelly—"

"Kelly and I hooked up once. When we were feeling reckless and rebellious about house rules." I stared at him, remembering Maddie seeing me dance with Kelly. "You didn't tell Maddie about that? You swore you wouldn't tell anyone."

"Relax. Your secret's safe." He grabbed a towel and mopped off. "I've never told anyone you actually hooked up. I didn't want you to lose your job. Not that it matters now. I may have mentioned part of the chase. You were hysterical, man."

He paused. "I told her stories about a lot of people in the house. Girls are always curious about what it's like for guys living in a sorority."

I silently cursed to myself. I should have been mad at Zach. But he was right—people were always asking about life in the house. And it was easier to make a joke of it than admit to the embarrassment of being in the servant class.

"Also, I also felt I owed it to Maddie. In case she accidentally met you when we were studying sometime and you turned on the charm and gave her the wrong idea. Girls like you, Seth. God knows why." He shook his head like it was a complete mystery. "I don't need you hooking up with one of my best study partners and making things awkward for all of us. Between you and me. Me and her. You and her. I'm crap at being the middleman."

"Why would it be awkward?" I sat next to him.

"I don't know." His voice was full of sarcasm. "Take the current situation. With you stressing about when to text her."

I shrugged and swallowed hard. "I *like* her."

"I like her, too. She's a sweet girl. Which means I'm gonna protect her from douches like you." He laughed.

"You need to work on your big-brother issues, Zach. You don't have to protect *everyone*. Certainly not from me."

He shrugged my insult off. "I like you, too, bro. Which is why I'm warning you. Maddie wants a reliable, steady guy. You have too many commitment issues for a girl like her. It's a match made in hell. Want my advice? Save yourself some heartache. Don't text her."

"Then I'll be working in hell's kitchen in cooking lab. We're lab partners."

"I told you not to switch labs." He slapped me on the back. "Hey. Sorry, man. I didn't mean to screw things up for you."

"I don't have commitment issues." I was defensive for good reason.

"You haven't had a girlfriend longer than two months since I've known you. Things start going well. And you bail on them." He gazed steadily at me.

"Most girls get possessive too damn fast."

"Uh-huh. I *have* found a study partner I want to hang with at least until I graduate. And you can't afford to piss off your lab partner. Especially this early in the semester."

He had a point. I ignored it and pulled out my phone. "Enough of this shit."

"Don't text her unless you think you can make this work for at least the semester." He was just goading me now. On purpose, judging from the smug look on his face.

"Fuck that."

Maddie

I had been stupidly checking my silent phone all morning. Which was dumb on so many levels— emotionally and logically. For example, I was an early riser. For a college student, anyway. I'd been up since nine. In the morning. Statistically, unless Seth had a major test to study for or a huge project to work on, he was probably still in bed past noon, like more than half the campus. I was handwringing over nothing.

I finally set my phone to vibrate. When it buzzed in my pocket, I practically jumped. And couldn't pull it out fast enough. My heart started pounding. When I saw it was from Seth, I broke out in a stupid, lovesick smile.

Hey, is it too early to text you?

Now, the girl's ever-present dilemma—text right back like I'm way too eager or make him wait? Crap, I couldn't help myself. Better to be too eager than too aloof, right? Better to show him more interest than less.

It's never too early to text ☺

After I hit send, I regretted that smiley face almost instantly. But it was too late to take it back. Was an emoticon too cutesy? Over-the-top eager, like a beaver? Crap. My turn to wait.

But not long. My phone buzzed almost immediately.

Want to study together?

Study? What were we going to study? It wasn't like cooking class was study-intensive. I took the offensive.

Sure. I have some Sensory Evaluation of Food and Wine lab homework I have to do. Want to help me?

It was the truth. I had a lab write-up due on Tuesday. But did that sound too flirty? Would he take it literally? Or like I was offering to sit around and drink wine? Crap. Sometimes this major was way hard to deal with.

He replied, *That will pair nicely with the studying I was going to propose—getting a jump on ideas for our HBM 225 final project. Have you read the course outline? We need to work on our food point of view. It's never too early to experiment. I have a meal I'd like to try out on you and get your opinion on. We can use my kitchen. Seven tonight at my place?*

I paused, confused and excited. Was he asking me out? Was he going to cook for me? Or were we really going to study? Did he mean for me to bring the wine?

There were thought bubbles on my phone. He was typing something. He texted again before I could reply. *Late notice, I know. If you're busy tonight, we can go for another time.*

I smiled to myself, full of hope. Was Seth just a little insecure? That couldn't be! Not the Seth Zach had described to me. Insecurity meant he liked me. He liked me! I replied before I lost my chance. *Tonight's great! Should I be studying red or white wine?*

Red. He gave me his address.

I knew where it was. I'd been to his complex before.

So he wasn't picking me up. Which made sense if he was cooking. Date or not date? Why did guys have to be so hard to figure out?

I typed my reply. *See you tonight.*

I made Olivia go with me to get the wine. Even though she was still hobbling around on her ankle, she was a good sport. I was no wine expert. I'd only had one lab, and it was just the intro. Part of our homework was to try a new wine from our list each week and write a report, kind of like a book report about wine. I went for broke and bought two that were on the class list, thinking I'd kill two weeks' homework at once. Both were local Washington state wines. I picked them in the most scientific way—I liked the look of the bottles and packaging.

I obsessed to Olivia as I got ready for the evening. Now who was the insecure one? "How do you dress for what might be a romantic dinner? Or could be just a study date?"

She rolled her eyes. "When in doubt, wear tight jeans and let your boobs and midriff show. In two words—look hot. No guy's going to complain about getting an eyeful of cleavage, and you have your bases covered." She pulled a top out of my closet and held it out to me. "Wear your jeweled bellybutton ring, the one with the blue stone."

"You're a genius," I said as I took the blouse from her.

I arrived at Seth's apartment with my stomach fluttering, and the wines, my lab notebook, and laptop in my backpack. As decoys or props or whatever. I was prepared for either dinner date or study date.

When he opened the door, something inside smelled delicious. But oh my! He was the main event. Dressed in skinny jeans, a white T-shirt, and beanie, he looked simply delectable. It always surprised me that his gruff was dark and sexy, although his hair, which peeked from beneath the beanie, was dark blond.

I inhaled deeply to cover my nerves and get a grip. "Yum! It smells good in here. I'm guessing your point of view is Italian?"

He grinned. "Good guess." He took my coat and backpack. "This is heavy. What do you have in here?"

"My homework. Wine. Remember?"

His eyes sparkled. "That's a real class?" He looked surprised.

"Duh!" I laughed. "And you have to be twenty-one to take it. Just like for the beer-making class. One of only a couple classes at the university where they card you to get in!"

"Wow! You have an exciting major. Why aren't people flocking to get in?"

"You've got me. It's the best one ever." I couldn't stop staring at him, or wanting to run my hands over his gruff. "Doesn't Zach ever talk to you about his classes?"

"As little as possible." He set my backpack on the sofa.

I looked around, taking in his apartment and trying to get a feel for his personality. It was a bachelor pad, but relatively picked up and clean. I'd never been to Zach's place before, certainly not while he lived in the basement of the sorority house, so I couldn't say what was Zach's and what was Seth's. Or whose influence was whose. There wasn't a lot of interior decorating going on, that was for sure. "Where *is* Zach?"

"Out with Alexis. Studying on a Saturday night? He couldn't be bothered." Seth grinned and headed to the kitchen. "I told him I didn't want him hanging around disturbing our concentration."

Be still my heart. I pulled the wine out of my backpack and followed him like a puppy, wanting to jump into his lap and shower him with happy kisses. It was a ridiculous image. Something about him made me want to touch him. I pictured myself coming up behind him, wrapping my arms around him, and resting my head on his back. I resolved to keep my hands, and my fantasies, to myself as I set the bottles on the pass-through opening to his kitchen. There were dishes and pans scattered everywhere across the counters.

"Wow! You're well equipped." The words just popped out.

He grinned wolfishly. "You noticed!"

Crap. I felt myself blushing from the innuendo in his voice.

He pointed to the wine. "Two bottles? An alky, are you?"

"More like uncertain whether this was a whole group study event or if you and I were going rogue tonight."

"Rogue?" The wolfishness reached his eyes. "I like the sound of that."

"So?"

"Just you and me, baby." He winked.

I laughed. "Baby?"

"Don't like it?"

I loved it. "The jury's out."

He spun the two bottles around and read the labels, looking surprised and delighted. If I were the type to get a big head, I would have congratulated myself on my selections.

"Excellent choices. Did Zach help you?" His eyes sparkled with some secret joke.

What had I missed? Maybe I was just wild with nerves.

"Zach? No!" I snorted, like Seth was crazy. "Zach has absolutely no nose for wine. The poor baby"—I used *baby* on purpose—"is a non-taster. Good thing he's great at microbiology and loves the food safety side of things. There's no way he could be in product development with a disability like that."

"Non-taster?" Seth grinned like I'd just given him ammo against Zach in the next macho fest between the two of them. "I had no idea. Is that what it sounds like?"

I couldn't resist ribbing him. "What? You haven't heard of it? And you call yourself an HBM major!"

"Zach has no taste! An insult, and yet the truth!" Seth said.

"Non-tasters can obviously *taste* things, just not as well as most people," I said. "Haven't you ever noticed that he wolfs his food?"

"Shit," Seth said. "You're right."

I nodded. "Non-tasters have fewer taste buds than about three-fourths of the rest of us. They're especially oblivious to bitter."

"Sounds like a good thing to me. Life shouldn't be bitter." He was so cute, completely adorable in his intentional misunderstanding. "You're a taster, I bet."

"No." I laughed. "I'm a *super* taster."

"More taste buds than average?"

I nodded. "Lots more."

He studied me in a way that made me blush, like he was trying to learn everything about me in a look. "Okay, then. We'll just have to keep bitterness out of your life."

His eyes narrowed, like he was thinking deeply. "You were a picky eater as a kid." He spoke like it was a statement of fact, not a guess.

"Oh, yeah. I was in trouble all the time with my dad, always sitting at the table after everyone else had left, alone with a pile of green peas in front of me that I refused to eat."

He laughed. "I hated liver." He paused. "Spinach. Cabbage. Kale. Asparagus. We should probably cut those out of our food point of view?"

He was so sweet and thoughtful. Not many guys would catch on so quickly.

"I would be eternally grateful."

His eyes sparkled. "I like the sound of that." He had a way of speaking that was pure flirtation.

I couldn't stop my heart from racing. I smiled to cover, and because it was impossible not to smile with the happy way my heart was dancing.

He picked up a cork puller and grabbed one of the wine bottles, shaking his head and laughing. "Zach *really* didn't help you pick this?"

I shook my head. "No. Absolutely not. You can thank my prof for making this selection. Both of those are on the wine list for class." I smiled at him and furrowed my brow when he continued staring at me. "What? Why are you looking at me like that?"

"Besides the fact that you're gorgeous?"

I blushed. "*What?*"

His grin deepened. "You really don't know?"

"No."

He laughed. "Of all the wines in the world, you picked this one. It's fate." He turned the label toward me and pointed. "I know the guy who makes this."

"Really?" I frowned, still puzzled by the way he was acting, as if it was really important.

"Yeah. He's *my dad*."

"No way!" Suddenly, I got it. No wonder he thought I was sucking up to him. "Your dad's a vintner?"

"No. A part-owner in this winery. He chucked his high-tech job in Seattle and moved to the wine country in Chelan after I graduated from high school. He was supposed to be retired, but he got bored. First he bought a hotel. Then this winery was up for sale. So he bought it, too." Seth shrugged. "I'm now the heir apparent for the family wine and hotel business."

"Seriously?"

He nodded.

He'd surprised me again. I'd gotten the impression from Zach that he and the other houseboys had to work at the sorority house because they didn't have any money. But a hotel in a popular resort area? It sounded to me like Seth's dad had plenty of money. And was willing to leave it to his son.

Seth pulled two wineglasses from the cupboard and set them in front of me. "Want me to open it?"

"Be my guest."

I watched as he expertly uncorked the wine and filled two glasses halfway. He pushed one toward me.

As I picked the glass up, I noticed writing and a logo on it. I turned it around, expecting the glass to be from his dad's winery. Instead it was inscribed with the date of last spring's Double Deltsie formal. "Yours or Zach's?"

When he caught my expression, he laughed. "Mine. The house always has extras left over. I grabbed a few."

"I see. *Not* a memento from a glorious sorority formal?"

His laugh made the whole room happy and sunny. "One of the girls go to an official sorority event with a *houseboy*?" He imitated the horror of one of the girls. "Are you kidding? That's social suicide. And completely against the rules." He grinned like the rules didn't matter to him. "You don't date the help." He lowered his voice. "Hanging with the houseboys is a backroom affair."

Crap, why had the way he said that both make me jealous and tingly at the same time?

"The class system is alive and well at the Double Deltsie house." I laughed. He was easy to tease and flirt with. "Why *did* you work there?"

His smile died and his face became a mask. "Long story."

"Sorry." I bit my lip. "I didn't mean to pry."

"No, it's okay." He picked up his glass and twirled it between his fingers. "My freshman year I was pissed at my dad. In a state of rebellion. That's what he said." He grinned. "The old man cut me off. He has the philosophy that I need to make my own way in the world."

He mimicked his dad: "'No one handed me anything. It made me tough. And resilient, boy.'" His laugh had a bitter edge. "I needed a job. I'd met Zach in a class. He was working in the house. He got me a job."

"Parents!" I rolled my eyes, but I couldn't imagine my mom ever cutting me off, no matter what I'd done. I was dying to know what he'd done to make his dad so mad. But I couldn't ask him.

Seth shrugged. "It didn't hurt that my mom was a Double Deltsie. Working in that particular house royally pissed Dad off."

My mouth just popped open. "What?" I was stunned. This gorgeous, regular guy's mom was one of the bitches from the most stuck-up sorority on campus.

He nodded, grinning like he enjoyed my look of shock. "Yeah, the girls never knew it. I'm a legacy. Of sorts." When he laughed, it still had the resentful edge to it.

Hadn't he just said life shouldn't be bitter?

He leaned across the counter and whispered, "Zach's the only other person who knows. You're sworn to secrecy now."

Our eyes met. Our gazes locked. I felt breathless reflected in his eyes and included in his secret. Paralyzed with emotion and wanting. He was so not the reliable guy Mom claimed I needed. But at that moment, he was everything I wanted.

"My parents divorced when I was less than a year old. Mom split. Dad raised me. I thought working at the house would bring me closer to her." He looked suddenly sheepish. And completely adorable and vulnerable.

Why were men so sexy when they let their vulnerability show? I wanted to wrap him in my arms and comfort him. "That's...that's so sweet. And awesome."

A timer dinged, breaking the spell.

"Shit! I almost forget the polenta." He grabbed an oven mitt and spun around to pull something from the oven. Their kitchen was small, like most college apartments. But compared to ours, spacious.

"You made homemade polenta." I watched as he pulled it from the oven, unable to keep the awe out of my voice. "Isn't that, like, really hard to make? You have to stir it forever and pray it doesn't get lumpy."

"I think you're thinking of risotto. Polenta is easy. Especially this oven recipe I got from Dad's chef at the hotel. It's practically foolproof." He set it on the counter.

"What can I help you with?"

"Nothing. I have everything under control. Relax and enjoy your wine."

I went to the sofa to get my notebook from my backpack. "Enjoy it! I wasn't joking. Drinking this wine is my homework. It's serious business. I have to sniff and swirl and write down all my impressions." I opened my notebook on the counter. "And sound like I actually know something about wine. Want to help?"

"Any way I can." He grabbed his glass of wine and raised it to mine. "To a successful night of studying." His words were simple and innocent, but his tone was full of promise.

I tapped his glass with mine. "To studying." I swirled, stuck my nose in the glass, and inhaled like I knew what I was doing. "Is this right?"

He was watching me. "Your form looks great to me."

I couldn't help smiling. "Your dad owns a winery. I thought you might know something about winetasting."

"Just a little." He stuck his nose in his glass, closed his eyes, and made an exaggerated sniff. "Do you want the aroma or the bouquet?"

I stared at him. "There's a difference?" I frowned. I hadn't known. "We haven't covered that yet."

"The aroma is the smell associated with the grape variety. The bouquet is the array of smells that are part of the winemaking process." He smiled. "Don't worry. Not many people know or care about the difference. Casual tasters don't make a distinction between the two terms. Dad has drilled them into me."

I wrinkled my nose. "We haven't gone over that yet. So...bouquet, I guess?"

He took another sniff. "I smell success. Award-winning undertones of..." He shrugged and pulled his cell phone from his pocket. "This is bullshit."

"What are you doing?"

"Texting Dad's vintner for the official word on what we're supposed to be smelling." He grabbed the bottle and spun it around to see the label. "What year is this?"

"That's cheating!" I tried to grab the bottle from him, but he held it out of my reach. "It's supposed to be *my* impressions. How will I learn if I don't do it myself?"

His phone rang with an incoming text. "Yeah, but it doesn't hurt to lead with a little professional help and impress the prof right away. We all know the drill. Impressions and reputation are everything. If a prof believes you're an A student, he'll give you the benefit of the doubt when he's grading your papers. Turn in a C paper. Get an A on it because he was sure you knew what you were doing. And were only a little distracted when you wrote it. Why do you think I want to impress Chef Steven first thing?"

He spun his phone around to show me the vintner's response. "Smell any of this?"

I read the text, closed my eyes, and inhaled deeply into my wineglass again. "Yes. Yes. Yes!"

When I opened my eyes, he was watching me with rapt attention. His eyes danced and he was smiling. "There's a reaction I'd like to see again." He shoved his phone back into his pocket.

I was warm all over as I scribbled my thoughts, actually the vintner's, in my notebook. "Knowing what I was looking for made all the difference." I looked up from my homework into Seth's eyes. "Do you always cheat on your homework?" I swirled the wine in my glass, looking for legs.

"Oh, sure. I just call up Stephen Hawking when I'm having trouble with physics. Or Donald Trump when I have a problem with a hotel management class." His laugh was infectious. "How many connections do you think I have?"

Everything he said and did charmed me. "Okay, so only half the time?" I held my glass up for him to see. "What do you think of these legs?"

"Stand up so I can see them and I'll give you my opinion."

"You're impossible," I said. "I really need to know this stuff." I stared at the legs in my glass again and recorded my lame observations. "What smells so good in the kitchen?"

"Chicken marsala." He grinned again, like everything was an inside joke. "Chicken something. I put my own twist on and substituted another wine, a Washington white with a pinch of brandy. The point of view I'm showcasing tonight is a Pacific Northwest-Italian fusion." He went to the fridge, pulled out a stoppered bottle of white wine, and showed it to me.

I started to laugh, too. "Your dad's. *Again.*"

"It's free."

"And yet you made me bring the wine?" I tried to sound playfully indignant.

"Hey, you just brought your homework." He lifted his glass and took another drink. "Dinner's almost ready. Want to help me plate?"

CHAPTER SEVEN

Maddie

We finished our glasses of wine. Seth poured us each another. I joined him in the kitchen. We each downed another glass while he cut polenta into squares and put them on the plates, tasted his chicken, and added a pinch of salt.

He handed me a knife and a bunch of Italian parsley. "Cut up the garnish?"

"Only if you show me how you want it."

Guys! He grinned like I'd said something dirty. Everything had a double meaning to them. Then he was behind me, with his arms around me. It was warm in the kitchen. With him pressed up behind me, I grew even hotter. He covered my hands with his and took control of the knife. Like the rest of him, his hands were strong and hot. They covered mine completely. My hands were as lost in his as I was lost in him.

"We want to mince it, leaving a few long stocks for flair." He pulled me close and smelled so good. His breath was hot in my ear. "Set a few pieces aside. We want some pretty leaves. Fold the rest of the parsley over in half. Then slow chopping strokes so no one gets hurt, keeping the fingers folded out of the way."

His idea of slow chopping was evidently very different to mine. He chopped quickly with fast motions. *Chop, chop, chop, chop.* I reflexively backed away from the knife, right into his hot front. My butt pressed up against his jeans. I felt his dick, long and hard, rubbing against me. Like a slow seduction. Much more slowly than the pace of the knife.

The wine had settled over me, leaving a pleasant glow, making me tingly to the tips of my fingers. Taking away my sense of balance, which was already off kilter from being wrapped in Seth's arms. I was lightheaded with the nearness of him. I spread my legs apart for balance. He took that as an invitation, and slid one of his legs between mine, rubbing me gently with his thigh.

Waves of pleasure built between my legs. My breath caught. I cleared my throat. "You're good."

"I try to be." His breath was hot in my ear.

"With a knife." I pulled my hands free from his and spun around, looking up at him, trying to resist him. Wondering if he would kiss me. Wondering what it would lead to if he did. I looked down and braced my hands against the counter. "We were going to plate?"

"Yeah. Are you hungry?" His voice was low and deep with desire.

Oh, yes, I was. For him. And nervous. And flustered. And confused. "Starving."

He grinned. "Good." He backed off and grabbed the plates of polenta. He put chicken and sauce on top of each, then sprinkled the parsley and laid a large stalk across each. He held them out for me to inspect. "What do you think?"

"Beautiful." I smiled at him.

"Yeah." His gaze was on me. He carried the plates to the table and set them in front of us. Then he refilled our wineglasses. "You first." He pointed to my chicken. "What do you think?"

I took a bite. The chicken fell apart in my mouth. I closed my eyes like I was deep in rapture as I tasted. "Awesome. Completely tender and delicious! I'd give it an A."

When I opened my eyes, Seth was staring at me like he'd rather taste me. "But will Chef Steven think so?" He took a bite. "Pretty good. I think it's the wine." His foot reached over and playfully rubbed mine.

"Yeah, must be the wine." It had gone to my head, just like Seth had. "How did you learn to cook like this?"

He began talking. And I was lost in him, wanting to know everything about him. We talked and drank the rest of the wine, as if we both wanted to know everything about each other. As if we would never run out of conversation. With none of the awkward silences that happen when you're not connecting with someone. Or you just plain run out of things to say. Can you fall in love with someone over dinner?

Because as we talked about everyday getting-to-know-you things, I really thought I was. Maybe it wasn't love yet. But I was falling for him. Headlong. We had so much in common.

"Siblings?" I asked as I cleared the table and he made soapy water to wash dishes. One of the many perils of college apartment life—hardly anyone had a dishwasher.

He shook his head. "Not living. I had a brother. But I never knew him. He died before I was born."

I set a plate on the counter next to him and rested my hand on his arm for comfort. "I'm sorry."

"Yeah. I wish I'd known him. I've always wanted a brother."

"What happened to him?" I didn't know if it was gauche to ask, but I couldn't help myself. I felt sad, and bad for bringing it up.

"Bicycle accident. He was twelve. He was on his way to school on a sunny spring day. A car hit him." He stared into the soapy water, playing with the bubbles as he slid a plate in. Looking like he didn't want me to see his pain.

"Dad doesn't talk about it much. My brother had massive head injuries. He was wearing a helmet. It came off during impact. His head hit a curb. He lingered for a week before Mom and Dad made the decision to take him off life support. Ultimately, his death broke up the marriage." He looked up, his hands full of bubbles. His eyes full of sorrow. "It's just a story to me.

You know how things are that happened before you were born. Ancient history."

I came up behind him, wrapped my arms around him, and rested my head on his back. The wine had taken away my inhibitions. I was pleasantly buzzed. "But your parents stayed together long enough to have you!" I sounded way enthusiastic. Because I was.

He snorted. "Yeah. Their replacement son. That didn't work out well. You?"

"I have a brother. Who followed me to school one day. He's a professor here."

"He's a professor? How *old* is he?" Seth wiped his hands on a towel.

I gave him a squeeze and reluctantly let go of him. "Thirty-four.

Seth paused. "Same age as my brother would have been."

"Really? Another thing we have in common," I said. "Most of my friends' brothers and sisters are much closer to them in age." I grabbed the leftover chicken. "Where do you want this?"

He gave me directions where to find a plastic storage container to put it in and asked me to put it in the fridge. His fridge was surprisingly full. And sitting right in front was a large bowl full of a lush spinach salad.

"Oh," I said, touched. "I'm sorry. You should have served this."

He turned around to look. "And forced you to eat the bitter stuff? I wanted you to enjoy my cooking." He shook his head. "It's okay. It keeps."

"But you went to a lot of work."

He slid the rest of the dirty pots and pans into the soapy water to soak. "Yeah. So why ruin the evening with bitterness?" He grabbed the second bottle of wine that was still sitting on the counter and lifted it toward me. "You still have more homework to do."

I was already feeling lightheaded from drinking my share of the first bottle of wine. A second bottle was such a bad idea. "You're right." I tossed him the cork puller. "Are you going to help me?"

He grinned that sexy grin of his as he opened the bottle and poured two glasses. "I can't text the guy who made this one. Sorry." He handed me a glass. "And I may not even be a super taster." He took a drink of wine.

I matched him. "We could find out. If you had blue food coloring." I didn't hold out much hope for that. What guy had blue food coloring lying around?

"We're in luck. I do." He went to the cupboard.

I giggled, like he was being absurd.

"What's so funny? I have it." He held up a bottle of it for me to see.

I reached for it. "I can't believe it."

"Green beer," he said cryptically. "For St. Patrick's Day. Add blue to yellow beer..."

"Ah," I said. "And here I thought you were also a master pastry chef or something. If you have a cotton swab, we're in business."

"Be right back." He returned a minute later with a handful of them.

I grabbed a piece of notebook paper and explained the experiment to him as I tore off a piece with a hole in it. "I'm going to swab your tongue with the blue food coloring. Put this hole over it and count how many taste buds you have." I squirted the food coloring onto the swab. "Stick out your tongue."

"Dad told me never to stick my tongue out at people, especially girls."

"Do you always do what you dad told you to?" I raised one eyebrow, challenging him.

He stuck his tongue out. As I swabbed it, he made a face. I laughed and put the paper over it. I didn't need to count the pink taste buds that now stood out. I could tell at a glance he was a regular taster. But I leaned in close and made a show of it, bracing my hands against his chest. "Twenty-seven. Twenty-eight. Oh, so close! But not a super taster. You missed it by this much." I held my fingers a tiny bit apart.

He pulled his tongue in. "How many did I need?"

"Thirty-five." I pulled away from him.

He grabbed his wine and took a drink.

"I'm impressed, though, by the way you combine flavors. Super taster or not, you have good taste." I took a drink of my wine, too.

He grabbed a cotton swab and the food coloring. "Let me count yours."

I hesitated.

"Fair's fair. I want to see a super tongue."

I giggled again and stuck my tongue out.

He leaned in close and swabbed my tongue. His face was inches from mine. "Your tongue looks like one big taste bud. Awesome." He grabbed my arms and leaned even closer. So close, our noses almost touched. He smelled like wine and cologne. His lips were full and tantalizing.

"Count," I said with my mouth open and my tongue out.

"This could take awhile." His voice was low and sensuous as he counted. "Thirty-four." Closer. "Thirty-five." Closer still.

So close, I closed my eyes.

"Thirty-six." He slipped my tongue into his mouth and sucked, pulling me against him, sliding his thigh between mine and rubbing me like he had before dinner.

Making me weak in the knees. I wrapped my arms around his neck and sucked and licked back. Pressing my lips to his, hard. Nibbling. Moaning softly as his leg rubbed between mine, making me wet with pleasure.

He lifted me off my feet, pressing his hard dick against me. I was drunk on him as much as on the wine. Everything about him turned me on. He wasn't at all like Zach had made him out to be. He was sweet and considerate. And totally hot.

I jumped into his arms and swung my legs around his waist. He carried me to the counter and set me on it, kissing me in a way that took my breath away. Then his kiss left my lips and trailed down my neck to the hollow where my pulse beat wildly for him.

I pulled off his beanie and ran my hands through his thick hair. He ran his hands beneath my blouse, up to the back clasp on my bra. I was glad I'd worn my pretty lace one. And the matching panties.

I should have stopped him. I didn't hook up with guys. It wasn't me. But I didn't. One more feel. Just one touch of his hot hands on my breasts. He unhooked my bra. Without fumbling. Then his hands were warm and firm on my bare back.

He kissed me again, picked me up, and carried me without breaking the kiss. I closed my eyes and let him carry me away him. I rode him to his dark bedroom. He closed the door with his foot, like he was practiced at this.

He laid me down on my back as the bed groaned beneath us. "You are so hot. So damned gorgeous." He cupped my breasts, pushing them up in mounds beneath my blouse. Then he was sucking on them through the fabric of my shirt and my lace bra while I trembled with pleasure.

I lifted his shirt and ran my hands over his back and then his chest. I felt the strong pulse of his heart and imagined it was mine. That it beat for me.

I didn't know what possessed me. Why I wanted him so badly. I was drowsy with wine and pleasantly buzzed. Tingly in all the right places. I wanted what I wanted. Any objections about moving too fast were dulled by the fizzy way the wine made my head feel.

I lifted his shirt over his head. He shrugged it off like he was eager to show off his finely sculpted chest and the excellent bulge of his biceps. I ran my hands over his arms—so toned and delectably touchable—and licked his nipple.

"This isn't fair." His voice was low and filled with desire. "I'm half naked. And you're fully dressed."

"Nothing's fair in love or war." I kissed him as he reached for the hem of my blouse. I fought him for a minute, teasing him while he cupped my breast and pinched my nipple gently, in a way that turned me on more. Finally, I gave in and let him pull it over my head. I slid my loose bra off. His pupils were dark, but his eyes went wide at the sight of my naked, peaked breasts.

"Beautiful." It was like he was mesmerized.

I reached up and pulled him against me, pressing him against my breasts and rubbing my crotch against the hard dick in his jeans as if there was no clothing between us. He moaned and kissed my neck, then rolled off me and reached between us to unzip my jeans.

He slid his fingers into the warmth between my legs. "Damn, you're wet."

I'd only meant to neck and pet. I was so close to climaxing with his finger stroking me. I wanted to feel him, too. I unzipped his jeans and pulled him out. He was long and hard.

I stroked him. Until his breath caught and it seemed like a contest between who could get the other to come first. He stroked me with his fingers. I pumped him with my hand. He kissed my nipple. I playfully bit his shoulder.

I ran my finger over the tip of his dick. It was wet and ready, pulsing.

He swore beneath his breath and slid my jeans off, then pulled something out of his pocket and held up a condom. He'd come prepared. Was this sweet and adorable? Or way too hookup-like for me? The wine interfering with my sense of reason didn't care.

He leaned down and whispered, his breath hot in my ear, "I can't hold on forever. Either keep stroking me like that or let's put this on and finish together."

I grabbed the condom from him, giggling though it wasn't funny. Or maybe it was. Or maybe I was more nervous than I thought. I made a move like I was going to toss the condom away, like I was throwing away temptation.

He grabbed my hand and squeezed, rubbing sensually with his thumb, holding my gaze, imploring me with his eyes. There was that vulnerable look again. It melted my heart and made me hot for him beyond reason.

It was too soon. Much too soon. Officially, this was still just a study date tinged with seduction. We were moving at lightning speed. I felt powerless to stop it. Like fate will be fate. Need is need.

But my head buzzed. I felt like I was thinking through a fog. His eyes begged me not to stop. Want. Want. Want. I *wanted* to feel him deep inside. I pushed away the voice of reason and ripped open the wrapper before I changed my mind. He kicked off his jeans and underwear. I pulled the condom out, pushed it onto his tip, and rolled it down over him.

He kissed me. I pulled him to me. He pushed inside me past my panties. I held him tight as he speared me, pressing me to the bed as he moved in and out of my wetness. Tense, like he was holding back, waiting for me. I held on to him. Tighter and tighter. Moving with him. Until finally, I let myself go and cried out with pleasure and let myself fly.

He was still and quiet for just a second. And then he thrust hard one more time. He groaned, and I knew he was flying, too. The tension left him. He collapsed on me, holding his full weight off and resting his head against mine and breathing hard. "Wow."

"Wow," I echoed back to him, and smiled. I could have said more, but what? That I might be falling in love with him? "Wow" seemed more than enough and far too little.

He slid out of me and lay on his back, grinning. He turned toward me and brushed a lock of hair out of my face as he kissed me again, tasting like wine.

His eyes were drowsy now, too, as he took the condom off and set it aside. He slid his arm around me and pulled me close. I nestled into the crook of his arm beneath his chin, listening to the beat of his heart.

We were both grinning. My eyes felt heavy. I shivered.

"Cold?" He grabbed a throw blanket and pulled it over us.

It smelled like him, his cologne, his body scent. I snuggled into him beneath it, coiling around him.

We lay in each other's arms, smiling with afterglow. Music pounded in the apartment next to us, trying to hide the rhythmic thumping of Saturday-night sex. The light from a streetlight filtered in through the blinds. I was so warm and cozy. And happy.

I blinked, trying to keep my eyes open. Seth kissed the top of my head. I thought I would just close my eyes for a second...

CHAPTER EIGHT

Maddie

I woke with a start to a blinding brightness. My head pounded. For a second I was disoriented. I couldn't remember where I was. I didn't think it was my bed. There was a weight like an arm across my waist. I covered my eyes with my arm and opened one eye slowly, peeking beneath my arm to the masculine arm around me.

Crap. What time is it?

I had the sinking feeling it was morning. And then I remembered the wine. And the sex. And Seth. And just closing my eyes for a minute.

I removed my arm from my eyes and looked at the guy sleeping naked next to me. Peaceful and relaxed in sleep, he was a total heartbreaker. At least, *my* heart was cracking in two. And I was still naked, too, except for my panties.

I had just committed the cardinal sin for someone who wanted a relationship, not a hookup. I mean, I'd slept with him on a mere study date. Okay, I had gotten dinner out of the deal. And I had enjoyed every minute of it. But I had a sinking feeling that this signaled the end of the sweet, attentive Seth. I had to get out of here.

I really didn't want him to see me like this, with bedhead hair, smudged makeup, and morning mouth. I slid out from beneath his arm and looked around for my jeans, blouse, and shoes. I scooped them off the floor and turned my back to Seth as I dressed like I was suddenly Miss Modesty personified. I put my jeans on. I was fastening my bra when his voice stopped me cold.

"Leaving without saying goodbye? I thought that was a guy thing. I'd like the view better if you'd turn around. And come back to bed." He patted the mattress—at least, that was what it sounded like. His voice was sexy, seductive in a totally tempting way that made me tingle all over.

"I didn't want to wake you." I tried to sound light and flippant.

"That's what they all say."

"Anyway, who says I was leaving?" I laughed, trying to lighten the mood, full of nerves and suddenly shy. I cleared my throat. "But I really should be going. I didn't mean to spend the night—"

"Don't go." There was that sexy vulnerability again. So sweet and charming. "I'm glad you did."

Damn, how did he do that? Sound so genuine. Like he was more than glad. Much more.

The bed creaked like he was getting up. Followed by rustling fabric. Like he was getting dressed, too. I imagined him pulling his jeans up over his lean hips. Tucking himself in. Reaching for his fly.

I was getting turned on. By the thought of him dressing. Because, in truth, I wanted to be the one running my hands over his body. I wanted everything— more physical intimacy, the emotional connection we'd had last night, the sweet murmurs of a lover.

I hurriedly pulled my blouse on. He came up behind me and wrapped his arms around me, still warm from the comfort of the bed. He'd put his jeans on, but no shirt. His chest rubbed naked and hard against my back. Like the bulge in his jeans pressed up against the back of my butt.

I wanted him. I wanted to do him again. But it was such a bad idea. I wanted more out of this...this thing we had going. More of a chase. More seduction. More romance. More time for feelings to grow. I was past the wild partying of freshman year and ready for something of substance. Like a real boyfriend. Not a study screw buddy.

"Let me make you breakfast before you go." He slid my hair over my shoulder. His breath was hot on my neck and sexy with morning hoarseness. I could have listened to it all day. "I'm used to making Sunday breakfast for girls. And good at it."

I hesitated, happy he wasn't eagerly shoving me out the door. Hopeful for all the wrong reasons.

What time was it, anyway? I had tons of things to do and none of them were Seth. Olivia would tease me mercilessly if she saw me doing the walk of shame. That's what everyone called it when they saw girls staggering home dressed in rumpled clothes from the night before. Not that anyone was actually shamed. But sometimes it was incredibly funny to watch hung over girls teeter home.

I ran my fingers through my tangled hair as I spotted a clock on Seth's nightstand. I held back a sigh of resignation. It was already late.

"I make great coffee." He ran his hand through my tangled hair and whispered in my ear, "I think we both could use some."

I don't know what possessed me. I nodded. "Sounds great. Bathroom?"

He pointed. "Zach and I each have our own. Just don't get any ideas about sneaking out the window." Then he laughed. "There isn't one."

He didn't offer me a shacker shirt. There was some prestige in a guy lending you his shirt so you could go home in something clean and, most importantly, different. And commitment. The guy would probably want the shirt back. So he'd have to see you again. It was a ploy. Like "accidentally" leaving something at your place. Did no shacker shirt mean total lack of commitment? Why did I have to analyze everything?

As I hurried into the bathroom, I thought, *Olivia will tease me mercilessly for hooking up with a lab partner.*

When I came out of the powder room, Seth's bedroom was empty and the smell of coffee and eggs made my stomach rumble.

I found Seth and Zach in the kitchen. And Alexis sitting at the table. She was leafing through an old sorority scrapbook with an intense look of concentration on her face. It was pretty obvious that's what the book was, by the overly large and decorative Delta Delta Psi letters on it. When she looked up, she wasn't particularly surprised to see me. Seth must have warned her I was here. Her lips twisted into an amused smile.

I wasn't sure what was so funny.

She patted the chair next to her. "Maddie! Come. Sit. I brought a show-and-tell!" Her voice was bright and way too sunny for first thing in the morning—even late morning, almost noon. She sounded absolutely delighted with herself.

I cautiously took a chair next to her. "What do you have here?"

"A secret." She held her finger to her mouth and glanced at the guys in the kitchen.

A cup of coffee sat next to her. She took a sip. "I was looking for a surprise for my mom. Until I stumbled on something juicier." She sounded like a spy about to reveal a top-secret cipher or something.

"I was looking through our archives and test files, hoping to find something of Mom's from her college sorority days. Spying on her, maybe. But I knew she'd get a kick out it if I could find something of hers, like an old test or report, and give it back to her as a Mom's Weekend present."

"And this is it?" I said, happy for Alexis.

She shook her head. "No. This is something else I found. It's totally unrelated to me. But connected closely to someone else here." She held up the scrapbook and slid a glance at the boys in the kitchen.

They were busy, and adorable, joking with each other as they cooked, anticipating each other's moves as if they'd been a team forever. She pointed to an old picture that was held in with photo corners. She leaned into me like I was her coconspirator and whispered in my ear, "What do you think? Seth has been holding out on us. He's as much a legacy as I am!"

I gasped softly, automatically. Which pleased Alexis tremendously, judging from her expression, anyway.

Seth hadn't wanted anyone of the girls to know. Now Alexis had gone and discovered it for herself.

I pulled the book to me and took a closer look at the picture the little sleuth had uncovered. When I saw it, I paled. For a second, I literally couldn't breathe. My chest felt tight, like my heart was cracking.

To the casual observer, it was just a sappy old dance picture. One of the old kinds where the girls had made the backdrop out of butcher paper and crepe paper ribbons. It looked completely tacky and fake.

The couple, dressed in outdated formal wear, stood in the center of an arch covered with flowers. The girl had long blond hair styled to curl away from her face, perfect makeup, and a dress that looked expensive and, judging by the quality, probably was the height of fashion for the time. She had the tiniest of waists and a quirk of a smile that was at once seductive and smug.

Possessive. As if she owned the guy and the world and everything in it. She was the *perfect* Double Deltsie blond.

He had his arm carefully posed around her, holding her as if she were as fragile as a rose in bloom, his large hand covering hers. The look on his face was carefully masked, trained into a forced smile for the camera that didn't reach his eyes. The look in his eyes was focused and fierce, almost like he was furious with someone or something.

And he was...*Ian.*

My hands started shaking uncontrollably. I made a fist to hide the trembling as I bent over the picture and tried to push disturbing, unbidden thoughts away. *Not Ian. Not Ian. Not Ian! Ian's real dad? But how could that be?* Dad *was our dad! Both our dad.*

The last thought made me almost physically ill, off balance and dizzy. Like the world had tipped off its axis and spun the wrong direction. I swallowed hard against the bile rising in my throat.

It was like looking at Ian dressed up for eighties day in high school.

"What year is this?" My words came out a croak.

Alexis didn't seem to notice. She clapped in that way people do when they're pleased with themselves, rapid, tiny claps of glee. "Nineteen eighty!" She pointed. "It says right below the picture."

I'd been so shaken that the caption had swum before my eyes. I focused, really concentrating now, trying to get the words to make sense. Someone had written a description beneath the couple in neat, loopy feminine script—*Colleen Smith with Rick Butler, Spring Formal, April, 1980.*

My mouth was so dry, I wasn't sure I could speak. *I'm staring at Seth's parents.*

"That has to be Seth's dad. He looks just like him!" There was absolute delight in Alexis' voice.

I nodded my agreement, reeling and sick, least of all from being hung over. Yeah, Seth looked like the guy in the picture. But Ian was an *exact* clone, down to the cowlick and dimple.

"Could be an uncle." I spoke on autopilot, defending Seth's secret like it was my own.

Alexis was undaunted and undeterred. She called out to him, "Seth, do you have any uncles?"

He looked up from his cooking, frowning slightly at the odd, out-of-the-blue question. "Yeah."

Alexis persisted, like a bloodhound on the scent. "Blood uncles?"

I tried to warn him with a subtle shake of my head, but he wasn't looking at me. He was staring at her.

"Mom's brother," he said. "Why?"

"No Butler uncles? Like, is your dad a twin?"

"No. What are you girls looking at?" He poured a cup of coffee.

"Nothing!" Alexis singsonged her answer and turned to me. "See?" Alexis whispered as she tapped the photo. "This *is* his dad. Has to be."

Seth came in and set the coffee in front of me. "What are you looking at?" He leaned over to see.

"You never told us you were a legacy, Seth." Alexis pointed to the picture. "If these aren't your parents, I'll turn in my amateur sleuth badge."

He stared at the picture in stunned, stony silence. "Where did you get that?" His voice held a dangerous edge.

"The house archives in the study room. It was stuffed in an old file cabinet that's full of ancient tests and study notes." Her face lit up. "Isn't this fun? I love history and looking at old pictures. These *are* your parents, right?" Alexis stared up at him, not understanding why he seemed upset.

He hesitated.

For an instant, I thought he would deny it.

But he nodded. "Yes." He spoke the word in a hard staccato.

"Why didn't you tell us your mom was a Double Deltsie?" She sounded genuinely curious and excited. And perplexed, because it was obviously glorious news.

"It's none of anyone's damn business." His words slammed into the pleasantness of the morning like a slap.

Alexis blushed, looking stunned by the sharpness and pain in Seth's voice.

Zach came in from the kitchen, carrying a pan of scrambled eggs and cheese, glaring at his roommate like he'd committed a capital crime. "Seth? What's going on?"

Seth winced. "Sorry, Alexis." He turned and stalked out of the room.

I couldn't take it anymore. I needed air. Things were falling into odd places. Snatches of things were coming together in a way that made me uncomfortable—Ian's cryptic reasons for taking a job here; Ian looking like Seth *and* his dad; our parents all being in school here together at the same time; both having older brothers the same age.

I jumped to my feet. "I have to go."

I grabbed my backpack, coat, and purse, and was out the door before anyone could stop me.

"Maddie! Maddie, wait!"

I heard Seth calling after me. I ignored him and kept going.

Seth

I chased after Maddie in my bare feet. Outside on the frozen pavement where a gentle snow was beginning to fall. I was so numb I didn't even feel the bite of the cold. Yeah, I'd acted like a douche to Alexis. And made Maddie uncomfortable. I had to explain. But only to her. Everyone else and their curiosity could go to hell.

Shit. Alexis didn't deserve my wrath, either. I watched Maddie drive away until she was out of sight. Alexis was still sitting at the table when I went back in. Zach sat next to her with his arm around her, glaring at me.

I took a deep breath. "I overreacted. I'm sorry, Alexis. Mom's a sore subject with me. Do me a favor—don't show that picture to anyone else. I don't want the girls to know and treat me differently. That's the last shit I want."

She stared at me and nodded. Without warning, she ripped the page out of the scrapbook and held it out to me. "Here." She shook it at me. "We all have crap we'd rather not talk about."

She shot a quick glance at Zach.

I knew what she was thinking. Zach had his own demons.

"Take this. Your secret's safe with me." She shook it again.

Grateful, I took it from her.

She stood and threw her arms around me, pulling me into a ferocious hug. "It's okay." Her eyes sparkled with sympathy when she looked up at me. "Friends?"

Girls, they could rip you up inside with their sympathy and understanding!

I nodded and swallowed a lump in my throat. "Yeah."

She squeezed me again before she let go. "What are you going to do about Maddie? You can't just let her go."

I shrugged.

"She's not another of your hookups."

There was that fierceness in her voice again. Like she was protecting me and Maddie. Making a statement of fact because things were so clear in her eyes.

"Make a romantic gesture." Alexis studied me. "Soon. As in before the day is out. Otherwise, she'll get the wrong idea."

She patted the chair next to her. "Come. Have some breakfast. Then you can shower and we'll think of something."

Maddie

I was still shaking when I got back to my place and parked in the space directly in front of the apartment. When I slid out of the car, I spotted Olivia in our kitchen window, which faced the parking lot.

She waved.

I waved back, knowing I was in for the college inquisition.

She was waiting for me in the two-by-three square of cracked vinyl we grandly called the entryway. "The shacker returns! Be glad you had such a short walk of shame."

Usually, I would have smiled and laughed at her teasing. Tossed it right back at her. Today, I fought back tears.

"That must have been some study date!" She whistled low, like, *wow*. "I want *all* the details."

She stopped short. "All right, what's wrong? What the hell happened? Am I going to have to kick him in the balls and make a eunuch out of him for you?"

That was so like Olivia, always coming to my defense. I was already an emotional wreck. I completely lost it and began sobbing my heart out.

She grabbed me and pulled me into a hug as I murmured incoherently about blowing things and going too fast.

Olivia was the best friend I'd ever had. She held on to me fiercely and stroked my hair like I was her child. "It can't possibly be as bad as you think. And if he's not the one, as in at least your next boyfriend, better to know now than after you've invested more time in him. You had some hot sex and a good time. Now you move on."

I kept blubbering. "No, it's much worse." I pulled back and wiped my eyes. "I think we might be related."

Olivia's eyes flew open so wide she looked like one of those big-eyed plush toy animals she had on her bed. "What?" She led me to the sofa. "Where did this crazy idea come from? Is that the wine talking? Tell me *everything*."

Even the dim light in our apartment hurt my eyes. I put my head in my hand and covered them. "Crap. I have a killer headache. Too much wine."

"Hang on. Have you eaten anything?"

I shook my head.

"You need to eat something innocuous." She went to the kitchen and returned with a glass of water, a generic store-brand cherry toaster pastry, frosted, our infamous bag of peas for icing wounds, and two ibuprofen. She handed me the bag of peas. "On the head. Cold on the head. Heat on the feet."

After I complied, she handed me the toaster pastry. "Eat this first."

"Yes, Mom." I wrinkled my nose, but after the first bite, the pastry tasted good and I felt less ridiculous about having a bag of peas on my head. I finished the pastry and took the ibuprofen. "What would I do without you?"

She smiled. "Whenever you're ready to talk..."

I nodded. "First, you have to swear, on your life, not to tell anyone about this. *Ever.*"

"That serious?" She pursed her lips. "All right, I swear. You can absolutely trust me."

Which I knew. Olivia had a sense of honor and loyalty totally uncommon to mankind. She was the *only* one I would trust with my torturous thoughts.

"You know how you were teasing me about Seth looking like Ian?" I told her the whole story.

"Coincidence," she said when I finished.

"No, you don't get it. I wish I had that picture to show you. Ian looks *exactly* like Seth's dad."

"In case you haven't noticed, there are common looks in this world." She bumped me playfully. "That's why we have that saying that everyone has a twin out there somewhere."

I shook my head. "Not like this."

She studied me. "What are you saying? That your parents adopted Ian?"

The thought had crossed my mind on the drive home. But it didn't make any sense. Why would Mom drop out of school to adopt a Double Delstie's baby? How could she have known then that Dad would get cancer and she would struggle for years and years to get pregnant? She'd never even mentioned someone named Colleen.

Then there were the pictures of Mom in the hospital with Ian, looking pale and delicate after giving birth. She couldn't have faked those.

I shook my head. "No. Ian is Mom's. I know she gave birth to him."

Olivia whistled like my assumptions were just fully dawning on her. "Wow! Way to make an accusation. Do you really think your mom had a thing with Seth's dad, got pregnant, and trapped your dad into marrying her to cover it?" Her eyes were wide. "That's ridiculous! Anyone with eyes could see how much your parents loved each other. Your dad was crazy for her."

I nodded. "I know. He *was* crazy for her. But you know Mom. She's...reserved. Now I'm wondering—was she as crazy for Dad? If it's true she had someone else's baby, it shatters everything. My childhood is nothing more than a myth."

Olivia gave me a sympathetic look. "Your childhood, your relationship with your mom and dad and Ian are all your authentic experiences. This changes *nothing*." Her undying protectiveness came out again. "Let's not jump to conclusions. You have no *proof* of anything."

"Yes, but—"

"No buts." Her tone was firm.

"Yes, there is a but. How can I date Seth now? With these suspicions hanging over my head? I can't very well ask him. That's like dropping a bomb. 'Hey, by any chance, did your dad knock up my mom in college and she have his kid?'" I sighed. "Like Seth would know, anyway. If Mom didn't tell me or Ian, why would Seth know?" I took another deep breath. "I mean, what if Seth and I share a brother?"

I couldn't believe what I was saying. Spoken out loud, it sounded preposterous.

Olivia gave my shoulders another squeeze. "So?"

I frowned. "How, can you be so calm! This is...this is disastrous."

She shook her head. "I don't see how. Let's play out the worst-case scenario—Ian is the son of your mom and Seth's dad. That makes Ian a half-brother to both of you. But you and Seth aren't related. And you weren't raised together like brother and sister in a blended family. What's the problem?"

She made a good point. But I was still leery.

"If Seth and I get past this, whatever this is, a bump? And get into a relationship, eventually it could all come out. Then what?"

"If that happens, you deal with the fallout." She shook me playfully. "Hey, maybe this is the good thing your intuition was telling you about! Found family members." She grinned like she was teasing me again.

I shook my head. "Right. I don't think so. If Seth knows anything about this, he's a brilliant actor. He looked at that picture, too. His only response was to get mad that Alexis had found out his mom was a Double Deltsie." I rearranged the peas on my head. "What would you do?"

She looked up in thought. "How much do you like this guy?"

"I've only known him a few days."

"You're hedging." Olivia sighed. "Don't BS me."

"I've never felt this way before."

She grinned. "That's better. That's what I thought!"

She sounded way too happy about it.

"Given that's the case, what would it hurt to give it a little more time? Find out the truth before you throw something away that has the potential to be life-changing."

Her smile softened. "You could be *completely* wrong, you know. Vivid imagination and all that." She paused. "Just see what happens, okay? I mean, if you feel this passionately about him, what can it hurt?"

CHAPTER NINE

Maddie

Olivia was right, but her point was probably moot. My promising beginning with Seth had spiraled into a disastrous end. I took a shower to clear my head. And stupidly checked my phone the minute I got out. As if I expected Seth would text me. How was I going to face him in lab on Thursday after running out on him? How would I ever explain?

I dressed, dried my hair, and settled down to study at the kitchen table. Or, more accurately, deride myself for overreacting and blowing things with Seth.

I carried on an internal conversation with myself, the equivalent of picking the petals off a daisy to decide whether I pursued him or not. A big part of me wanted to take a chance on love, throw caution and convention to the wind, and text him. Guys weren't the only ones who could put themselves out there.

On the other hand, if my vivid imagination had any merit to it, I was flirting with danger each time I flirted with Seth. There was no way in the world I would ever intentionally do anything to hurt my big brother. Or Mom.

I racked my brain, trying to come up with an innocuous, totally stealth way to find a way to find out if Mom had ever even met Rick Butler. I guessed I could ask her directly. Toss his name out there and watch her reaction. Mom had always been honest with me. I'd thought.

Someone pounded on our front door. I jumped, startled out of my thoughts. Olivia was expecting one of her lab partners, but she was up in her room getting ready to go out. I was closest to the door and in a total state of dress.

"I'll get it!" I yelled to her.

I threw the door open without a second thought. And there stood Seth, holding a wine bottle with a single red rose in it like this was a scene from an Italian restaurant.

He held it out to me, a heart-melting look of apology on his face. "You forgot your homework. I thought you might need this for proof of tasting or something."

He looked completely adorable, almost like the bottle was his heart in his hand. And a red rose? Who could resist that?

As I reached for it, our hands brushed. The passion I felt for him surged through me.

I'm doomed in love.

I stared at the rose. At the bottle. Looked back into his eyes.

"Thanks," I finally managed to stammer. "Repurposing thrown away objects, that's sweetly green of you."

He grinned and my heart became a puddle.

I smiled back at him, feeling unreasonably happy to see him. "The prof hasn't mentioned bringing in the bottles."

He stood awkwardly in the doorway.

Maybe I should have invited him in, but I was still debating whether it was wise to jump off this precipice.

He stuffed his hands in his pockets. "Want to get some coffee? I hear it's good for clearing hangovers."

"Are you implying I got drunk last night?"

"I'm saying I did. And I want to talk to you. And apologize and explain."

"You don't have to apologize. I should be the one apologizing for running off." I stepped back and gestured toward the interior of my apartment. "You could come in. I can make you coffee here."

Olivia appeared at the top of the stairs. "Is Cody here already?" She stopped short when she spotted Seth.

He saw her and whispered, "I'd rather go somewhere neutral. And publicly private, if you know what I meant."

"That sounds ominous." I gripped the wine bottle tightly, like I was in danger of dropping it.

His eyes twinkled. "Just fair."

Olivia cleared her throat. "Hey."

I turned to her. "Olivia, I don't think you've met Seth, my cooking lab partner." I didn't know why I introduced him so coyly. "We were just going for coffee." I winked at Seth. "I'll get my coat."

Seth had driven to my place. Even though it wasn't a long walk to The College Grind, it was on the opposite end of campus. Up a hill and then down another hill. And then back down one. He insisted on driving there. It was, as usual, packed. And smelled deliciously of warm beverages of all types.

"On me." He stepped to the counter. "Order whatever you want."

Coffee sounded surprisingly good. I ordered a mocha and a sandwich and offered to pay for the latter. But he wouldn't hear of it.

We waited for our order and found a table out of the main traffic. My favorite battered green one. I always grabbed it when I could. It was a good place to study and people-watch. The tables were an eclectic mixture. I didn't know why I liked that one so well. It just seemed...lucky. I took its availability as a good sign.

We sat in awkward silence while we each sipped our coffee and I picked at my sandwich. Then we both spoke at once and laughed.

"I need to apologize first," he said.

"No, I do. Really." I twirled my coffee cup. "I'm usually not flighty. But I guess in this case I was, like, literally a flight risk. You were right not to trust me." I gave him a shaky smile.

I took a deep breath. "It's just...things were moving too fast. And I got scared—"

"Wait!" His smile was killer. "Isn't that my line?"

I felt myself blush as I smiled. "Is that how you feel, too?"

He shrugged. "Maybe. Yeah."

I was actually relieved. "I don't know..." I couldn't find the right words. "I'm not looking to rush into anything. But I'm not looking to just hook up, either." I paused. "Does that make any sense?"

He smiled like he understood and was as relieved as I was. "Absolutely. I like you, Maddie. Probably way too much. I'd like to get to know you better."

The puddle that was my heart beat a little faster. "I'm not usually a flight risk, though."

His smile reached his eyes. Like he understood.

I had that sense again that I'd known him forever. And that filled me with joy and scared me to death at the same time. Maybe it was because he reminded me so much of Ian.

"I can't blame you. I was acting like a douche toward Alexis."

"She caught you by surprise. You didn't want anyone to know about your mom."

His eyes lit up. "Not a good excuse." He frowned and took a deep breath. "I need to explain about Mom."

I reached across the table and covered his hand with mine. "No, you don't. I understand family pain."

He held my gaze. "You don't understand. I *need* to talk to someone about it."

How did he do it? Reel me in more and more with everything he did? Be vulnerable and intimate and sexy all at the same time? Make my heart swell for him with a cocktail of emotions I couldn't separate and give names. And didn't understand at all.

I squeezed his hand and smiled encouragingly at him.

His returning smile was filled with relief. "Only Zach knows this shit. Mom's a touchy subject with me. You should know why, in case it comes up again."

His Adam's apple bobbed. "She abandoned me when I was just a few weeks old. Put me in my crib. Covered me with a blanket. Left me for Dad to find screaming when he got home from work. Walked out, locked the door, and didn't ever come back."

Too late I realized I'd let my horror show.

He covered our hands with his other hand and squeezed like I needed reassurance. And maybe I did. I couldn't even imagine.

"Yeah." He nodded.

"But why?" I was still stunned. "How could she?"

If eyes really are mirrors to the soul, his pain was soul deep and bared there like he wanted me to see it. Like he wanted me to run if I was going to.

He sighed. "Dad said she left because she loved me and thought it was best. I didn't understand. Until I got older. And found out she suffered from postpartum depression so bad she was suicidal. She'd been having thoughts of killing both of us."

I gasped involuntarily.

He smiled sadly. "I know, right? Hard to take." He took a deep breath. "Dad says she left because she was afraid she'd act on her thoughts." He snorted. "That doesn't explain why she never came back."

I bit my lip and pulled my hand free to reach across the table and stroke his cheek. "I'm so sorry. Where did she go?"

He shrugged. "Nobody knew. She vanished into thin air. Didn't tell anyone. Not even my grandparents. Everyone says Dad went crazy with worry about her. She was the love of his life. Seeing that picture of Alexis', and how happy they'd been in college, just reminded me of all I cost them."

I bit back my thoughts that they didn't look all that happy in that picture. In fact, I guessed they'd been fighting. But I couldn't say that. "Seth, don't. It's not your fault—"

He caught my hand and kissed my palm, pressing it against his lips as if he desperately needed the connection with me. Finally, he let it go and guided my hand to the table, still held tightly in his.

"Dad filed a missing person report. Hired a private detective to find her. Put his life on hold to care for me and find her. Meanwhile, the police suspected him of foul play."

There weren't words.

"It took him six months, but he finally found her living with some other guy in California. She wanted a divorce. Dad gave it to her. When I was eighteen and leaving for college, I pressed him about it. Yelled at him and accused him of not fighting for her."

He took another deep breath. "Dad said he tried. But she wouldn't." He swallowed hard again. "I heard, through a gossipy great-aunt of mine, that she refused as long as he kept me. She wanted him to give me to her parents to raise. At least for a while. He wouldn't give me up."

"Your dad must love you a lot." My words didn't seem to comfort him. "Is that when you were fighting with him and he cut off your college funds?"

Seth nodded. "Yeah. We really went at it, trying to hurt each other. I was furious at him for getting her pregnant with me and putting us all through this. He never fought back and defended himself."

Seth looked away. "Finally my grandma set me straight. She couldn't stand the rift between us. She made a special trip to campus to talk to me in person." He paused. "She told me that after my older brother was born, my mom had spun into a severe depression. So severe that when she finally came out of it, my parents decided it was too dangerous to have more children.

"But when my brother died, Mom was inconsolable. He'd been her life. She wanted another child to replace him. She begged Dad."

Seth got a faraway look in his eyes. "He offered to adopt. But she wanted her own biological child. That was the only way to replace her boy. Finally, against Dad's better judgment, he relented." Seth looked absolutely miserable. "And then there was me."

My heart broke for him.

"I was supposed to be the child that saved her and their marriage. Instead, I was the baby who broke up our family and drove my mom almost mad."

"No!" I leaned toward him. "You can't think that! You didn't have a say in any of it. They knew the risks. They must have tried to treat her—"

"Yeah," he said. "That's what I tell myself." His voice broke.

I bit my lip, unsure whether I should ask what was on my mind. "Where is she now? Do you ever see her?"

"She's dead, Maddie." His tormented eyes filled with incredible sadness. "When I was eight, she remarried, got pregnant, had a stillborn baby, and committed suicide four days later."

I paused, struck dumb with sorrow. What a tragedy.

"I'm sorry." It was the only thing I could think of to say.

"Yeah." He paused. "You and I have a connection, Maddie. Now that you know the worst about my family, what do you say? Can we start over? Just take it slow and see where it goes?"

What could I say? He'd just bared his soul to me. And proposed exactly what I'd wanted. I couldn't very well dump my crazy, unfounded suspicions on him now. Or tell him to take a hike. And so I did what my heart demanded, on all counts. I leaned forward and kissed him gently, as if he might shatter.

He pressed his forehead against mine. "I'll take that as a yes."

My heart pounded in my ears as I thought quickly. "Yes, on one condition."

"You have a condition?" He sounded genuinely surprised.

"No posting about us on social media."

"You want a secret relationship?" He sounded uncertain.

"In a way, yes." I laughed to lighten the mood. "For good reason. My older brother is here at the university." I licked my lips. "He's what you might call overprotective. I don't want him coming down on your ass. It's just best for now if he doesn't know about us."

Seth tipped my chin up so that our eyes met. "I don't need any big brothers in our business. Deal."

He kissed me again, with the sweet gentleness of starting over.

CHAPTER TEN

Maddie

And so our relationship started off again slow. With slow, tender kisses. Lingering and slow to leave each other's presence. Delaying our goodbyes until goodbye faded and joined with good morning. Slow lovemaking sessions that left me eager and trembling and each of us breathless and begging for completion. With wanting him all the time. With being slow to admit I was in love with him.

Seth's power was in his vulnerability and ability to make me laugh. In the way I felt connected to him. We talked about everything, as if we had known each other forever. As if we were connected by an unbreakable bond. Like family.

I ignored the little warning bells that popped up in moments of quiet. *Maybe he is family.* I ran over them with music. I even started studying to music instead of the quiet I'd always preferred, just to drown out the doubts.

I opened up about the feelings of loss since my dad died. Told him things I'd only shared with Ian and Olivia. Shared my fears.

I told him about Mom and Ken. "Mom's settling for Ken. I know it. I have to pretend to be happy for her." I took a deep breath, trying to find the right words to express what I felt. "It's just that she loved Dad so much. He was the love of her life. And I think Ken is only a good friend."

"Can't a person have more than one love of their life?" His tone of voice was serious. He wasn't mocking or making fun of me.

"Isn't that the definition of 'the love of your life'? Emphasis on the 'the.' One." I brought up their engagement picture on my phone and showed it to him. "This is them."

Partly, it was to throw Seth off the scent. He wanted to know everything about me. I wouldn't show him Ian's picture. Not that he'd asked. But if he did, I would find a way to avoid it. Just in case. But there was no harm in Mom's.

"Your mom's gorgeous." He bumped me with his shoulder. "She looks a little bit like mine did."

"Really?" I stared at Mom's picture, mentally comparing her to the brief glimpse I'd had of his mom. Chilled by the thought because of the implications—

did his dad have a type of woman he preferred? Were both of our moms it?

"That's a compliment to *both* of you," he said. "You look like her. I'm sure you've been told that a million times before. You could be her clone."

He was right. People told me that all the time. I would even go to school and people who'd never met her would tell me they'd seen my mom at the grocery store or wherever. That it had to be her.

I almost opened my mouth to say, *What you see is what you'll get if you stick with me for another thirty-plus years.* But that was way too committed for both of us. I wasn't thinking that far into the future. I wasn't thinking into the future at all. Because the future meant making decisions and potentially dangerous revelations. I was living purely in the moment. And I liked it that way.

"You *really* think our moms look alike?" I almost willed him to change his mind.

"Not exactly alike." Seth studied the picture. "Same coloring, shape of face, and build. How old is your mom?"

"Fifty-four."

"Wow. She doesn't look it. Looking at her, I would guess early forties. At the oldest." He frowned like he was thinking. "She's the same age as my dad." His voice became soft. "The same age Mom would be."

My heart stopped even though it was a totally innocuous statement. And broke a little for him. I was sure he was picturing what his mom would look like if she were still alive. I felt a well of longing for Dad.

I squeezed Seth's hand. "Judging from her off-spring, I'm sure she'd still be a total hottie."

His smile lit up my world, even when it was tinged with sadness.

"Back to guessing ages. You would be wrong, oh great age-guessing swami," I said, deflecting. "Don't ever go into age-guessing as a profession. You suck at it."

He shook his head like he wasn't listening to me. "No, seriously. I bet people tell her that all the time." He grinned at me. "And confuse her for your older sister," he said with a wicked gleam in his eyes. "If you age like her, you'll be hot in your fifties."

I rolled my eyes.

He looked like he was still thinking. "She went to school here, didn't she?"

Oh, crap. I didn't like where this was going. I nodded. "For a year." I pointed to her smile in the picture on my phone. "See that? And the way she's leaning away from Ken ever so slightly."

Seth squinted at the picture like he didn't see it. "She's leaning away?"

"Ever so slightly," I said. "That means there's no passion. Just friendship."

"Friendship isn't enough?" Seth was sitting next to me. He ran his hand up my thigh. The look in his eyes was absolutely teasing.

And took my breath away.

He knew it would never be enough for us.

"You know it's not." I kissed him.

He took another look at the picture of Mom and Ken. "Man, I think my dad would really go for your mom."

Again with the heart stop. He didn't know what he was saying.

"I should introduce her to my dad. Test your theory. See if he can use the old Butler charm and steal her away from her dear old friend Ken. Dad's a lady-killer." He winked. "Or so I've been told."

"No!" The word exploded out of my mouth and hung in the air.

Seth's eyes went wide. "Chill." He looked perplexed by my reaction. "I was just joking, Mads."

I laughed nervously to cover. "Do you want us to end up as brother and sister? Don't even joke about something like that."

I shuddered for exaggeration, trying to get past my overreaction.

He laughed and kissed me lightly. "You're putting the cart way before the horse. And even if something crazy and outlandish, and I might add, totally improbable, like our parents marrying and making us step-sibs did happen, it wouldn't change a thing between us."

He bumped me playfully with his shoulder. "Think of the perks. We could spend our breaks under the same roof." He wiggled his eyebrows and smiled, full of innuendo and desire.

I laughed, hoping he was right. That nothing changed between us.

Having each lost a parent was another bond. Seth shared his grief over being motherless. That was what *slow* meant to us—falling headlong.

Even Ian commented on how happy I seemed when I met him at the SUB for lunch. And suspected a guy was the reason.

"I want to meet this guy." He dumped his tray and stacked it above the garbage can.

"I didn't say there is a guy," I said as we walked into the common area.

"There is."

"When I'm ready." I wasn't sure I ever would be.

"You used to talk to me about your crushes." Ian looked almost hurt.

On impulse, I hugged him. Fiercely. And rested my head on his chest, letting him wrap me in his brotherly embrace.

"Yeah." I listened to the beat of his heart. "And I will again. I promise. It's just—"

"I wouldn't approve of this guy?" He caught me by the arms and tipped my chin up so I had to look him in the eye. "Baby sis?"

I led with the truth. "He's a lot like you."

He smiled. "What's that supposed to mean? Is that a good thing or a bad thing?"

"It means he's different." Which was true in so many ways. "And easily scared by the threat of commitment." I tried to sound jokey.

"Like being introduced to your brother?"

I nodded.

"Sissy, if that scares him off, he's not worth keeping."

I nodded. "I know. But it's too soon. We've been seeing each other for less than a month."

Ian nodded and pulled me back into a hug. He kissed the top of my head. "Understood."

Olivia liked Seth immediately.

"I see what you mean about him looking like Ian!" she said when I got home from that coffee date with Seth. "They look like brothers."

I shook my head. "That's what I said! But you're not supposed to tell me that. I'm already freaking, remember?"

"He even sounds a little like Ian." She had a tease in her voice.

I gave her a deadpan look. "You're supposed to be on my side, not scaring me."

"I'm not scaring anyone. I still think it's just coincidence."

"Nice cover."

Within a few weeks, I spent so many nights with Seth that Olivia complained she never saw me anymore.

"You can stay here, you know. Once in a while," she said.

"No. This is a you and me place," I told her. "Zach has Alexis over all the time. And they each have their own bedroom *and* bathroom."

But we spent a lot of time at my place, too.

In the kitchen, Seth and I were more creative than the rest of the class combined. And so in tune that even

Chef Steven noticed. He started calling us his MadSeth team, which he thought was a hysterically funny pun because it sounded like "mad chef."

And, I thought, maybe he was right. This was mad.

It was reckless and careless the way I carried on. We held hands and kissed in public in the SUB, at The College Grind, in the mall between classes. We couldn't keep our hands off each other.

I spent night after night at his apartment. We were affectionate in Chef Steven's kitchen. In short, we were extremely public. But I was deliriously happy. So what did I care? Happier than I ever remembered being. Truly happy for the first time since Dad died. In a way where life seemed bright and bubbly again.

Seth

A few days before Valentine's Day I was walking to class when my phone rang. "Morgan? It's been a while."

I was surprised Morgan hadn't been in touch before. She and I had been pretty tight at the Double Deltsie house. Her boyfriend Dakota was Zach's good friend from high school. He hung out with us at our place from time to time, but Morgan never came with him.

"You could always stop by the house and say hi." She had a direct, sparkling way of speaking that sounded sexy and bitchy at the same time.

I fired right back, "Your boyfriend hangs out at our place. You could always come by with him and see Zach and me, baby."

She laughed. "Yeah, but Alexis is there most of the time, too, I hear."

"She's your little. Are you afraid of her? I thought you two made up."

Morgan sighed. "Oh, we have. But, you know, as her big I like to give her her space."

"Intellectual alibis are shit, Morgs. Come over some time for my sake, then. I miss you."

She laughed again, that effervescent, rich laugh that finally sounded happy. And sober. I was glad for her. Morgan could be a real bitch when she was drunk. Sober, she was pretty sweet.

Morgan had been through a bunch of shit in the last few years. A year ago, if anyone had told me that dating Dakota Bradley would help her clean her act up, I would have told them they were full of crap. After I told them there was no way in hell she'd ever date him, period.

Dakota was Zach's best friend from high school— and an arrogant frat boy, in my original opinion. After I moved in with Zach, I had to tolerate him. But as I got to know him, he was growing on me. And no one could deny he'd been good for Morgan.

"What's up?" I asked.

"Does something have to be up?" she said. "I can't just call?"

I laughed now, too. "You can, but you seldom do."

"Okay, you caught me. I just ran into someone by The College Grind who reminded me so much of you, I actually called out to him thinking he *was* you. You have a doppelgänger on campus, Seth! It wasn't until I got close that I realized my mistake. Anyway, seeing him reminded me how much I miss you. I just had to call and share. And catch up."

"What? I have a twin." I frowned. I didn't know why I didn't find it amusing. It should have been. "And here I thought I was a unique, special snowflake."

"Not a twin." She paused. "More like an older brother."

I swore I heard confusion in her voice.

"When I called your name out to him and he didn't answer, I caught up to him and grabbed his arm. He introduced himself. He's a prof!"

"A prof? There has to be a way to use that to my advantage."

"Shut up! You would think of that first." She giggled. "And not how embarrassing it was for me. Or it would have been, if he hadn't been so damn gracious and charming. Like you, Seth. He even has your single dimple."

I smiled at her flattery. Morgan and I had always flirted with each other. But it didn't mean anything. "And you see, that's why Dakota doesn't like me. Because his girl thinks I'm charming."

"He likes you just fine. Now that you aren't a houseboy."

"You wound me, baby. Being a houseboy is honest work."

"Sometimes," she said.

Yeah, we'd pulled a few stunts. "Does this prof have a name?"

"Oh, crap." she said. "He told me. But I'm spacing on it now. I'll think of it. Eventually."

CHAPTER ELEVEN

Maddie

I was studying at my kitchen table when my mom called.

"You must be busy!" she said in falsely cheerful voice. "You haven't called in a while."

I felt a stab of guilt. I'd been avoiding talking to her. Because of Seth.

"Well, you know, it's my killer junior year. You've warned me since I was in high school that this is the worst year of college. That the professors are determined to make your life hell, flunk you out, and guarantee you don't get more than four hours of sleep a night. Looks like your dire predictions are pretty much coming true. All I do is study." I laughed, but it came out nervously. I crossed my fingers, hoping she didn't notice.

"Did I say that?" She laughed again because she knew she had. "I thought maybe there was a boy involved in your neglect of your mother."

Oh, crap! I hoped Ian hadn't said anything to her.

"Any plans for Valentine's Day?"

"Stop prying, Mom," I said with as much good humor as I could manage. But as I'd learned from reading a ton of spy novels in high school, when lying, it's always best to lead with as much of the truth as possible. "But I do have a date with my cooking lab partner."

Mom perked up. "Really?"

I knew immediately I'd made a mistake. Ian hadn't told her a thing. She'd been fishing and I'd just swum into her net.

"It's nothing serious, Mom. Just a date."

"Hmmph," she said. "Still, it sounds promising. Is he handsome?"

"Very."

"Always a plus," Mom said. "And I suppose he has a name?"

"Seth, Mom. And that's as much intel as you're getting out of me. Don't make too much of this."

She laughed again. "Sorry. Hey, I'm actually calling about spring break. It's only a month away. There's a big annual bridal show I'd like us to go to. And I thought I'd set up some dress-shopping appointments while you're home. Wouldn't that be fun?"

My heart lurched. "You've set a date?"

"More like a season. We've decided on a summer wedding. Next year, after you graduate. Then we'll both officially be empty-nesters. Footloose and fancy free."

I was her reason for waiting? I really didn't understand it. Deep down, I felt she was stalling.

"You didn't have any big plans for spring break, did you?"

"No," I said, slowly. I wasn't the party-like-crazy type of spring break girl.

"Good! Then it's settled. I'll buy the bridal fair tickets."

"Mom? Did you ever date a frat guy?" The question popped out of my mouth before I even thought.

Seth's dad had been in a frat. My dad hadn't. If Mom had never dated a frat guy, problem solved. So simple, right? In retrospect, the question was brilliant.

"Oh, boy!" She sounded wary. "This Valentine's date of yours isn't a frat boy, is he?"

Like a lot of independents, Mom had never liked the Greeks. But then, both she and I were introverts. Introverts didn't really thrive in the extroverted Greek system.

"No."

She let out a sigh of relief. "Then why the question?"

"No reason. Just wondering about your college experience. You never talk about it."

"There's not much to tell," she said.

I persisted. "So? Frat boys?"

"No."

I should have been satisfied. Totally relieved. Except that...she had hesitated before answering. And her voice had been soft and unsure. Like she was lying and felt guilty about it.

On Valentine's Day, Seth sent me a red rose in class. One of the clubs on campus sold and delivered them as a fundraiser. It came complete with a chocolate heart. If that had been the only rose he sent me, I would have been happy. But that night, he showed up with another dozen.

"That makes thirteen," I teased him. "Isn't that unlucky?"

I was feeling superstitious. Things had been going too well.

"A baker's dozen unlucky? In what universe?" He pulled me into his arms and kissed me.

He was confident that way. He liked to laugh in the face of fate. But he didn't know what I knew. If he had known, would he have been so glib?

I didn't like to think about it. Was I keeping a secret from him? Or just keeping my unfounded suspicions to myself? I liked to think the latter.

He took me to a little Mexican restaurant for dinner. Then out for red drinks at a local bar. He seemed nervous, like there was something on his mind. Half a dozen times he started to ask me something, then stopped himself short.

He had something important on his mind. A surprise, maybe? The evening had already been perfect. But I was greedy, and more was always better.

Midway through my second cherry martini, he took my hand and looked into my eyes.

I saw myself mirrored there, holding my breath as if I was waiting for a proposal. But it was *way* too soon for that. Even so, I couldn't breathe.

"What are you doing for spring break?" His eyes were serious, and he seemed more nervous than I'd ever seen him.

I spoke without thinking, or paying attention to the signals he'd been giving me all night. "Going to a bridal fair with my mom. This is one of the big bridal shows. One of the best. It's held, like, twice a year, and she's dying for me to go with her. Doing some wedding dress shopping. She absolutely insisted I come home for it. She has this romantic notion of picking out her dress with her daughter. And I'm probably checking in on my internship—"

His face fell. His grip loosened on my hand.

Which is when I realized this *was* the big question. The surprise. And I'd just trampled all over it.

"But that won't take the *whole* week?" He looked hopeful again.

I tilted my head. "No. Why?"

He broke into the most adorable, wobbly, hopeful grin. "Come home with me. For as many days as you can spare. I want you to meet my dad."

I swore his voice shook.

My hands certainly did. And my mouth went dry. "I...I..."

I didn't know what to say. We'd just cruised past the one-month mark. Zach's warnings about Seth rang in my ears. How he bailed on relationships at the one or two-month mark. This was Seth's statement of commitment.

I wanted to go. And at the same time, I wasn't ready to meet his dad. Not for the usual reasons. I wasn't ready for what I might find out.

Seth stared at me, waiting expectantly for an answer. My hesitation was hurting his feelings. I was trapped and I knew it.

I forced a smile and put a falsely bright note in my voice. "Yes!"

He pulled me into a kiss. "You had me worried for a minute. Zach warned you that I'm not the committed type. But he should have warned me about you. I've met my match." He squeezed my hand.

"Meeting your dad is a big step." My voice trembled.

"Yeah." His eyes sparkled. "It is." He paused. "I've never taken a girl home to meet Dad before." He grinned. "I'm scaring you! Don't worry. Dad will *love* you." He swept a lock of hair out of my face and touched my cheek. "Just like I do. I love you, Maddie."

He'd never said *I love you* before. Some people were casual about it, throwing the phrase around lightly. But not me. Not us.

My eyes filled with tears of joy. "I love you, too."

I'd been trying to fight it. But sometimes you can't fight destiny. What were we going to do?

The Friday night a week before spring break, the food science club sponsored a pub crawl. Complete with T-shirts. Of course, I invited Seth. Zach came along. Alexis wasn't twenty-one yet, and the club was strict about that, no fake IDs allowed, so Zach came solo.

A pub crawl was our version of a frat party. We wore T-shirts made specially for the event and went from bar to bar drinking. Only we called it tasting. Like it was part of our food sensory class. Our ale sensory unit. Being food nerds, we also talked about the brewing process and the flavors of the beer and ales. Showing off our knowledge. Half the guys in food science brewed beer in their bathtubs. I was surprised Zach and Seth hadn't tried it yet.

We were a largish group, about thirty of us. The night was pleasant for early March. We walked between bars. When we invaded some of the smaller ones, we practically took them over. By the time we got to The Night Crawler, I was feeling a pleasant buzz.

In the spirit of crawling, I crawled into Seth's lap at the table we commandeered and looped my arms around his neck. I kissed him, fully, tasting the beer on his lips, pressing against him. He was so hot when he was buzzed, too, and his hands roamed all over me. And the bulge in his jeans rubbed against me. I was ready to go back to his place.

"One more round," he whispered directly in my ear. "And we're out of here."

We ordered a sampler platter of regional ales.

As a group, we were loud and laughing. Yelling over the music as we pounded down shots of ales ranging from light to dark and full.

Seth nuzzled my neck. Life seemed perfect until the door opened and let a cold breeze in. An ill wind that blew my brother in. Ian stood at the door with a group of profs and students, looking for a table.

Noooo! No, no, no, no!

I froze. And watched in horror as he scanned the room. My heart stopped while his gaze skimmed over us. Fortunately, Ian had elements of an absentminded professor. When he focused on something, he ignored everything else. He missed us and waved to some guys at a table in the corner. I had to do something. But what?

My skin prickled. It was like I was in a science fiction movie. The kind where someone travels back in time to an earlier part of their life. But if they run into their younger self something horrible happens in the time/space continuum and it's death for everyone.

I had that same feeling now. I couldn't let Ian run into Seth. But he was blocking the door and our table was in the path to both the bar and that corner table he was focused on.

Ian started walking our way. I grabbed Seth's face and kissed him. Fiercely, blocking his face with mine, with one eye open, watching my brother and his group as they walked by. Necking, the new way to become invisible.

I released Seth when Ian was comfortably settled at the bar with his back to us.

Seth's eyes were round with desire. "Don't stop now." He tried to find my lips again.

I dodged him, reached into my purse, and threw a twenty on the table. "We have to go." I caressed Seth's cheek and put all the come-on I could manage in my eyes and voice.

"Now?" His eyes sparkled wickedly.

I leaned in and whispered, "Yes, now. I need you. *Urgently.*"

"Urgently?" He got a sexy grin on his face.

This wasn't a slow seduction. This was an emergency situation.

"That's what I said. This is a need emergency."

His coat was slung over the back of his chair. I pulled his beanie from his coat pocket and tucked it on his head, covering that crown of blond hair so like my brother's.

I slid off his lap and grabbed his hand. "Let's go."

A couple of the guys we were with made lewd remarks and whistled.

"If I were you, man, I wouldn't hesitate." One of them winked and punched Seth in the arm.

What I wouldn't put up with!

As Seth stood, I took his hand. He slid it free from mine. "Don't lose the mood. I'll be right back. I have to take a leak."

Stupid, stupid beer! What could I say to that? Like, no, no bathroom for you! Hold it. You absolutely have to dance all the way back to your place?

He brushed my lips with a kiss and sauntered off, passing just to Ian's left to the small hallway that led to the men's room as I held my breath.

"Hey, Maddie, chill!" one of our group said. "He'll be right back."

But Zach, who knew me best, stared at me. "Are you okay, Maddie? You look like you've seen a ghost."

More like a shadow. "I'm fine. Drank a little too much too fast."

One of the other guys slid his chair away from mine. "If you're gonna puke, don't do it on my shoes."

I frowned at him and tried to mask the horror and relief I felt.

Before I could fall into my seat and cover my face or use one of the guys as a human shield from my brother, Ian turned around, laughing. A group of girls who had been inadvertently running interference between me and my brother and blocking his line of sight moved toward the bathrooms. Leaving Ian a wide-open view of me. There I was, standing out.

Oh, no! He's going to come over here!

I was suddenly stone-cold sober. I had to cut him off at the pass. All right, this wasn't a Western bar, but terminology aside, the idea was the same. I had to stop him from coming to our table. If my friends and class-mates met him, they'd see the resemblance between Seth and him. How could they not?

And then they'd comment on it. I would never hear the end of it. They would insist on the two of them meeting. And highlight the similarity with way too many drunken jokes. And even if I managed to get him away from the table before Seth got back, Seth would be furious with me if he knew my brother was in the pub and I purposefully didn't introduce him.

I acted on instinct. I was at the bar in as few steps as I could manage. I gave my brother a bear hug that made him go "umphh" with the force of it. I neatly spun him back around to face the bar before any of my companions got a look at him. And took up a spot on his right so I could watch for Seth.

My fellow pub crawlers were drinking their ales now, totally preoccupied and getting hammered by the minute. One tragedy averted.

Ian held me at arm's length. "What are you doing here?"

"Pub crawl."

He glanced at my T-shirt and nodded. "Is that what you foodies call it?" He laughed. "We call it Friday night fluids lab."

He still had his coat on, but it was unzipped so I could see his plain shirt.

"No official T-shirt? You're not as organized and official as we are," I teased, trying to keep the nerves out of my voice.

"Mom says you're only home part of the week of spring break. Something about a food science trip to the Methow Valley wine country for a few days? Do you have an official shirt for that, too?"

Yes, that was the lie I'd fed my mom so I could sneak away to Seth's. The food science club was always taking trips to food companies, dairies, or wineries at the end of vacations. Wineries hired a lot of food scientists, so it was a natural. And not at all unusual or suspicious.

"No, no shirt. But we're designing an apron to sell to raise funds for the club." I gave him a playful punch. "But you, you're going to Hawaii! No fair."

"Life's not fair, sis. That's the way it is." He laughed. "A couple of the guys got here early and saved us a table. Want to join us?"

I caught a glimpse of Seth heading back to the table. "Thanks," I said, thinking on my feet. "But this is one of those *Let's not step on each other's toes* situations. I have my club and you have your group. I was just about to leave, anyway." I went up on tiptoes and kissed his cheek. "Let's get together before break."

One of the guys Ian was with tapped his arm and said something to him, distracting Ian just long enough.

"Catch you later!" I said to him, and dashed off.

I managed to intercept Seth, grab my coat, and pull him out of the bar before he had a chance to glance back at Ian. I was so relieved, and euphoric, about having avoided a disastrous chance meeting that my knees almost gave out.

Laughing, I caught Seth's arm and pulled him along.

We ran laughing, tipsy, high on love, hand in hand to his apartment complex up the hill from The Night Crawler.

His apartment was dark and empty. He shut the door and locked it as I shed my coat and shoes and pulled him toward his room. Once inside, I had my T-shirt off before he got the door closed.

"Hey! That's my job."

"Then get over here and do it!" I unzipped my jeans and shimmied out of them.

He threw his arms around me and unfastened my bra. I helped him slide it off my shoulders.

"Now this is a sight I like." He pushed my breasts together until the nipples touched, and he licked them while I moaned softly.

"No teasing." My voice was breathless as I pulled at the hem of his T-shirt, the large twin of mine.

He helped me pull it off and tossed it aside.

I couldn't get him out of his clothes fast enough, kissing him as I disrobed him. Pressing my kisses to his lips, his neck, his chest.

When he was naked and silhouetted in the light that filtered through the thin curtains, I playfully shoved him on his back on the bed. It was crazy, maybe, but the feeling of physically controlling him turned me on. It was only an illusion. He could have overpowered me at any time. But he let me have my way as I climbed on top of him and mounted him.

"No foreplay?" He grabbed my hips as I rode him.

"Isn't that what the whole night has been?" My eyes were adjusting to the dark. I loved looking at him as I moved with him. Loved being on top, breasts bouncing, and seeing the desire on his face. Hearing his moans.

"Keep doing that and I won't be able to hang on long." He pushed up into me with a powerful thrust.

"Neither will I." I leaned down and covered his mouth with mine, running my tongue along his lips.

He tasted seductively like beer and partying. I loved him. I wanted him and no one else. And I was so afraid it would all come crashing down. That our families would fly apart and ruin this beautiful thing.

I broke the kiss. "I love you."

I meant it with all my heart. I loved him like I had never loved anyone.

He caught me off guard and flipped us over, pounding into me as he pressed my arms above my head. "I love you, too. So. Damn. Much."

I gasped with every thrust. Until the waves building in me crashed and the climax that came made me gasp with its power. He kept thrusting, and the aftershocks of pleasure kept coming until tears slid down my cheeks and he collapsed on top of me, hot and sweaty.

His hair smelled like pub food and smoke, fresh air, and wintry nights. I held on to it, trying to memorize everything about this.

"Wow." He took a deep breath. "Pub crawls are my new favorite thing if they always get you this hot."

He had no idea what really drove me.

A tear of both joy and fear slid down my cheek.

"Hey, are you crying?" His voice was incredibly tender as he wiped it away.

"That was so powerful."

The look of satisfaction and love on his face was priceless. Like this had never happened to him like this before, either. So powerful it rocked the foundations of my emotions.

He slid out of me and rolled beside me. "We're going to have to go back to The Night Crawler again. Soon."

"No!"

He leaned up on one elbow and frowned as he looked at me.

"Don't go there again. Not ever. Not without me."

His frown deepened, like he didn't understand me.

And I couldn't explain.

"What we had tonight is such a beautiful thing. Let's not...let's not ruin the memory." It was lame, but it was the best I could do.

I couldn't chance Ian and Seth bumping into each other. I was going to have to do something. Come clean soon. Without ruining everything. But how?

CHAPTER TWELVE

Maddie

A grand deception requires a grand plan. When Mom asked if I needed money for the food science trip, I told her I'd worked off my fee by putting enough hours in at the university-run ice cream shop. Which is what we commonly did. To avoid any objections, I stressed how important it was to my future career to make contacts in all the food industries.

I asked Zach to cover for me if Mom got suspicious. And I threw Mom under the bus by telling Seth that lying to Mom about having to go on a food science trip was the only way I was going to get away with leaving a few days early. Like she was a real bitch or something.

"I'm not ready to tell her about you," I said truthfully. It was the *only* truthful part of my story, but there it was. "She'll read too much into this trip."

Seth hugged me close. "Wow, you really are more commitment averse than I am. Should I be worried?"

"No!" I pressed my head to his chest. "Not at all." I tried to laugh it off. "It's just, Mom will object to me going to a guy's house that she hasn't even heard about. Right now, I don't need the hassle. She's stressed about wedding stuff and...it's just better this way. Trust me."

Friday afternoon, I loaded up my car and headed to Seth's to say goodbye. Olivia and I usually traveled together, but she had flown out earlier in the day to join her family for a week in Cabo. Ian left for Hawaii the next morning.

Zach was driving Alexis home. The three of us were headed to Seattle. Seth was going to the Chelan area. We were going to caravan until Seth peeled off our route and headed north.

They were waiting for me in their parking lot, loaded and ready to go.

I clung to Seth. "I'm going to miss you."

"Six days. And then spring break *really* begins." He kissed me.

"Hey, break it up and let's roll!" Zach slapped Seth on the back.

Seth shoved him away and looked me in the eye. "I'm going to miss you, too." He opened my car door for me. "Drive safely." He closed the door and blew me a kiss through the glass.

And we were off. Two hundred miles into the three-hundred-mile drive, we pulled off to gas up before heading over the mountains. A quick fill up and passionate kiss and Seth and I parted ways. He headed north. Zach, Alexis, and I headed west. I drove the last hundred miles with my music blaring, trying to drown out the thoughts that kept popping up. *This isn't going to work. You're going to ruin everything.*

When I arrived around eight, Mom and Ken were waiting in the living room with the lights on and the blinds open. As soon as my car was in the driveway, they were out on the front porch.

Mom pulled me into a hug the second I stepped out of the car, and then peppered me with questions. "How was the drive? How was the weather over the mountains? How was the traffic? How did you do on your test this morning?"

These were the everyday questions that kept my mom worrying. In her mind, I would always be her baby. A beginner driver in a sea of dangerous traffic and frightening weather conditions.

"I feel good about my test. An A- at worst, I think. Traffic was your usual spring break rush to get out of town, an endless stream. Some maniacs and some idiots."

Which was one of Dad's references. Maniacs were drivers who wanted to go faster than you. Idiots wanted to go slower.

"Weather was fine. Road conditions great."

Which she would have known, because my mom was a consummate weather watcher and would have been checking the DOT mountain pass reports and traffic cameras about every half an hour.

Ken had been standing back, politely watching the reunion. He came forward, gave me an awkward hug, and grabbed my bags when I popped my trunk.

I was hyperaware of Ken. Watching him and Mom like a cat watches prey. Trying to decide how each felt about the other, as if I was some kind of relationship expert. But, corny as it sounded, for the first time ever, I felt like I knew what love was. What it really felt like. The scorch of burning passion. The pang of longing when you were apart. Two hours away from Seth and I missed him already. I texted him that I'd arrived safely.

He texted back, *Home, too, and missing you. I'm a poet and didn't know it!*

I had to suppress a smile.

Mom caught me anyway. You know moms. They have eyes in the backs of their heads and a sixth sense for when you're hiding something from them. She raised one eyebrow. "Good message?"

I shook my head. "Just Zach and his girlfriend saying they got home safely, too."

She didn't look completely satisfied with my answer. "I made cake!"

Ken nodded. "And it looks delicious! I've barely been able to keep my fork out of it."

Ken was in his late fifties. Slender, for the most part. But paunchy in the middle. Out of shape. Average height. Thinning gray hair. Glasses that were serviceable, not stylish.

The best way to describe Ken was bland and average, with a twist of nerd. He was an engineering technical fellow at a large airplane manufacturer. Wind tunnel studies were his specialty. Yeah, boring. And he looked the engineering part, if you know what I mean. On a scale of one to ten, even narrowing the field to guys his age, he maybe rated a four, possibly a five if I were in a super-generous mood.

As he slid past Mom with my bags, the difference between them was startling. Although he was only a few years older than she was, he looked a good ten or fifteen years her senior.

Even casually dressed, Mom was slender and toned, stylish in skinny jeans and an oversize sweatshirt. Her hair balayaged to a beautiful blond that fell to her shoulders, cut in an age-appropriate yet youthful style. An easy ten to his four. A mismatch that gave Ken all the prestige.

I frowned. Ken had been one of Dad's good friends, a longtime bachelor. He was a nice guy. But as a love interest?

"Let's eat!" Mom held the door open for Ken.

I followed Mom and Ken inside.

In the kitchen after he deposited my luggage, I watched Ken watching Mom while she sliced a chocolate layer cake. Their relationship had bloomed since I'd gone to college my sophomore year. I hadn't thought too much about it. Fortunately for me, they kept it private and weren't too mushy while I was around. There was no doubt, watching Ken, that he was a man besotted, in love, head over heels. Now there was a picture. Aren't our heads pretty much always over our heels?

Mom cut him a thick slice of cake and served him first.

He beamed, absurdly pleased. Like he was king for a day.

The thing was, I knew Mom's cake-cutting operandi. It's much easier to get a thick first piece out of a cake than a thin one, like she and I liked. If Ian had been here instead of Ken, he would have gotten the first slice. Any guy, really, would have done.

Mom, on the other hand, treated Ken like they were an old married couple. With consideration and attention. Friendly, but where was the heat? Not that I wanted to see a manifestation of it. But, you know, a glimpse of it would have been somewhat reassuring.

You know how a memory can hit you out of the blue? Strike you and bring up an emotion that has no name but is as clear to you as daylight? One that puts you in another time and place.

I remembered her serving cake to Dad on his last birthday. It was just a snatch of a memory. Nothing special. Just the way she put the cake on the plate, flipping it so the frosting was on the left side of the plate, like he preferred. The way she set the fork alongside.

Just like she was now. With the same look on her face as she assessed the crumb of the cake, as if she was pleased with her baking efforts. The way her face changed to simple kindness as she handed it to Ken, in the way she had to Dad.

I was struck, feeling it almost physically. *She's looking at Ken the same way she used to look at Dad.*

I used to think that was the look of love, romantic love. I mean, everything your family does seems like the norm, the way it is for everyone. Because that's all you know. So that's the way two married people looked at each other in my world.

I'd grown up since then. Now that look was upsetting, illusion shattering. Not because Ken had replaced Dad as the love of her life. But because she wasn't looking at Ken like a woman in love.

It took me a second to breathe again. I remembered Dad on his deathbed, clutching my hand.

"Take care of your mom, Maddie, my baby girl. She's going to need you. And Ian. She's the love of my life." He sounded almost sad.

I had thought, at the time, it was because he was dying. And everything was sad and especially poignant.

He squeezed my hand. "And you two are the love of hers. Hold on to each other."

At the time, it seemed reassuring. It was clear to me now what was missing. He hadn't said he was the love of hers. He'd left himself out. Intentionally. Maybe it wasn't his to tell. Or maybe he knew he wasn't and couldn't lie about it, even with death beckoning.

"Maddie?" Mom was holding a piece of cake out to me.

Startled, I reached for the plate. "Sorry. I zoned out. My brain's fried. Tests. Long drive. Long day." I sighed to cover my real thoughts.

"Completely understandable." She smiled sympathetically as she put a hand on my shoulder. "And under ordinary circumstances, I would let you sleep in tomorrow as long as you like and just catch up on your rest. But tomorrow's the bridal show!" Her exclamation point seemed forced. "We want to get there early before it gets too busy." She patted me. "Sorry. You'll have to keep your zoning out and fatigue to a minimum."

I smiled to reassure her that I was excited for her. It was like we were playing charades. "Are you telling me to eat my cake and go to bed?"

She laughed. "I'm saying I need you fully rested for a day on your feet!"

Across the table from me, Ken was beaming.

Bridal fairs are not for the faint of heart. We pulled up to the Tacoma Dome at minutes before nine. I yawned, still not fully awake even after drinking a tall mocha.

Mom put the car in park and thumped the steering wheel. "This is it!"

She sounded determined more than excited.

I got out of the car and followed her into the event center. There were booths as far as the eye could see, hocking everything from cakes to venues. Flowers, groom's gifts, DJ services, catering, wedding interior design, cakes, and destination honeymoons.

There were brides, brides, brides everywhere, with their entourages in tow.

At the door, a bridal show employee handed us a map and a goodie bag to hold all of our brochures and samples. "Be sure to enter all the drawings! The grand prize is an all-expense paid wedding!" She looked pointedly at me.

I turned to Mom as the crowd carried us inside. "Where do you want to start?"

"Venues." She took a deep breath. "Without a venue, everything else is moot."

I scanned the room. "The booths don't appear to be in any order. We'll have to work our way around the room. To the left or to the right?"

She bit her lip, looking overwhelmed already. "To the right. We'll just go booth by booth."

Walking through the event hall was like being in wedding wonderland. A kind of fantasyland where every booth was another wedding theme. Like you could just step into a booth with a groom and be done.

Some of the booths were decorated with chandeliers and flowers, tables with elegant place settings. Any theme of wedding you wanted, you could find a sample setup of it here.

The first booth we came to was a bakery. Four-tiered cakes covered with the most beautiful gum paste flowers sat in the center. All around them were tables filled with little plastic cups, and I mean tiny, containing bite-size pieces of cake.

"Cake at night. Cake first thing in the morning. It seems to be the theme of my life. I can't escape it."

"We can bypass it," Mom said.

"Not on your life." I stepped forward and read the sign cards. "Chocolate ganache. Raspberry lemonade. Pink champagne!"

One of the women manning the booth approached us. She smiled at me. "Try as many as you like." She handed me a brochure. "Here's our price list and a bit about us. Is this your first bridal show?"

"Yes." I nodded, relieved at her sympathetic smile.

"Have you set a date yet?"

I turned to Mom.

"Summer next year."

"Excellent!" The woman smiled at me. "Plenty of time for planning. Have you booked the venue? Will your wedding be local?"

"Oh!" I finally got it. I pulled Mom forward. "I'm not the bride. My mom is." I pointed to Mom.

"So sorry!" The woman laughed. "One should never assume. But really, you two look like you could be sisters."

And so the flattery and upsell of Mom began as the lady grilled her about what she was looking for and whether she'd picked a bakery yet.

At booth after booth, I was mistaken for the bride and Mom for the mother of the bride. It was a natural enough assumption. There weren't that many fifty-something-year-old brides in attendance. Finally, a woman at one of the photography booths gave Mom a big sticker that said "bride" and a "maid of honor" one for me.

"That should do the trick," the lady said. "Now, have you selected a photographer?"

She'd been nice enough to give us the stickers, so we sat through her speech, entered her drawing, and took her card with a promise to keep her in mind.

"Was it like this when you married Dad?" I asked Mom when we finally took a breather and found a bench to sit on for a few minutes to try and clear our minds from the sensory overload of the show.

"No." She stared out over the booths with a faraway look in her eyes. "We had a small, casual wedding."

Beneath the tiredness, I thought I detected an edge of bitterness and resignation. Not what I expected. Not what I'd hoped for.

"I was pregnant with Ian." She turned to look at me. "I'm sure you've figured that out by now." She sighed. "I had to get married...quickly. Before I showed much more."

It was as if the "quickly" was an afterthought to cover the accidental resentment that had slipped into her voice. *I had to get married* meant something else entirely. Suspecting what I did, I felt the horror of it.

"I wore a loose gunnysack wedding dress. Thank goodness for the flowing, hippie-like styles of the day." She reached over and brushed my hair behind my ear like she had when I was small.

"It wasn't the wedding you dreamed of?" I watched her closely.

She twisted a brochure she'd been holding. "Not exactly, no."

"You wanted a fairy tale wedding?"

"I wanted a fairy tale." She didn't elaborate.

This time, the omission of the word "wedding" was telling. It was like she was lying while trying to be completely truthful. *Lies of omission are still lies, Mom.*

"I know." I sighed. "Dad shouldn't have died. Prince Charming doesn't die in the fairy tales."

Her eyes went wide. She looked startled that that was the way I'd taken her statement. Like that wasn't what she'd been thinking at all.

"No, Mads. He shouldn't have died." She sounded fierce. "He was a decent, loyal man. He deserved better."

Decent. Loyal. Both true and both damningly faint praise. There was no glowing remembrance in her voice, just regret.

I hadn't noticed before that she always referred to Dad in those terms. *My good friend. Loyal. Decent. True. Kind.*

"Love isn't like it's portrayed in fairy tales. Friendship and reliability count for more than romantic notions of princes on white horses."

What she was saying made me incredibly sad. I thought of Seth and wanted to scream at her that she was wrong. The guy you loved could be your good friend, too. They didn't have to be mutually exclusive.

I blurted out what I was thinking: "Why did you marry Dad?"

She cocked her head, studying me as she considered her answer. "Because of Ian. I didn't want to raise my baby without a dad. Some women could. But I wasn't that strong."

I was parsing absolutely everything she said. I couldn't help myself. But it was blatantly obvious that she hadn't said, "Because I loved him madly and couldn't imagine life without him."

Which is what I wanted to hear. And I noticed, too, that she called Ian "my baby" not "ours." And "without *a* dad" rather than "without *his* dad."

Subtle distinctions? Maybe. But totally damning.

Before I could ask another question, she reached over and patted my knee. "Let's try on some dresses. Both of us! Won't that be fun? What do you say?" Her voice was falsely bright.

I nodded. I would have done anything to please her and lighten the mood. "Yeah."

The biggest, best wedding dress booth was in the back of the main showroom near the restrooms, which doubled as changing rooms. It was like a mini wedding dress boutique—racks and racks of dresses, round platforms to stand on before three-way mirrors. And signs advertising one-day special bridal fair discounts if you buy now.

I stared over the racks. "I had no idea there were so many shades of white." I pursed my lips. "What color are you looking for? White white? Cream? Pinkish white?"

"Cream. This is my second marriage." She sounded definite.

"I don't think anybody cares about that these days, Mom. Get whatever color you want. Go wild. Get a light pink or even lavender. Something fun."

She shook her head. "Those are for the girl brides. I need something sedate and classy. Something that hides my matronly figure."

She made herself sound a million years old.

"You don't look matronly!" I gave her my chastising stare, the one that was the complete mimic of hers.

She laughed. "Compared to you, I do."

We began cruising the racks, and even though I had a maid of honor sticker prominently displayed, I got more attention than Mom did. I gave up and pretended we were mother and daughter brides. I ended up with a half a dozen dresses to try on. Mom found two.

We shuffled into the restroom and each shimmied into our first-choice dress as far as we could without help. Mom didn't actually need much help with her long cream sheath dress with a draping back. It was plain and classy. No corset top. A zipper. Very few buttons. I helped her straighten it in the back as I held the white gown I was wearing in place over my chest with one hand.

"You look beautiful!" I told her.

The look on her face said she didn't believe me, that I was just humoring her.

"Turn around." She made a spinning motion with her finger. "I'll lace you up. And then we'll flatter each other silly."

The dress I wore buttoned in back up to the waist and had a corset top. I held my hair up out of the way.

"Suck it in like an old-time Southern belle." Mom grabbed the laces.

I laughed. "If you plant your foot on my back so you can lace all my breath out of me, I'm going to disown you as a mother."

She laughed. "While I'm wearing this dress?" You have to be kidding."

"Don't lace me too tight. If I'm getting married, I want enough room to eat the chicken dinner."

We were suddenly having fun, laughing and joking with each other as she tugged and pulled. I flashed back to shopping for my prom dress. How proud Mom had been. How sad that Dad wasn't there to see it.

When she finished, I grabbed her hand and pulled her out of the bathroom to the podium in front of the three-sided mirrors that were set up in the booth.

"Get up and take a look at how gorgeous you look!" I took her hand and helped her step up. "See for yourself that I'm not lying!"

She stood sideways and looked at herself from every angle. Her face softened, but I saw the critical look in her eyes.

I was so caught up in Mom's experience that I barely noticed one of the ladies from the boutique come up next to me.

She gasped. "You are the most beautiful bride we've had all day! That dress is perfect on you. I swear. I would love to use you in our brochure."

Mom turned, beaming from the compliment.

Which is when we both noticed the woman was talking to me.

I blushed. "Oh, I don't know—"

"Don't be modest! Your groom is a very lucky man," the shopkeeper said. "Here, let me tie the bow better for you. This is one occasion where it's absolutely essential to look good from the back. There's a trick I can show you." She spun me around and untied the bow Mom had made.

I caught Mom's expression. Tears glittered in her eyes as she looked at me. And something else. More regret? The desire to be young again? I couldn't tell.

The shopkeeper faced me toward the mirror. As I caught my reflection, I pictured Seth walking down the aisle toward me. My eyes teared up. Because the odds of that ever happening were becoming thinner and thinner. Not that I was ready to think of marriage. But I didn't want to lose him, either.

Crap, I was in so much trouble.

CHAPTER THIRTEEN

Maddie

We came home from the wedding fair exhausted, with a bag full of samples, giveaways, and business cards. We trooped into the house.

I dumped the contents of my bag on the kitchen counter. "What am I going to do with all this stuff?" I pushed aside a pink pen with the name of a caterer on it.

I picked up a pair of treat boxes shaped like a headless groom in a black tux and a headless bride in a white dress with a pink bow, and clunked them together like they might be kissing. "I don't play with dolls anymore."

Mom laughed.

I pulled out a photo strip of Mom and me wearing mustaches and feather boas. We'd stood in line for the photo booth inside a stall that sold fun things for your guests to do. Like take silly pictures with props in a photo booth.

"I think you should definitely get this! Girls with pink mustaches as a souvenir of your wedding? Who wouldn't want a reminder like this, huh? Silliness to the core. No matter what you have to sacrifice in your budget to make it happen, you *must* have a photo booth."

Mom smiled. "I'll keep that in mind."

I fell into a comfy chair in the family room across from the kitchen. "I hope you win something from the wedding fair. Like one of the boudoir photo sessions."

"Madison Foster!" Mom put her hands on her hips and tried to look stern. But her lips twitched like she was trying not to laugh.

"What?" I said innocently. "You looked gorgeous today. You're going to be a beautiful bride."

She came into the family room and sat on the sofa. "No, *you* made a beautiful bride." Her eyes filled with pride, but she wounded wistful. She got a nostalgic look on her face. "If only I were young again..." She sighed. "Seeing you in that dress you reminded me of a much younger me."

I seized my opportunity. "You were a beautiful young bride, Mom. Can we look at your wedding pictures to Daddy?"

She looked startled. "Maddie—"

"Please, Mom. I know it's hard. And maybe it's not super tactful of me to ask to see them now. But I miss Dad so much. Just one look?"

It had never occurred to me before to question why she never kept her wedding pictures up.

She sighed and got up. "They're in the closet in my room."

I followed her upstairs to her room and sat on her bed while she looked for them. I rarely went in there. I noticed, as if struck, that there were no pictures of my dad up. Given she was going to marry Ken, maybe that was natural. But still...

She pulled an old photo album from the top shelf of her closet. "We practically eloped. So we didn't have a professional photographer. There aren't many pictures."

She opened a page of the book and pulled out a four-by-six snapshot and handed it to me.

My parents looked very young. I loved my dad, adored him, really. But looking at my parents' wedding picture, I was struck by how mismatched they were. He was a tall, gangly nerd. Beaming from ear to ear like he'd just scored the fantasy girl of his dreams.

Even pregnant, Mom was absolutely gorgeous. Way out of his league, looks-wise. A ten to his four. Like she and Ken were.

She looked peaked and pale. Which you could chalk up to morning sickness and being in the early stages of pregnancy. But the sad, haunted, betrayed look in her eyes?

My imagination was running wild. I had to be making all this stuff up out of worry, right? Imagining looks in eyes. Why was I suddenly seeing things I'd never noticed before?

The nineteen-year-old girl in the picture looked like she would rather be anywhere but there. Resigned. Determined. Sad.

Dad had his arm around her, pinching her dress with his fingers where his hand rested around her waist like he would never let her go. And she was leaning away from him. Ever so slightly. But it was there. Just like with Ken. Her body language was undeniable.

I looked up at Mom with a question in my eyes.

She sat down beside me. "Not the best picture of me. I was so...sick that day."

And there was my imagination again, imagining she really meant *heart*sick.

I reached for the photo album in her lap. "Are there any more pictures?"

As I pulled it from her, I startled her. She jumped and the photo album fell from her lap. As we both reached for it, a letter envelope fluttered out.

I leaned forward to pick it up at the same time she did. She snatched it up. But not before I got a look at the return address scrawled in the left-hand corner in a distinctly masculine block script.

Rick Butler.

My world spun. For a second, I felt dizzy, nauseated, and sick. Like I'd been spinning and spinning and suddenly come to a stop. *This can't be!*

My mouth went completely dry, but I managed to speak. "What's that?"

"Oh, nothing. Just an old letter from a friend." She snapped the album closed. "That's enough reminiscing."

She held out her hand for the wedding picture.

I handed it back to her and watched as she put it and the letter back in the album.

"We should call Ken. Make him take us out to dinner and bore him to death with bridal show talk." She was trying hard to be lighthearted.

I told myself to breathe deeply. I was still reeling with shock and needed time to process. I needed to talk to someone. Like Olivia. Before I exploded. Even if I had to call her in Mexico.

"You and Ken go. I promised the girls we could get together tonight after I got back from the bridal show. You don't mind, do you?"

She stared at me for a minute, like she was trying to determine if I was feeling all right. "No. Not at all. Of course your friends from home want to see you. Are you okay?"

"Fine," I said, with that same note of false brightness in my voice.

But later, after Mom and Ken left, I sneaked back to her room and found her photo album. Yes, snooping was despicable business. But I had to know what was in that letter. Had to make sure I wasn't imagining things. I grabbed the album.

The picture of Mom and Dad was there where she'd stuffed it between the pages. But the letter from Rick

Butler was not, no matter how many times I shuffled through the pages.

It was pretty clear Mom didn't want me, or anyone, to see that letter. I could have turned her room upside down looking for it. But she could have hidden it anywhere. Or even destroyed it. I'd reached a dead end.

"Rick Butler, damn you," I whispered. "Did you break my mom's heart? What kind of a douchebag are you?"

I shivered, full of dread about going to Chelan. Yet I had to know. I had to meet this man that I suddenly hated on principle. I could find an excuse not to go. But that would hurt Seth. And damage our relationship. Morbid curiosity combined with irresistible passion was a potent force driving me toward some inevitable fate.

But before anything else, I had to talk to Olivia.

I pulled my phone out of my pocket. But it felt like the house had ears and anything I said here would be held against me and reported to Mom. So I went to the coffee shop on the corner and called Olivia.

She listened while I told her the whole story. And had the good sense not to tell me I had an overactive imagination.

"You love Seth, right?" she said in her circumspect, intellectual, I'm-your-friend-and-I'm-right-about-this voice.

"Yes, of course."

"Then you have to go. You don't know what happened all those years ago. Rick Butler may not be the douche you think he is. But the point is, you can't ask your mom what happened without blowing your family apart. Like she'd tell you the truth, anyway. I mean, what if she destroyed that letter?"

"Yeah, I know." I nodded my agreement, even though we weren't Facetiming and she couldn't see me. "She certainly hid it from me."

"So you need to find out from Rick what happened. While not tipping Seth off. Until you can figure things out."

"Oh, great," I said. "Nothing like asking the impossible."

On Friday morning, I hugged Mom, jumped in my car, and headed to Seth's two hundred miles and four hours away. Fortunately, the two mountain passes I had to drive over were all clear and the roads good.

I had those four hours to think. My mind wandered toward worst-case scenarios and a complete family meltdown. Even the music I blasted didn't drown it out.

I had never been to Chelan before. It was a quaint tourist town on the lake. I stopped to gas up and get last-minute directions and texted Seth that I was minutes away. Just outside of town toward Wapato, the hills around were more arid-looking but still dotted with green.

Vineyards on the hills were coming to life with budding leaves. The lake below was a deep blue. The scenery spectacular. It was easy to see why Rick Butler loved it enough to move here. Though I considered Seattle pretty awesome and beautiful.

The Butlers lived in a house on acreage on the edge
of the vineyard. Land in the Chelan area was expensive,
and Rick Butler owned a lot of it.

I followed the GPS on my phone through twisting
country roads, up a hill, through a wrought iron gate
past a sign welcoming me to the winery and listing the
tasting hours. Past the winery and tasting room, a
heavy, classic building sat on the edge of the hill with
balconies jutting out over the hillside, facing the lake
below and a view east to the surrounding hills. Up a
private drive through fields of grapevines.

As I turned the last corner, a large, modern, villa-
style house with windows and balconies galore came
into view. My heart pounded into overdrive.

Seth waited for me on the front porch.

I had a vision of his father, old and paunchy. Gray. A
worn-out, sagging version of Ian. I thought I'd find
some satisfaction in that. That Mom remained pretty
and young-looking while Rick Butler had aged terribly.
That she would be way out of his league now.

But then, I thought of Ian or Seth in thirty years,
aging badly, no longer hot and handsome. The vengeful
thought became a lot less satisfying.

Seth bounded down the steps as I pulled to a stop in
the circular driveway. Mom lived in a nice, middle-class
house. Dad had left her enough insurance money to
keep her comfortably middle class. But Rick lived in
splendor. The house was obviously high end and pro-
fessionally landscaped.

Which peeved me even more. How could he make
his son work in that horrid Double Deltsie house when

paying for his education would have been like handing out pennies?

Seth was at my car door, opening it for me before I could unbuckle my seatbelt. He was beaming. The look on his face totally priceless as he pulled me from the car and into his arms.

"I've missed you, Mads." He pressed me close and kissed me, a quick, ardent kiss where his tongue slid into my mouth, tantalizing me until I trembled.

"I can't wait to show you around." He let go of me and grabbed my hand. "Dad is eager to meet you."

As we turned toward the house, a man came out the front door. My heart did a major thud and skidded to a stop. Our eyes met. Time stood still.

He paled. I swear he did. Like he was seeing a ghost.

I was, too. Seeing a ghost, I mean. A ghost of things past and future.

"Dad." Seth pulled me by the hand toward the man. "This is Maddie."

"The infamous Maddie." His voice was warm and deep, like honey in the sun. He recovered quickly and put on a welcoming smile that lit up his face as he extended his hands and took mine in both of his.

I knew what he'd seen in me—Mom. Little Laura, as my grandpa used to jokingly call me. And it had stunned him. If I'd needed any more confirmation our parents knew each other, I certainly had it now.

My forced smile wobbled as I looked into his eyes. I had the feeling he was assessing me as much as I was him. It was natural he would size up his son's girl-friend. But this was more. I tried to guess what his stunned reaction meant. How had he felt about Mom? He obviously remembered her. Good? Bad?

His hands were warm. His grip firm. "Welcome."

"Nice to meet you, Mr. Butler." In so many ways. And in others, it was a complete lie. Life would have been so much simpler if I hadn't.

"Please. Call me Rick. Mr. Butler is my granddad, not me."

Such simple, ordinary words. So much charisma. In his voice. In the way he held my hand. In his smile and even in his very demeanor. Some people just have it, that special magnetism. Successful politicians. Rock stars. And Rick Butler.

With his money and confidence, he would have been alluring even if he had gone to seed. But he hadn't. The man who could very well be my brother's father was tall, toned, and fit. Younger-looking than his true age by at least ten years, just like Mom. Her equal.

Looking at him, I was both entranced and filled with bitterness. There was no way a young Mom could have resisted him. My stomach burned with the very real fear that he'd charmed her into his bed, gotten her pregnant, and abandoned her. And that those events, thirty-five years ago, were going to ruin my life now.

This man was my boyfriend's father. And possibly my brother's. Life was such a mess.

CHAPTER FOURTEEN

Seth

I didn't understand Dad. He couldn't keep his eyes off Maddie. Yeah, she was hot. But I didn't need Dad looking at her like he thought so, too. And flirting with her. He talked and joked with her as I got her bag from her car and carried it into the house. He kept talking while I was trying to excuse Maddie and me and show her to her room. And show her how much I'd missed her.

What was wrong with the old man? He'd never acted like this with the girls I dated in high school.

And Maddie? She stared back at him, not exactly sure about him, clinging tightly to my hand as I carried her suitcase upstairs to her room.

"Your dad is—"

"Making a fool of himself." I set her suitcase at the foot of the bed.

She laughed. "I was going to say charming."

"When he wants to be." I paused. "Don't let him scare you off."

He'd already won her over.

She smiled and stepped into me, so close her breasts brushed my chest. *Go to hell, Dad. This girl is mine.*

"This is a gorgeous house." She looked up at me, moving her lips inches from mine. "I missed you so much."

I was hungry for her. Desperate. I kissed her and pressed her to me. She kissed me back with enough passion to turn me to a hot burn and let me slide my hands beneath her blouse and play with her breasts.

Finally, she stepped away, breathless, and tucked my hands in front of me. Her eyes wide and a smile on her face. "I need to freshen up. Is there a bathroom in this place?"

"You have your own private bathroom." I pointed the way.

She smiled. "Meet you downstairs?"

"I was hoping we'd stay here."

She lifted one eyebrow. "With your dad down-stairs?"

I sighed, resigned that she wanted to make a good impression. Good thing I had other plans for later, away from the house. "See you down there."

Dad sat in the living room staring into space. He looked up briefly when I walked in.

"What's Maddie's last name again?"

"Foster."

He nodded absentmindedly, like he was deep in thought. "Foster, Foster, Foster...*Foster.*" He frowned like he'd remembered something unpleasant and un-thinkable. He muttered to himself before looking at me again. "She's a gorgeous girl."

I nodded. "Duh! What did you expect? Your son has excellent taste."

I expected him to laugh or joke or tease me about it.

Instead, he nodded. "Very pretty. And sweet. Intel-ligent."

"And mine," I said.

He looked startled, like I'd misinterpreted his inter-est in her. But damn it, Dad had never flirted with my dates before. Maddie was different. Special. What the hell was he doing?

Maddie cleared her throat behind me. I practically jumped. How much had she heard?

She came up behind me and put her hand on my shoulder, facing Dad.

"Am I interrupting?" Her voice was soft and con-cerned.

Dad's eyes lit up.

I pulled her even with me.

"No. Of course not." Dad didn't look the slightest bit rattled. But he studied her closely. "I was asking Seth the usual fatherly questions about you." He smiled, putting on the charm for her.

Then Dad did something he rarely did. He hesitated. Like he was nervous. What the hell?

"You remind me of someone, Maddie." He shifted in his chair, another sign of nerves.

I slid my arm around Maddie and felt her stiffen.

"Oh?" She sounded almost too casual, like she'd almost been expecting this question. And was not at all surprised, just leery. "I get told that a lot." She glanced up at me. "I must have a common look."

If she was looking to me for confirmation, she was crazy. Maddie's stunning looks were anything but ordinary.

What the shit is going on?

"This probably sounds like it's coming out of left field." Dad cleared his throat. "You look a lot like a girl I went to college with." He paused. "You're not by any chance related to Laura Glenn?"

Maddie trembled. I felt her weight in my arms like her knees were weak. She slid her arm around my waist. I tightened my grip on her.

"Small world!" she said. "Laura's my mom. She only went to the university her freshman year. Before she dropped out to *marry* my dad."

I didn't understand the tightness in her voice. Or why she sounded defensive.

Dad's expression was masked. "Laura was beautiful. You look like I remember her."

Pieces fell into place. Like why Dad reacted to Maddie the way he did.

"How did you know Mom? Were you in class together?" Maddie's question was innocent enough. Natural. But she lifted her chin and there was a challenge in her voice.

Dad met her eyes. "We dated. For a while." He paused. "I haven't seen her since...a few days after Mount St. Helens blew up. That was?" He looked up like he was thinking and trying to remember. "Nineteen eighty?"

Shit. I'd never seen Dad act like this. It was clear to anyone watching that Maddie's mom been special to him.

My stomach tightened and burned. This meeting wasn't going at all like I'd planned. I find out that my dad dated my girl's mother in college? Like father, like son?

"You dated someone besides Mom in college, Dad?" I challenged him. He'd bragged about going out and partying in college, seeing girls. But not about an actual relationship with anyone but Mom. "You never *mentioned* it."

Dad shrugged. "I wasn't a saint. I dated a lot of girls I've never mentioned." His voice was tight. He turned to Maddie. "Laura married Bruce Foster?"

Maddie nodded. "Bruce is my dad." There was that edge of defiance in her voice, like she was sticking up for her dad and mad at mine.

There was something going on that I didn't understand. The two were playing a game of cat and mouse. Parry and feint. Dancing around something just below the surface.

"Did you know him, too?" Her eyes snapped, like she defied him to say anything bad about her dad.

Why would he?

Dad held her gaze. "Bruce was all right."

Damn it. Faint praise. All right? All right? I tried to warn Dad off. He ignored my cues.

"I met him once or twice. Briefly. They were friends, as I recall. He used to help Laura with her chemistry. Science wasn't her thing. Your dad was good at it." Dad made being good at science sound like an indictment. "How *are* your parents?"

Shit, Dad was stepping in it.

"Dad passed away four, almost five, years ago. Cancer." Maddie's voice wobbled.

"I'm sorry." Dad's face softened, like he was sympathetic for Maddie. He looked thoughtful. "Laura's a widow, then. Has she remarried?"

"She's engaged."

Why did Maddie sound so fierce?

She smiled too sunnily. "I spent most of the week working on wedding stuff with her."

"But she's doing okay?" It was like he had to know, wanted to be reassured. "Life turned out okay for Laura?"

Maddie studied him. "Yeah, she's great."

I didn't understand Maddie's nerves. Or why she didn't elaborate.

"Good." Dad nodded like he was thinking. "Tell her...tell her hello from me, will you?"

Maddie hesitated. Which was odd. It was a simple request. Why should it be a problem?

She finally nodded, hesitantly.

I took her hand, eager to escape. "We should get going." I squeezed it. "I have a busy day planned."

Maddie

Seth's dad is Ian's dad. Seth's dad is Ian's dad.

The phrase repeated over and over in my mind as Seth pulled me outside by the hand.

He didn't speak as he led me to the attached garage where a pair of bicycles leaned against the side. He tossed a helmet to me. "It's a gorgeous day. I thought we'd bike to the lake and take the boat out."

His voice was hard. He was obviously upset, but was he angry with me?

I barely had time to strap my helmet on before Seth was on his bike, cruising down the driveway.

I threw my leg over the bike and headed out after him. "Hey! Seth! Seth! Wait!"

He took off, as they say, like a bat out of hell, pumping and cruising down the twisting lane.

My helmet was jammed on my head, with my hair sticking out beneath. The ends blew in the wind as I pumped furiously to keep up with him.

The wind in my face felt good. I just needed to breathe and think. It would have been perfect, except Seth was upset with me. I just knew it.

We flew past the winery, down the hillside road to the main road, which was, mercifully, mostly flat. Just a few gently rolling inclines. I had to work to keep up with him. He ignored my calls for him to slow up.

He was a full block ahead of me by the time he turned off the main road toward the lake. I made the left turn and cruised past hotels, cafes, condos, and local convenience stores until I found him standing on the porch of a quaint, romantic boutique hotel at the edge of the lake. His bike leaned against the rail.

I leaned my bike next to his, hung my helmet over the handlebars, and joined him on the porch. "What's wrong?"

"You tell me." His eyes and voice were hard as he grabbed my hand and pulled me into the hotel.

Through the lobby. Into the kitchen where everyone seemed to know him. And directly to a large refrigerator.

"Ah, so *this* is the girl!" A large man in a chef's apron smiled at me, studying me with blatant curiosity.

"I'm Maddie." I held out my hand for him to shake.

"Caesar." He took my in his two meaty ones and squeezed warmly. "This one has been so excited that you're coming! Our Seth is a charmer, like his dad. Girls always hanging around him. But I've never seen him this way about one before! Dedicated. Committed." When he laughed, his voice filled the room with good humor. "Almost like this time the girl has the upper hand."

He leaned into me and whispered, "Use it to your advantage. Tame this cocky young buck."

Seth glared at him. "Our lunch?"

The chef dropped my hand and wagged his chubby finger at Seth. "Patience!" Caesar returned his attention to me. "You had a good trip?"

"Very pleasant," I said. *Up until a few minutes ago.*

"Don't let Seth hotdog on the lake. This one likes to make a wake." He opened the commercial fridge and handed a large cardboard picnic box embossed with the hotel's logo to Seth. "Have fun, you two kids. But not too much!" He laughed again, large and booming.

"Thanks, Caesar." Seth took the basket with a scowl on his face.

"Where's your sense of humor, man?" Caesar winked at Seth.

Seth grabbed me by the hand again and pulled me outside, across the beach, to the end of the dock and a waiting speedboat. He tossed the picnic box in without a word and offered me his hand.

I scrambled over the edge of the boat and into the passenger seat next to the driver.

"Life jackets are in there if you want one." Seth pointed to a storage compartment at the back of the boat as he untied the boat from the dock.

He jumped into the driver's seat and backed us out, slowly and carefully. As if Caesar or Rick were watching and grading his boat-driving skills. He took it easy near shore, past the buoys. Then he gunned it.

I jerked back in my seat. We flew up the lake away from town. The day was sunny, and warm for early spring. But cool on the lake with the spray coming up.

He wove and turned. Cornering so fast that I screamed. First in fear, then in delight. Up the lake until the bare hills became dotted with trees and then heavily forested and dark in deep green foliage. The air became cooler as the lake became shady.

The large, expensive homes became fewer and fewer, replaced with smaller cabins and cottages. We passed a mail boat making its daily rounds. Seth waved to the mailman.

Neither of us spoke. But in the fresh air away from the town, a calm settled over both of us.

I was wearing a lightweight sweater. I shivered and cuddled up next to Seth for warmth. I couldn't stand him being cold toward me. He peeled off his sweatshirt and put it around me, still looking straight ahead, his eyes on the path up the lake.

Finally, he pulled up to a dock jutting out in the shady lake from a small beach. A small, rustic cabin sat above it.

"Dad's fishing shack." Seth grabbed the dock and tied the boat up.

"Your dad owns half the town."

He jumped out of the boat onto the dock and offered me a hand up. "Hardly."

"A hotel, a winery, a fancy home, and a fishing cabin?" I arched an eyebrow. "He does pretty well."

"Yeah." Seth reached into the boat for our picnic lunch.

I followed him up the dock that bounced gently in the ripples from the lake. Across the shore. Up a set of wooden steps to the balcony deck of the cabin that overlooked the lake.

Seth plunked onto a wooden bench against the wall of the cabin and stared out over the water. "It's peaceful here. Secluded. I like to come here and think sometimes."

I sat next to him and folded my hands between my legs, though I ached to touch him. I'd been nervous about meeting his dad. I'd known enough to be wary about what could happen. I'd even worried Rick would notice my resemblance to Mom.

But from my perspective, one level, things had gone relatively well with Rick. I'd gleaned valuable information. On another level, Seth's reaction scared me. I swallowed hard.

He sighed. "This isn't going like I'd planned."

My eyes misted up. He'd planned a romantic reunion and I was touched. And saddened.

He turned to look at me. "What was going on between you and Dad?"

I swallowed hard. "What do you mean?"

He frowned. "Don't pull that crap with me. What is that shit? Did you know our parents knew each other in college?"

I suspected. That, and so much more. But know for sure? No. I crafted a partial truth and shook my head. "Mom never talks much about her college experience. Except in general terms, like how much she hated her science classes. Your dad was right about that. And how hard the classes were. And about my Dad. And how he saved her butt more than once."

I thought about what I'd just said. Suddenly seeing that Mom could have meant much more than I'd always thought.

"It shouldn't matter, right? That our parents dated." I begged him with my eyes not to care and slid my hand to rest on his thigh.

If he was so upset about this, what would he do when he found out about Ian?

"It's weird. Creepy." He sighed again. "Am I the only one who thinks so? Like something in my family's
DNA is genetically programmed to be attracted to your
family's." He shook his head.

"It's...a strange coincidence." I wondered if there
was a way to exonerate myself from the guilt of the secrets I was keeping from him. Or, more accurately, the
suspicions. Because even now, all I had was damning
circumstantial evidence.

"Then why were you nervous and angry at Dad back
at the house?"

Damn! He was too perceptive. Almost like he saw into my mind. Was I that easy to read?

"I wasn't nervous."

He shook his head like he didn't believe me. "You
think he hurt your mom."

I was too slow to deny it.

"My dad was a player in college. No doubt about it."
He snorted. "He liked the girls and they liked him. If
you can believe his bragging. Mom and him were on
and off again all the time." He took my hand in his.
"I'm sorry if he hurt your mom or treated her like a
douche."

He squeezed my hand, almost desperately. "I'm not
my dad. I would never hurt you. I know you've been
worried over what Zach's told you about me getting
cold feet and bailing on relationships after a month or
two." He squeezed my hand even tighter. "I'm not bailing on you. I'm in this relationship one hundred percent.

My heart felt tight. My eyes misted over again. He believed what he said. But he had no idea how much he would be tested.

"Our parents dating back in college is like an echo through time," I said before I could stop myself. I knew so much more than he did about the true situation. "Are we doomed to fail, too?" I was thinking out loud again, voicing my fears.

"I love you, Maddie. I'm not letting you go."

I caressed his cheek with tears standing in my eyes.

He leaned in and kissed me.

I slid over into his lap, straddling him. "I love you, too." Desperately.

He couldn't know how afraid I was that I would lose him.

He stood with me wrapped around him. I slid my legs down him until they touched the deck floor.

He grabbed me by the hand, leaving our lunch sitting on the bench as he pulled a key from his pocket. He held it up. "Let's go inside."

The lock was sticky. He had to rattle the key to get the door to swing open. And then we were in. The cabin was cold from standing empty and unheated.

He closed the door and pulled me through the living room into a bedroom with a log frame bed. I kissed him as he fell back onto the bed, pulling me on top of him.

His hands were warm as they slid beneath my blouse and caressed my bare skin at the small of my back. Everything in me tightened at his touch, aching for release.

I needed him. Simply needed him. The reassurance of being with him. The bonding.

I felt the long, hard bulging in his jeans as I lay on him, straddling his hips with my thighs, rubbing against him.

I ran my hands through his hair. "Why do you have to be so gorgeous?"

He smiled. "Why do you have to be so beautiful?" He took a breath. "I missed you, Maddie. So damn much. I thought I would go crazy if the week lasted much longer. And then we got off on the wrong foot earlier. I've been planning this all week. Shit, since I first asked you here for spring break. Did you think about me?"

"Every minute." And more. I couldn't tell him I worried, too. That I was so afraid our parents' relationship had doomed our love all those years ago, well before we were born. I reached for his fly and unzipped his jeans.

He covered my hand with his. "Did you think about this?" His eyes were dark and round as he looked up at me. "Did you think about having sex with me?"

I slid his dick out of his fly and stroked him. Hard. I leaned in close, so that our lips were separated by a whisper. "More. I *dreamed* about it."

He smiled, slowly and seductively.

I closed the gap between our lips and kissed him again. Softly, running my tongue over his parted lips with the lightest of touches. He liked it when I took charge and teased him.

I nibbled at his lips, stroking him until I could feel him holding back. Until I felt the first tremors of pulsing in his dick and knew he was completely at my mercy and on the edge.

"You're killing me, Mads." His voice was ragged. "Either finish me by hand or get serious."

I kicked off my shoes. "Oh, I'm serious."

I released him, unzipped my jeans, and slid them and my panties off.

He slid a finger inside me. "You are thinking about me."

I gasped. I was ready for him, too.

Another time I would have lifted his shirt. Run my hands over his flat abs and muscled chest. Sucked on his nipples. Not now. I needed him too badly, emotionally and physically.

"I would rather have your dick inside me," I whispered into his ear.

He pulled his finger out. I stroked him a final time and slid onto him.

He didn't wait for me to ride him. He thrust up into me until I gasped and moaned.

I was so ready for him, it took only a few pulses until I gasped and the climax crashed over me.

He moaned and grunted, pushing up into me, holding my hips firmly in place, riding his own crest of pleasure.

Finally, I collapsed onto him, pressing my head against his chest, listening to his heartbeat.

He grabbed my butt. His hands were warm.

"Your butt is cold." He kissed the top of my head.

I smiled, so happy in the moment. "It's out in the open air. The cold air."

He pulled the edge of the comforter over me. "Better?"

"Mmmmm."

He wrapped his arms around me and slid out from inside me.

"You planned this all along," I said.

He laughed. "Maybe."

"I could stay like this forever," I said. And then my stomach betrayed me by growling.

He shook me playfully. "Until you died of hunger. I guess I should feed you." He put a note of mock exasperation in his voice.

"I guess so," I said. "I drove hundreds of miles across dangerous mountain passes to see you. That's enough to work up an appetite."

"Not to mention what we just did." His dick was growing hard again between my legs.

"Not again."

"Just once more?"

Eventually, we got up and got dressed. We ate lunch in the sunshine in the corner of the deck. Caesar had packed us a magnificent lunch. Sandwiches on focaccia bread, hand-cut potato chips, cold soup in Mason jars, and thick chocolate cookies that we ate with a bottle of wine from Rick's winery.

I swore that nothing had ever tasted so good. After lunch, Seth showed me around the woods, pointing out spring wild flowers. I found a first bloom of a rare pink lady slipper nestled beneath a clump of bushes.

"I'm going to press this and keep it forever," I told him. "Do you have any wax paper?"

He found me some inside the cabin. We found a couple of heavy books and pressed the flower between them.

Seth put the books in the boat. "Dad won't mind if we borrow these books from the cabin for a few days." He hesitated. "Speaking of Dad, he would like us to have dinner with him at the hotel tonight." He paused again. "I made the arrangements before you came. If it's too awkward—"

"No!" I took Seth's hand. "It's fine. It's good." I paused. "Seth?"

He looked at me like he knew what I was going to ask from the tone of my voice.

"Do you think your dad and my mom ever...did what we did earlier?"

"You mean pick wild flowers?" He acted too innocent.

I bumped him with my shoulder. "Only euphemistically."

"Shit, Mads. I hope not. I don't want to think about that."

I was trying to prepare Seth, gently, for the shock that I couldn't hide forever.

"Are you curious about what really happened between them?" I needed an ally. It occurred to me that working together, we might get details out of Rick that my mom would never give.

"Not to that level of detail." He made a point of shuddering.

"Shut up!" I kissed him lightly. "Me, either. But I would like to know more. Like how long did they date?"

Seth frowned. "Leave it be, Mads." He kissed me before I could protest. "We should get back."

CHAPTER FIFTEEN

Maddie

We ate dinner at sunset in the dining room of Rick's hotel. It was Friday night and the restaurant was busy with locals and tourists. People spending the weekend in Washington wine country. People whose children were on spring break. But we had a prime table with a view of the lake and sunset.

I dressed for dinner in a spring dress I'd bought on one of my many wedding shopping trips with Mom. A nod to her guilt that so much of my time at home was about her. Seth sat next to me. Rick across from me.

Rick was on his best behavior—laughing, joking, being generally charming. I saw now where Seth got his friendly, easygoing nature and natural charisma. Seth had his arm possessively looped over the back of

my chair. Like he was making it clear to his dad that I
was his.

Rick studied me as if he was looking for Mom in me
and seeing her in almost every aspect. I studied him,
too. With every passing moment in his presence, seeing
him as he was now, and imagining him as he'd been at
Seth's age, I knew there was no way Mom could have
resisted him. Just like I was powerless to resist Seth.
No matter how loyal, intelligent, and supportive Dad
had been. Compared to Rick Butler, he hadn't stood a
chance.

It was hard to imagine Mom young and passionate,
in the same state as I was—desperate in love. Wanting
to hold on with everything she had. Wanting Rick in
the way I needed Seth. It was so unlike the woman
who'd raised me. The sensible, calm, unromantic woman.

The woman who had only let Dad kiss her on the
cheek as they left for work in the morning. The woman
who'd given him a peck on the mouth—so quick and
perfunctory—when they both came home at night. The
wife who was solicitous and loyal, but whose eyes had
never sparkled with passion toward him.

I had always thought Mom wasn't the romantic kind
by nature. That she'd always been the way I knew her
to be. But being around Rick, I was beginning to wonder if what I'd seen of her was more of a shell. A woman whose passions had died. A woman who'd settled for
friendship, loyalty, and security at the cost of her heart.

It was almost unthinkable. And heartbreaking. But there it was staring me in the face in the form of Seth's dad.

Maybe I didn't know Mom at all. Maybe she'd kept a big piece of her from all of us. Maybe that explained the worried looks Grandma used to give her. Or the way Grandpa complained Mom had become too serious. What had happened to his darling, fun-loving girl? Mom blamed the change on Dad's cancer. Fighting that for years took its toll.

I'm sure it had. But maybe there was *more* behind it. Like an incurably broken heart.

Sitting across from Rick, I thought, *Crap! What if he's the cause? What if he can fix it? Can I chance what I have with Seth to give Mom her heart back? What if seeing Rick again will make things worse for her?*

Rick asked me all the usual polite questions about my classes and college life. "Favorite class?"

"HBM 225! Cooking with Chef Steven." I slid a sideways glance at Seth.

He beamed and stroked my bare arm with his fingertips.

"Because of my boy!" Rick's laugh boomed. "That's sweet. Now." He leaned across the table like we were sharing an intimate secret. "What's your *real* favorite?"

I laughed, cupped my mouth so Seth ostensibly couldn't hear, and whispered, playing along, "HBM 225. Second favorite—microbiology."

Rick leaned back and shook his head, his eyes twinkling. "Good answer. Diplomatic." He addressed Seth. "I like her."

"That makes two of us, Dad."

I furiously tried to think of ways to draw him out and get him to spill details Mom had locked away. But how did I steer him in that direction?

"Your favorite class?" I asked Rick, taking the chance that he and Mom had had one together.

"Couldn't name one. There were too many to count—math, history, science, computer programming. I loved them all. Damn, I was a nerd. I lived for learning."

The way his eyes danced, I couldn't tell how far he was pulling our legs, or how much truth he was telling. Or what he loved learning about. I got the impression he was talking about more than classwork.

I couldn't imagine him as a nerd. I knew for a fact he wasn't. Not judging from the college dance picture I'd seen of him. Self-perception, though, was a flawed mirror.

"I loved college. Period. The camaraderie of the frat. The new experiences. The girls." He winked at me. "Enjoy what you have left of it. It's the best time of your life!" His smile was infectious.

"Shit, Dad," Seth said. "You mean it's all downhill from here?"

"Shut up, kid." Rick grinned. "You're always nailing me on semantics. I should have said 'one of the best times.' Life is a pretty fantastic adventure. But college!" Rick shook his head. "On your own for the first time. Finding yourself. Total freedom. Absolute pressure. Surrounded almost exclusively by your peer group. Won't happen again! Not like that. That's why I say enjoy it. It slips away all too quickly. Like life. Suddenly you look in the mirror and see a middle-aged man looking back." He sounded resigned and suddenly reflective and nostalgic.

"That won't happen to me!" I couldn't let Rick's good mood slip.

He looked at me like, *Oh, yes, it will.*

"Maybe an old woman, but not an old man." I liked teasing him.

His eyes lit up again. "You've already been hanging out with my boy too long." Rick was clearly teasing. "I'm glad you're here. The boy can't shut up about you. Now I see why."

Seth rolled his eyes. "Dad—"

Rick laughed. "How did you two meet, anyway? In class? Through Zach? Isn't he friends with both of you?"

"Dad—"

"What? I don't remember you spilling the deets, Sethie."

"Sethie?" I turned to Seth. "Cute!"

He scowled at his father. "You're trying to embarrass me now, *Daddy.*"

Rick roared. "Is it working? Wait until I drag out the naked baby bathtub pictures of you. He was adorable, by the way."

"I would *pay* to see those!" I loved the way the two of them bantered back and forth and ribbed each other. It reminded me of the way Mom and Ian got along.

"What?" Rick put on a totally innocent look. "Your mother's probably asked how you met Seth, right?" His gaze bounced between us, landing on me.

I squirmed and shrugged noncommittally.

"She hasn't commented on the coincidence of the Butler last name?" Rick was clearly prying now, trying to draw me out.

Did she remember him? Had she asked about him? The questions were there in his eyes.

So the games begin again, I thought.

When I hesitated, Rick continued, "Butler is a common enough last name, I suppose."

"I haven't told her Seth's last name." It was the truth, and a damned partial lie again. I hadn't told her anything.

I don't know why I felt compelled to put Rick at ease regarding Mom. To not hurt his feelings with the thought she'd forgotten all about him.

Rick frowned. "I see."

Beside me, I felt Seth stiffen. I shouldn't have felt guilty. I didn't want to hurt his feelings, either. He knew I was keeping our relationship from my family, and was in agreement with me.

"It hasn't come up yet. I'm..." I paused. "Mom has the tendency to get way ahead of herself when I tell her about guys. It's better to share as little as possible with her until...we've only been dating a little over a month."

"And yet Seth brought you home to meet me." Rick's gaze was intense. "You're the first girl he's brought home from college."

If Rick meant to hang me out to dry and condemn me, he was doing a fine job.

I squeezed Seth's leg and switched the subject back to his original question. "We met in class." I beamed at Seth like I adored him. Because I did. "I was single and looking for the next boyfriend. I knew, just knew, that something life-changing was going to happen this semester. I figured that meant a new guy. I mean, had to be." I squeezed Seth's hand.

He relaxed and beamed at me.

"And I had this feeling that cooking class would be it. So I got all dressed up and strutted into cooking class, totally trolling for fresh blood."

"And there was my boy with his eyes popping out!" Rick took a sip of wine. "Do you remember exactly what she was wearing, Seth? Was she bathed in a golden romantic glow?" He laughed like he was laughing at himself.

"I remember every detail." Seth squeezed my hand back as he described the outfit I was wearing and how he'd spotted me sitting in the auditorium.

"I remember exactly what your mom was wearing the first time I met her, too, Maddie." There was that nostalgic look in Rick's eyes again. "Then again, it was pretty dramatic." He paused. "Did Laura ever tell you how she and I met?"

My heart thudded to a stop. This was information I desperately wanted. I didn't want to shut him up by offending him and telling him she'd never mentioned him, period. So I simply shook my head.

"Really? Huh." He shook his head like he couldn't believe she wouldn't have.

I thought he was being incredibly arrogant.

"I'm surprised. A brush with death isn't something you forget." He shrugged and poured himself more wine.

"What?" I couldn't believe what I was hearing. "A brush with death?"

"Yeah, Sethie here should thank me. Without me, there would be no you."

Or Ian, I thought.

Rick raised the wine bottle. "More?"

I laced my arm through Seth's and hung on tightly.

Seth slid his glass over. I covered mine with my hand. I was still nursing my first glass and dying to hear his story with a clear head.

"The first time I met your mom, I saved her from being blown up by a heartsick, maniacal bomber." Rick's eyes lit up, like the memory was still an absolute adrenaline rush.

"What? Bullshit, old man!" Seth shook his head. "How come I've never heard about this before?"

"Maybe you never asked." Rick winked at his son, seemingly unoffended and nonplussed by Seth's disbelief.

"What? How?" It seemed too fantastic to believe.

Was Rick really—like, literally—my mom's hero?

Rick nodded. "You never heard about the big spring dorm bombing of nineteen eighty?"

We shook our heads.

"Ah, well, I suppose they don't advertise it for obvious reasons. It was all over the national news when it happened." He looked lost in thought for a second, like he was traveling back in time.

"I was working on a lab report with my lab partners Steve and Sarah in Sarah's dorm room at Cole Hall. You know the one," he said to Seth. "The old concrete one at the top of Stadium Way. It was only a few years old then. Nice, sturdy modern construction. Which saved a lot of lives and property.

"Sarah lived on the fifth floor. Had her own single room. We studied there a lot. We could blast our music. It was private. No roommate to disturb.

"We heard a commotion in the hall. Some jerk screaming obscenities at some girl Sarah knew who lived near the end of the hall near the stairs.

"'That has to be Becky's ex.' Sarah was shaking. Which was uncharacteristic. Usually, she was fearless. 'He said he'd kill her if she ever broke up with him.' She looked at us with round eyes. 'She broke up with him last week.'

"Well, shit, I thought. I'm not going to let some jerk terrorize a defenseless girl. I stepped out in the hall to tell him to can it and get lost.

"I stopped short just in time. He was armed to the teeth with shotguns and rifles. And had something strapped to him that looked like a homemade bomb. I stepped back in the room and locked the door.

"'Call the cops,' I told Sarah as calmly as I could." Rick paused and took a sip of wine. "She grabbed the phone just as we heard sirens. A dozen or more cop cars and fire engines pulled up. Along with the bomb squad.

"Cops got out with bullhorns and started yelling directions for everyone on all floors but the fifth to evacuate. They told those of us on the fifth floor to stay put and wait for help.

"A ladder truck pulled up at the opposite end of the building and raised its ladder to help two girls out.

"'We'll be last', I told Steve and Sarah. There was a large evergreen outside Sarah's room. 'To hell with waiting,' I told my lab partners. 'I'm not waiting to be blown up.' The three of us decided to climb out the window.

"I was good at climbing trees and not afraid of heights. I went first and tested the tree out. I decided the nearest branch was sturdy enough to hold one or two of us at a time and the climb down would be safe. Safer than staying inside.

"Steve guided Sarah out the window. I grabbed her from my perch on the branch and helped her to the trunk. I was going back to help Steve when the most beautiful girl I'd ever seen leaned out the window next to Sarah's room. 'Can you help us, too?'

"Her eyes were the deepest blue. Round and large. But not afraid. Why hadn't I ever seen her before?'" He took a deep breath, lost in the memory.

I was lost in his story, picturing Rick Butler coming to an impressionable young Mom's rescue. Imagining Seth rescuing me in a similar situation. The bond would be unbreakable.

"The sun lit up her flowing hair like a halo. There was no way in hell I could have said no. Fortunately, there was another, equally sturdy branch near her window. I climbed out it to help her.

"'I'm Laura,' she said, as calmly as if she was introducing herself at a party." He smiled at the memory. "'And this is Mary.'

"Mary was hunkering inside the room. It took some doing, but Laura and I coaxed her out. I helped Mary to the center of the tree where Steve waited to help her down while Laura waited for me to come back for her.

"Sarah was already gamely scrambling down. By the time I went back for Laura, she was climbing out on the branch herself. She wobbled. I caught her hand and helped her to the tree trunk.

"'Do you always skulk about in trees helping damsels in distress?' she asked me.

"'Always. It's a calling. My superhero power—tree climbing. I haven't seen you here before,' I said to her.

"'You wouldn't. This is the first time I've visited Mary. We were supposed to be studying. So much for that. You don't live on the fifth floor, I hope?'

"The dorm was coed by floor. The fifth was obviously a girls' floor. 'I'm a Tau Psi,' I told her.

"'Too bad,' she said. 'I don't much care for frat boys.'

"She scrambled down the tree like a seasoned tomboy. The tree was large and the bottom branch was trimmed a good six feet off the ground. I swung down first and held my arms out to catch her as she hung from the bottom branch, and I helped her down.

"I remember everything about that moment as if it was yesterday. The smell of her perfume. The look in her eyes. The way she smiled down at me. The way she felt in my arms—" He stopped himself short, as if he'd said too much already.

"You saved her? Wow!" I was picturing the scene. Mom in his arms. Danger in the air. Rick playing hero. Mom a hero, too, for making sure Mary was safe first.

I agreed with Rick. He wasn't being arrogant at all when he wondered why Laura hadn't told me about her adventure. Who wouldn't tell such a story? Why hadn't Mom ever mentioned she'd almost been blown up? And that a guy had saved her. It was as if she was trying to completely erase Rick from her life. Trying to forget he'd ever existed.

I had to know the rest. "Then what happened?"

"I took Laura's hand. The cops were directing students into the street and the far parking lot. Hand in hand, we ran toward the crowd. We'd just reached the street when the bomb went off, deafening us for a minute."

He turned serious. "Windows blew out. Glass rained down, just missing us. I wrapped my arms around Laura to protect her from the debris. But damn if that solid concrete dorm was still standing when the smoke cleared. Barely damaged. Except for the fifth floor."

He took a deep breath. "The rooms we'd been in were badly burned, completely destroyed. But only one person died—the bomber." He paused again.

I had no words.

Rick looked me right in the eye. "Do you know what Laura said to me when our ears stopped ringing enough so we could hear again?"

"Thanks for going out on a limb for me?" I said, fearing what she really said.

His eyes went wide with surprise and then he broke out laughing.

"You're your mother's daughter, all right. No," he said. "She said, 'Do you think my prof is going to believe the excuse that a bomber blew up my homework?'"

My eyes welled with tears. "That sounds exactly like her." I was so proud of both of them.

I just couldn't get over it. He'd risked his life for Mom? I pictured it all too clearly. Rick with his cocky frat-boy attitude and long, sexy hair. It was like the prince coming to rescue Rapunzel from the tower. I had the feeling he was sanitizing the account for our ears. I imagined him coaxing the girls down with a lot of flirting going on. Laughing at danger. Putting them at ease.

After that, even if he hadn't been totally hot, she would have been hard-pressed not to develop a hero-worship crush on him.

"I took Laura out for ice cream," Rick said as an afterthought. "Because that's what you do to calm nerves after nearly being blown up. And she refused my offer of a beer at the frat." His smile turned sad. "That was the beginning of a whirlwind romance."

He must have seen the look of shock on our faces.

He couldn't have guessed the real reason for mine. I was becoming convinced he'd been in love with Mom. Really in love. The look in his eyes when he talked about her. The romantic way he remembered their dramatic first meeting.

So what had happened to break them apart?

"You can look up the old news reports about it," Rick said. "Probably have the news story on microfiche at the college newspaper archives."

"And I thought mass campus killings were a modern-day phenomenon." Seth laced his fingers through mine, holding on protectively.

"Human nature hasn't changed." Rick picked up his glass again. "Explosions seemed to be the theme that school year. Just five or six weeks later, Mount St. Helens blew up."

I made a mental note—Mom and Rick Butler had dated for about six weeks. Okay, not an eternity. Not a long-term thing. But, evidently, not inconsequential, either. I had to keep Rick talking.

"Dessert, anyone?" Rick asked. "Caesar will be insulted if we don't indulge."

I nodded. "Sure, why not?" I didn't want to insult Caesar. Plus, the cookies he'd packed us for lunch had been delicious. "We studied the eruption in, like, the fifth grade." I leaned back to let the waiter clear my plate. "What was it like in person?"

The waiter set a dessert menu in front of me.

"Gray." Rick didn't bother looking at the dessert menu. "The crème brûlée is superb. So are the chocolate lava cake and the early spring rhubarb cobbler. We grow the rhubarb at the winery."

"You'll have to be more specific," I said. "About the eruption."

He ordered coffee for the table. "That. Not as spectacular as the old news footage. I'd gone home for the weekend. Which made Laura unhappy. I left home in Seattle to drive back to school shortly after the mountain erupted. Drove all the way across the state in an ash cloud.

"Poor visibility. We crawled along. I was concerned the ash would clog my air filter. Cars were stalling out along on the freeway. Took me forever, but I made it back as the worst of it hit the university. Day turned to night. The birds roosted. It was eerie. Back at the frat, they'd thought ahead to buy beer. Got as many kegs as they could get their hands on and prepared for a long volcano party.

"I tried to call Laura. But the phone lines were busy, totally overloaded. So I disobeyed university orders and went out in the ash to her dorm to rescue her from certain boredom.

"The girls were scared. But there was really no reason. I convinced Laura to come back to the frat with me and party on." He paused.

I tried to imagine Mom at a frat party. She hated the Greek system. Never said anything good about frats or the guys in them.

"Mom wouldn't go to a frat party. She doesn't like frats or frat guys. She's always warned me off them." I didn't know why I felt I had to challenge him.

"You don't know your mom as well as you think."
Rick looked out over the lake, like he was getting control of his emotions.

When he looked back at me, he was grinning. Arro-
gantly. "Is that what she told you? Damn. Could have
fooled me. She liked frat boys well enough in those
days."

He had the nerve to laugh.

"Dad." Seth had a challenge in his voice.

Rick ignored it. "We partied all night. When the
sun came up the next day, the world was covered in two
to three inches of gray ash. Like fine, powdery snow,
only dirty.

"The university canceled class. They never did that.
Not even the day the dorm blew up. Or the many times
they received anonymous threats about someone poi-
soning the dorm salad bars with cyanide stolen from
the chemistry department.

"Then they issued us facemasks. The kind doctors
or maybe, more accurately, furniture makers or something wear. Because the dust could be dangerous to our
lungs. Give us lung cancer when we were older." He
laughed. "Hasn't come true yet. The truth was, it was
just dust. Like the kind you get on your car from driving along a dirt road on a dry summer day. Just pulverized mountain.

"We wore them for about a day until everyone discarded them as a nuisance. Made your face hot and it
was hard to breathe. Damn funny for a while, though,
seeing everyone on campus wearing a white mask over

their mouths. Couldn't recognize a damn person." He shook his head like it had all been folly.

"The university and town sent the street sweepers out to get rid of the dust. Which mostly just made a dust storm in the wake of the sweepers. Many people scooped up jars and vials of the stuff to keep as a souvenir. I didn't bother.

"The second day, a breeze kicked up and blew the dust off the trees. The stuff blew around everywhere. Some of it sifted into the grass. After a few days, it finally rained. We were never so glad about a rain shower. Washed most of the dust down the drains. But not all. Remnants hung around and blew around in dry weather for years.

"The middle of the state got a lot more ash. Thicker ash. A good ten years later they had to close I-90 because of an ash storm caused by wind."

Something about his tone. His eyes lost their look of humor and happy memories. It was as if the ash coming had put a gray cloud on everything.

Seth grabbed his water glass. "Dad, didn't you marry Mom that summer?"

"In Seattle. We didn't have a problem with the ash there. It missed us."

I frowned. "But you were dating my mom when the mountain erupted? Then..." I couldn't help frowning.

Seth shot me a look warning me to back off. I opened my mouth to go for it anyway.

Rick beat me to it. "So what happened?" He sighed. "Colleen was pregnant with Seth's older brother. She told me a few days after the mountain blew up.

"Colleen was always...fragile. She wanted the baby. Wouldn't hear of aborting or giving it up. She needed me. I broke up with your mom and did the right thing by Colleen and my baby. I married her."

CHAPTER SIXTEEN

Maddie

Somehow, I made it through the rest of dinner and the evening. Though I didn't know how. I was reeling. Since I'd first suspected Rick Butler of fathering Ian, I'd assumed he was a complete douche who'd walked out on Mom when he found out she was pregnant. How was I supposed to deal with this new information?

He'd gotten two girls pregnant? At the same time! And married the first one who told him. Out of a sense of duty. No wonder Mom never mentioned him. He'd broken her heart. I was sure of that.

I should have hated him. But I couldn't. Not after he'd saved her. And spoken so fondly of her. He wasn't the douche I'd thought he was. Or wanted him to be.

And now, an even more terrible thought occurred to me—did Rick even know Mom had been pregnant, too? Was she really the villain, keeping the baby a secret from him?

He sure didn't act like he knew.

And what about my dad? What had she told him? He'd always claimed Ian as his own. Had he known the truth? Or had Mom convinced him the baby was his?

The thoughts kept swirling in my head like an ominous cloud on the emotional horizon. I didn't know what to think or believe.

Through dessert, I listened to Seth and his dad banter back and forth. I didn't know whether they noticed my relative silence.

After dinner, Seth took me out to sit on the beach and look at the stars.

He slid his arm around me and held me close. "You're awfully quiet."

"I'm thinking." I bit my lip. "Does it bother you that your dad married your mom out of a sense of responsibility?"

"You mean does it bother me that Mom trapped him into marrying her?" He sounded bitter, and yet almost amused at the same time. Like it was what it was. "Not really. I've always known she was pregnant when they got married. When I think about the way things are, it makes total sense. From my perspective, they've never been in love. Always been divorced and bitter toward each other.

"I always thought it was because of my brother's death. Now I know there was more to it. Does that make a difference to me?" He shrugged. "Not really. The outcome is the same."

I had to test him, dip my toes in the waters of coming clean. "Seth, at some point...what happens if your dad and my mom meet each other again? I mean...if you and I...you know, continue on together, they probably will." I was making a mess of things. I shuddered involuntarily and tried to cover and act like it was because of the cool evening.

He pulled me closer. "It will probably be awkward as hell. But whatever happened between them was years ago. They should be over it by now."

I nodded uncertainly. "Maybe."

"Don't worry about it," he said. "We'll deal with it when we have to."

I had the feeling, though, that "when we have to" was much sooner than he imagined. I was thinking about Ian. And how strange he'd acted when I asked him why he'd chosen to come to the university. Did he suspect what I did? How would he have known?

I had to talk to him. I needed to tell him what I suspected. I needed his advice and opinion. But I didn't want to hurt him. How could I tell him without hurting him or Mom? Or Dad's memory?

But if I didn't and he accidentally ran into Seth? Or insisted on meeting him? And eventually, probably sooner than later, he was going to insist on meeting Seth simply because he was my boyfriend. What did I do then? How would I explain? To either of them.

I was the victim of a sliding, accumulating set of circumstantial evidence. Should I have gone to either Ian

or Seth with my suspicions the first time I met Seth
and noticed he looked a lot like Ian? When I found out
Rick and my parents were at the university at the same
time? When I saw that picture of Rick and realized Ian
looked like a young Rick? When that letter fell out of
Mom's photo album?

When was the accumulation of evidence enough?
Okay, now. Now it was enough. But before—when exactly had it crossed the line?

I looked at Seth. I wouldn't lose him. I couldn't. But
I felt like fate had already doomed us. How would he
react if, when, I told him I thought we shared a brother?

Seth

I had planned everything about Maddie's visit. I was
determined to show her how romantic I could be. And
impress her. To show her how committed I was to her.
Because, damn, I'd never wanted to impress a girl so
badly before. Or show any kind of commitment.

I was failing. I could feel it. Dad was interfering in
ways I'd never imagined. She hadn't acted the same
since that story he'd told about saving her mom. And
seriously, what guy could compete with that hero shit?
What was I supposed to do? Hire a bomber so I could
save Maddie like Dad had her mom?

He had to tell that story and one-up me. Dad, the
accidental hero.

Since then, Maddie had been preoccupied. Half a
dozen times, she started to tell me something. And cut
herself off.

On Saturday afternoon, I took her on a tour of the local wineries. I'd planned it carefully, starting with the least impressive winery. Ending at Dad's. After closing. Kind of like tasting dry wines first and ending with sweet.

"All this winetasting should get you extra credit," I told her.

"And drunk," she teased back, but it was forced, like she there was something heavy on her mind. It weighed down everything about her.

Basic tasting was free at all the wineries I was going to take her to. So, yeah, you could say it was a cheap date. If I'd played it that way.

After tasting the standard four offerings at the first winery, Maddie slung her purse over her shoulder. "On to the next one!" That false perkiness sparkled in her voice.

"Not so fast." I grabbed her hand. "What was your favorite?"

She paused and looked upward, like she was thinking hard. "That's tough. I liked the last two."

I prompted her. "You like the sweeter wines?"

"Dry to sweet!" She laughed and nodded. "When you put it that way, yeah, I guess I do. At least here I did."

"Choose carefully." I squeezed her hand.

She looked at me like she wondered what I was up to. "I liked the last one. The dessert wine."

"Excellent!" I pulled her to a display of wines and grabbed a bottle of the one she liked.

"What are you doing?"

"Buying a bottle of your favorite."

"You don't have to. I wasn't begging—"

"I want to." I had an excellent plan to show my romantic, committed side. "We'll save it and drink this bottle of wine on our next month anniversary."

Her eyes misted over. "That's so sweet."

After I bought her favorite at the second winery, she caught on. "How many wineries are we visiting? How much wine are you going to buy?"

"Enough to have a bottle a month through our one-year anniversary." I kissed her quickly and more passionately than I intended. My heart pounded in my ears. "I've never made it to a year with a girl."

She turned her gaze on me, her eyes wide and misty. "Oh, Seth." She hugged me, clung to me.

I was almost embarrassed that she was so moved by my plan. And pleased and incredibly happy.

We ended the day at Dad's winery at sunset. I let us in with a key. I'd ordered dinner from the hotel and bribed one of the waiters I knew to set it out for us on a table on the balcony. With a red rose in a vase.

Maddie gasped when she saw it.

At first, I thought she was pleased and overwhelmed. Damn, I was good with the romance. But she had paled and was trembling.

"What?" I put my arms around her. "What's wrong?"

"Nothing." She bit her lip. "It's so...perfect. Like...you aren't...this isn't..."

I stared at her, trying to prompt her. "Isn't...?"

"You aren't going to propose?" She winced.

I laughed. "Shit! No. I'm not that committed. *Yet.*"
She looked relieved, and smiled. "Good."

"Good?" I stared at her, trying not to be hurt. "You mean you wouldn't marry me?"

"I didn't say that. I don't know. I really don't. Maybe. Someday. But right now, it's too soon to tell." She paused, looking like there was something she wanted to say. "We don't know everything about each other. Maybe there are secrets..."

I laughed, trying to lighten the mood. "It's not good to know everything. They always say you shouldn't lose the mystery." I paused, studying her. "You have secrets? Anything you want to tell me?"

She bit her lip, looking like she was struggling with herself over something. "We all have secrets." She put her hand on my arm. "To be perfectly clear, you aren't proposing?"

I shook my head. "No. Guess I overdid it with my wine buying? Came off too serious?"

"No. It was perfect."

Why did she sound so damn sad, then? I was screwing things up. I didn't understand her.

She relaxed and dropped her hand from my arm to study the table. "Wow, when you do propose...to someone"—she sounded almost sad and extremely cautious—"it's really going to be something. How are you going to top this? She's going to be very lucky."

Shit. I didn't like the way she practically assumed that girl wouldn't be her. Neither of us had any idea what the future held. But the way I felt now, she had every chance of being the girl I'd eventually marry.

I caught her hand in mine and squeezed. "Let's pick out the wine for our one-year anniversary. Dad gave us full run of the cellar."

I caught her chin in my hand and stared into her eyes. "I love you, Mads. I wish I could prove it to you somehow. I want to be your hero."

Although it had been on my mind, I didn't know why I said it. It slipped out.

"Be careful what you wish for." She reached up and stroked my cheek. "You don't have to pull me from a burning building to be my hero. You just have to believe me. Believe that I would never intentionally do anything to hurt you. Believe me when I beg you to."

A shiver ran down my back. What was she telling me?

She grabbed the wrist of my hand holding her chin and turned her mouth to kiss my hand. "Let's go pick out that wine."

CHAPTER SEVENTEEN

Maddie

Rick saw us off the next morning. He walked us to the driveway and helped load our bags in our respective cars.

He hugged me, which caught me off guard. "Say hello to your mom for me. Next time you talk to her."

He was clearly issuing a challenge. He wanted me to tell Mom who Seth really was—Rick Butler's son, the man who had saved her life and killed her heart. Hardly a good bargain for her.

I shrugged, noncommittal. If he wanted to know if she still remembered him, he could hunt down her contact information and cold call her. The thought sent a shiver through me.

Mom was notoriously private. She kept off social media. But how hard was it to find anyone these days?

I didn't want him to be the one to tell Mom about Seth. And for his part, Rick didn't know what he was asking. Or potentially walking into. Though he had no idea, he was bargaining for another son and a total disruption to too many lives. Things were quickly spiraling out of control.

I had to get back to school. I desperately needed to talk to my brother.

Rick hugged Seth. "I'll see you in a few weeks when I'm in town to set up the winetasting event." He slapped Seth on the back like a proud dad.

And we were off. Four hours of alone time to think about what I should do. And dread the consequences. Everywhere my mind turned I ran into a no-win scenario.

Olivia was already at the apartment when I arrived. She bubbled with news of her trip and asked me questions about Rick and Seth and my stay with them. It was a relief to be able to talk candidly with someone else. I told her everything.

She agreed with my conclusion. "You're absolutely right. You have to tell Ian."

I nodded. Now that I was back in town, I was filled with dread at doing what I knew was the right thing.

Olivia handed me my phone. "Call him. Now. And schedule some face-to-face big-bro time."

His phone rang and rang. He didn't pick up. He was like that when he was busy or didn't want to be interrupted. He'd go old school and off the grid.

I left him a voicemail. "I have to talk to you. As soon as possible. In person. It's urgent."

I looked at Olivia for confirmation.

She hugged me. "You're doing the right thing. You'll find a way to tell him."

My phone rang in my hand with the ringtone I used for Ian. I took a deep breath and picked up. "Hey. Thanks for calling me back."

"You've heard." Ian sounded protective and furious at the same time. More upset than I'd heard him since he left his last position. "How much?"

"Uh—" *Heard what?*

"You warned me this department had problems. That they were overly sensitive to issues of sexual misconduct. But I can't believe this! For some anonymous shithead to accuse me of inappropriate sexual behavior with one of my students! I will kick his ass when I find out who the coward is."

My heart thudded and stopped cold. I felt the blood drain out of my face. *Oh, no! Not again.*

Beside me, Olivia listened in to my side of the conversation. "What's going on?" she mouthed.

I held up a finger to silence her.

He cursed beneath his breath. "Don't worry. I'll get this straightened out. The department chair wants me to meet him in his office tomorrow at ten to hear my side."

"Oh, no!" I said, aloud this time. "Ian—"

"Don't worry." His tone became big brotherly. "I'm innocent. I don't have anything to fear. The truth will win out. Given the Dr. Rogers case, they're being cautious. This is just an informal one-on-one."

"But who's accused you? What are they claiming you did, exactly?" I had a horrible, sinking feeling.

"Someone has supposedly seen me carrying on all over campus and at the bars with a chemistry student." His voice shook. "The chair of the chem department wants to voice his concerns in person. Those are all the details I have."

The pain in his voice broke my heart.

"That's not fair. You have the right to meet your accuser. Or at least know who it is."

"Since when has life been fair?" He sounded almost resigned.

How could I tell him about Seth now? It would have to wait until after his meeting with the dean.

He sighed. "Don't tell Mom, okay?"

I sighed. "Okay." But a sick feeling was settling over me. "You'll let me know how the meeting goes? Maybe you should get a lawyer—"

"I'll let you know." He paused. "Was there something else you wanted to talk to me about?"

I bit my lip and glanced at Olivia for strength. She nodded and motioned to the phone. "Make a date to see him," she whispered.

"Yes," I said. "Actually, I want to catch up. Hear about Hawaii. And...I need some big brotherly advice. Can we meet for coffee after your meeting?"

"Advice, huh?" He sounded intrigued. "About what?"

I sighed and laughed nervously. "Boys."

He laughed. "I thought I gave you that talk years ago."

"Shut up, Ian. This is serious. I really need to talk to you. As soon as possible."

"Okay. Okay. I'm beat today and have to get ready for my eight o'clock class tomorrow. My meeting shouldn't last more than an hour. Then I have a break. Want to meet at eleven? We can catch an early lunch."

"Sounds good," I said. "Meet you at your office?"

"Awesome. See you tomorrow."

After he hung up, I explained to Olivia.

She got a funny look on her face. "I hate to bring this up." She hesitated. "But it just occurred to me. What if someone's seen you and Seth together and mistaken Seth for Ian? They look a lot alike and you've taken a lot of chemistry. It's not a stretch for someone to get confused and think you're one of Ian's students. And Seth is Ian. And, well, you get the idea."

I stared back at her. "Crap! I was thinking the same thing. And hoping I was just being paranoid." I paused. "Until we know more, it's just speculation. I'll bring it up with Ian tomorrow. After I tell him about Seth."

Seth

On Monday morning, Zach and I carpooled to campus. We parked in our usual lot and hiked up the hill to the mall toward class. We each had a cup of coffee. It was the only way I was going to stay awake for a ten o'clock class.

Morgan walked by. Her face lit up when she saw us. "Zach! Seth!" She threw herself into me and gave me a gigantic hug. "How was your break?"

We made small talk for a few minutes.

"On your way to class?" Morgan asked.

I nodded.

"I am, too. First day back after spring break sucks. There isn't enough coffee." Morgan's eyes lit up. "Oh, I almost forgot to tell you. I remembered!"

I frowned, puzzled. "Remembered what?"

"The name of that prof who looks like you!" She pulled her phone out of her pocket.

I'd forgotten all about it.

"I even found his picture so I could prove how right I am. You two could be brothers. Here's his official university photo on the website." She flipped the phone around so I could see the screen. "Ta-da! Dr. Ian Foster, chemistry professor!"

I froze. *Ian Foster?* Maddie's last name was Foster. And her brother's name was Ian. And he was a professor.

"Let's see that." I took the phone from Morgan with a high degree of skepticism, expecting to see some guy with a similar haircut and build. Same color eyes. That kind of thing.

When I took a look, I went cold. "Shit."

Morgan clapped her hands like a delighted child and nodded. "He's like your older twin or something. Am I right or am I right!"

Zach crowded behind me and peeked over my shoulder to get a look.

"Whoa!" Zach said. "Morgs is spot on." He huddled closer. "You know who he really looks like, though?"

I didn't answer. I couldn't.

"That picture of your dad Alexis found in the sorority archives." He shook me by the shoulder. "Wait a minute! Isn't Maddie's older brother's name Ian?"

I nodded.

"If I were you, I'd head over to the chem department and meet this guy," Zach said.

"I have class." I spoke on autopilot. This was just eerie.

Zach enlarged the text on the phone and pointed. "Dude, he has office hours next period, right after your class."

Maddie

I'd rehearsed and rehearsed what I was going to say to Ian. But how do you bring something like this up? *Hey, big brother, I think I may be dating your little brother. The one you had no clue even existed. Let's tell Mom. Won't she be surprised?*

There was no way. Simply no way to be tactful and diplomatic when delivering news like this. Olivia and I had tried every permutation. I was going to try to be gentle and ease into it. But I was so afraid I would just blurt it out. I was more nervous than I ever remembered being as I climbed the steps in the chem building and made my way into the office.

Tessa, the chem department office administrator, looked up as I came in. Usually she was quick with a smile. Today she looked surprised, not in a good way, and a little wary.

"Maddie!" Her smile looked forced. "Good to see you. Which chemistry do you have this semester? Who are you here to see?"

Her questions seemed innocuous enough, but there was an edge of morbid curiosity to them I'd never noticed in her before. Like she was on the trail of a scandal. Maybe the whole department was simply paranoid. More likely, she knew about the allegations against Ian and was gently fishing for more information.

I was always impressed by the way Tessa remembered everybody, even those of us who weren't chem majors. Then again, I had spent an inordinate amount of time in these offices getting help for the numerous chem classes my major required. I almost had a minor in chem.

"I'm not in chem this semester." I forced a smile. "Thankfully."

"You aren't?" Tessa frowned. "That's a first. I could have sworn you were."

I shook my head. "First semester since I started college that I'm completely chem-class free."

She laughed nervously. "So what are you doing here?" A pregnant pause. "What can I help you with?"

"I'm here to see my brother, Dr. Foster."

The look on her face was priceless.

"Foster! Of course." She paused. "Foster," she said more softly. "I thought it was just a coincidence."

"It's a common name," I said. "Is he still in his meeting?"

"Yes." She popped out of her chair. "You can wait here or by his office." She pointed toward the chair's office. "I'll just go check on it and let him know you're here."

Odd.

I shrugged. Ian's office was locked, which was usual procedure when profs weren't in. There was an empty chair by the door. I took a seat and prepared to wait.

Just then, the main door to the chemistry department offices swung open. I looked up just in time to see Seth come in. I swore to myself. There was nowhere to hide. He didn't see me at first.

When he spotted me, his face clouded with confusion, followed quickly by something that looked like horror.

He knows!

I sprang to my feet. "Seth!"

He frowned and came toward me. "Maddie? What are you doing here?"

The door to the department chair's office that Tessa had disappeared into opened. Dr. Blanchard and Ian came out.

Dr. Blanchard shook Ian's hand. "Thanks for coming in. You have nothing to worry about." He spotted Seth and me.

Ian looked over at the same time. When he saw Seth, the color drained from his face. "What the hell?"

Dr. Blanchard looked equally stunned. "Your brother?"

Ian turned to me with a look on his face asking me to explain. "I don't have a brother. That's my sister. Maddie?"

Seth's gaze bounced between us.

My mouth went dry. I had to force the words out. "Ian, Dr. Blanchard, Tessa, this is my boyfriend, Seth. Seth, this is my brother Ian."

Drop-dead, stone-cold silence hung in the air. Then, to my horror, Dr. Blanchard started laughing. Gently at first, then into a roar, like this was the most hilarious thing he'd ever seen.

I didn't get it at first.

"Ian, they say everyone has a twin in the world. There's yours!" He pointed to Seth. "The resemblance is uncanny. If I had to pick which one of these two is your sibling, hands down I would have bet my life on Seth. Your sister bears only a slight resemblance to you."

He grabbed his sides and wiped his eyes. "If we needed any more evidence, this seals the deal. You accuser mistakenly took Seth and your sister for you and a student." Dr. Blanchard patted Ian on the shoulder again. "This is one to go down in the books. What a lucky coincidence they're both here. Case closed!"

No, Dr. Blanchard was wrong—this was no lucky coincidence. This was utter disaster. The worst timing in the world. A catastrophe. And the case was anything but closed.

Dr. Blanchard shook Ian's hand again. "I'm sorry to put you through this, Ian. Glad your good name is cleared." He looked at us. "Nice to meet you two."

He disappeared back into his office, leaving the rest of us in stunned, awkward silence. Tessa went back to her desk and ostensibly back to work. Though I had the feeling she was still spying on us.

Ian walked over and unlocked his office door, studying Seth the entire time. "Let's talk. Come on in. I'd like to get to know my sister's boyfriend." He ushered us into his office. "Tessa, I don't want to be disturbed."

Which elicited a most curious look from her. It was like he'd issued a challenge to her sense of curiosity.

Ian locked the door behind him. The three of us stood staring at each other. The two guys I loved most in the world were looking at me with hurt and questions in their eyes.

"Well, looks like your meeting went well," I said. "Good that's all cleared up. Mistaken identity, who knew?"

"Maddie, you had something urgent to tell me?" Ian pointed to Seth. "I take it this is it?"

I nodded lamely and tried to smile.

Seth was deathly quiet, the kind of quiet that usually indicates rage. The scary quiet. Ian seemed to be taking things better, so I engaged with him first. "Ian—"

"You're dating a guy who looks just me. I guess I should be flattered?"

"Ian." I screwed up my courage. This was where my world could fly apart. One way or the other, I was doomed. "This is Seth *Butler*. His dad is Rick Butler?"

I studied my older brother, looking for glimmers of recognition.

"Butler?" Ian cocked his head like he was thinking and trying to place the name. "Is that supposed to mean something to me?"

I nodded. I prompted him. "His dad dated our mom in college?"

I glanced helplessly between Seth and Ian. Surely Seth had to be piecing this all together by now? But what in the world was he doing here in the first place?

The two guys sized each other up.

Ian looked suddenly uncertain, like things were beginning to dawn on him.

"Ian, I think..." I took a deep breath, feeling sick inside. "I believe..." Tears formed in my eyes.

This wasn't how it was supposed to happen. This wasn't how Olivia and I had rehearsed things.

"I think you two are brothers." I spat the words out as fast as I could.

There. I'd said it.

The words hung in the air, undigested for a second.

"Shit!" Seth was wearing his beanie. He pulled it lower on his head with a nervous gesture. "You really do look like Dad."

Ian ran his hand through his hair and studied Seth as if he was scrutinizing his own reflection in the mirror.

"I don't know for sure," I said, ping-ponging my gaze between them, looking for signs of hope. "It's all circumstantial. All the evidence just sort of piled up bit by bit."

I was pleading with them, but neither one of them was listening.

Seth turned to me, hurt shining in his eyes. "How long have you known? Why didn't you tell me? Were you using me for fun? How could you, Maddie?"

He turned abruptly on his heel and stormed out.

"Seth! Wait! I can explain." I started after him.

Ian grabbed my arm. "Let him go."

I started bawling.

Ian shut and locked the door again and pulled me into his arms, cooing to me like I was still his baby sis. "It's okay. He needs time to process. Give him a little space. He'll come back."

He guided me to a chair and gently sat me in it, and poured me a glass of water from his water cooler.

He handed it to me. "Drink this."

"Water, it cures everything." I wiped my eyes with the back of my hand and sniffed.

Ian handed me a tissue. "Water is calming."

He pulled up a chair next to me.

"Are you okay?" I said through my sniffles. "This isn't the way I wanted you to find out. I didn't ask Seth to come here today. I don't know why he was here." I wiped my eyes. "I was going to tell you and ask your advice about what we should do and how I should tell Seth."

Ian nodded.

"You're taking this well," I said.

He nodded. "I'm not completely surprised. I mean, I am totally surprised that my sister is dating my brother."

"Yeah, that's crazy," I said. "Completely insane. A trick played by fate. Almost Oedipal."

"Not quite." He took my hand between his. "You and he aren't blood related." He stated it as simple fact. "I'm not surprised that I have a brother or that Dad isn't my biological dad. I've known he wasn't for a while now."

"That's why you came here," I finished for him. "That's what you hinted at, about finding out more about Mom and Dad's story."

"I always knew you were bright, sis." He squeezed my hand.

"What made you suspect?" I asked.

"Little things. The way I looked nothing like Dad or any of his side of the family. The way Mom treated me differently from you. The way you were Dad's obvious favorite. The stories I overheard from Mom's sister and from Grandma about how surprised they were when she married Dad. That he didn't seem like her type. That she'd never mentioned him during the school year and the courtship was so quick. About how the quiet ones could surprise you, but he never seemed the type to knock a girl up. And hadn't she been so crazy about that frat boy? What had happened between them? Why didn't she act all gaga like that about Bruce? Maybe she'd grown up and gotten past the silly stage.

"The way Mom and Dad never talked about college or how they met. When asked, they were totally vague." He paused, looking thoughtful. "You know how a lot of little kids think they're adopted? Even ones who aren't?"

I nodded.

"I've had that feeling forever, that I was adopted."

I nodded. Ian and I were both intuitive that way. In fact, my feeling about this semester being life-changing was right on target. Just not in the way I'd thought it would be.

"Then one time I overheard Grandma speculating to her sister, Great-Aunt Rebecca, about how she'd always wondered if I really was Bruce's son. That sealed it for me. I was positive I was half adopted. That I wasn't Dad's." He hesitated again. "I have a confession. I did something crazy, Mads."

I looked at him, surprised. "What?"

"I had a paternity test run on myself."

I was sure my eyes went wide. I was stunned. "What?"

He nodded.

"When? How? Dad is...gone."

He looked apologetically at me. "A few years ago. You can't tell Mom. I just had to know. I got a DNA sample from Uncle Will. The paternal DNA can be matched to a male relative. If he was my blood uncle, we'd share the same male DNA from our Y chromosome."

"And you didn't?"

"No."

I was dumbfounded. "Dad's brother agreed to that? How did you approach him? How did you talk him out of it? And swear him to secrecy?"

He shrugged. "I didn't ask him. I stole it."

I just stared at my brother, in awe of him. "Like, pulled a hair out of his head?"

"Something like that." He looked like he was trying not to grin over his cleverness.

"And kept it a secret for years?"

He nodded.

"And didn't tell me?"

He shook his head.

"Were you *ever* going to tell me?"

He looked almost guilty. "No. Not unless I had to. Bruce raised me like his own. He claimed me. He's the only dad I've ever known. He *is* my dad. He didn't want anyone to know I wasn't his biological son. I felt I owed him that respect and loyalty." His eyes misted over. "I loved him, too, Mads."

Fresh tears welled in my eyes. I realized something else. "I'm only your half-sister."

"You're my sister. Period." He paused and looked at once hopeful and sheepish. "Do I have any others?"

I smiled through my tears at him. "If you're hoping for a better sister, you're going to be disappointed. If I'm right about Rick Butler being your dad, I'm the only one. And, by the way, he was a frat boy. Just another bit of corroborating evidence." I bit my lip. "You had another half-brother besides Seth."

"Had?"

I nodded. "I'm sorry. He passed away years ago. When he was twelve." I hesitated. "He was almost exactly your age."

Ian took a minute to take that in. "My suspected father got two girls pregnant at once?"

I nodded. "And, from what I've pieced together, married the first one who told him she was going to have a baby—Seth's mom, Colleen." I took a deep breath. "I wanted to hate him, but Rick is a good guy."

"You've met him?" Ian looked surprised.

"I spent the last weekend of spring break with Seth at his dad's. Mom doesn't know. I lied to her about where I was going. I suspected things. I had to find out."

Ian whistled softly. "Now I'm impressed."

"If it's any consolation, I don't think he knows about you. That you exist at all. That Mom was ever pregnant. I don't think she told him."

"We're talking like he's a sure thing," Ian said.

"The evidence is circumstantial, but pretty monumental and convincing. I'll tell you everything I know. How this all happened. How I found out. How I started dating Seth."

I broke my hands free from his and scooted close enough to throw my arms around his neck. "Just please don't judge me. This all piled on me one bit of circumstantial evidence at a time."

"I would never judge you, baby sis. You know that." He sounded fierce and protective.

I believed him. Ian had always been my rock.

"I love Seth! I need your help to get him back. He had no idea he had another brother. No idea that brother is my brother, too. It's all such a mess."

Ian stroked my hair. "He's had a shock. He needs time. If he's really my brother, he'll come around. I've had a couple of years to digest the information that Dad wasn't my biological dad."

I gulped and nodded, trying to smile. "I have to text him and offer to explain." I felt even paler. "And warn him that Rick doesn't know about you."

"You're right," Ian said gently, seemingly unconcerned his dad might accidentally find out about him. "Text him and then we can talk. We have all day."

CHAPTER EIGHTEEN

Seth

I raced out of the room, out of the offices, out of the building. Out into the fresh, cool spring air. To the edge of the mall. I had to get away.

I ran to the parking lot and collapsed against my car. How could Maddie do this to me? How long had she known?

I have a brother. A living older brother.

The thought was startling. Did Dad know? Had he kept it from me, too?

Maddie had hurt me. Hurt me so bad. To the core. Buying wine ahead for our one-year anniversary. What a douche I was.

My phone buzzed with a text. *Maddie.* My heart felt tight in my chest. I almost ignored the message. But

Maddie was impossible for me to resist. Deep down, I wanted her to explain. I wanted her to be innocent. A victim of circumstance. I wanted to believe she hadn't meant to hurt me. But how could I trust a girl who didn't share important crap like this? We were supposed to face things together.

Shit, I still needed her.

I'm sorry. I didn't mean for you to find out like this. I learned the truth bit by bit, piece by piece until it became a mountain of evidence. I only came to the full realization over the weekend. I had to talk to my brother before I went to you with my suspicions. I was meeting him at his office to tell him and get his advice when you walked in.

Ian didn't know anything about you or us. He's totally innocent in this. He's always believed my dad is his dad. From what I've pieced together, I don't think Rick knows Ian even exists, either. Please, let's talk about this before you tell him.

Just know, you and I aren't related. And I love you.

I swallowed a lump in my throat. I wasn't in the mood to talk. I slid the phone back in my pocket without answering and pounded my fist against the hood of my car.

How was I supposed to deal with this? I had been dating my brother's sister. My girlfriend and I shared a brother. What kind of crazy shit was that?

I needed to think. I just needed to think.

Maddie

After I left Ian, I went back to my apartment and told Olivia the whole sad story.

"So Ian suspected your dad wasn't his and took the whole thing well?" She sounded dumbfounded.

I nodded. "He's always been intuitive. I think he likes the idea that he has a little brother, too. He's always wanted one. Though maybe not this way." I couldn't keep the bitterness out of my laugh.

"And Seth didn't take it so well?" Olivia frowned.

I shook my head. "I wish I knew why he'd come to the office. It was totally unexpected and caught me off guard. I thought by going to Ian and telling him, I had everything under control." I sighed and gave her a sad look. "You and I never practiced this scenario."

"Fate can be a real bastard!" Olivia spat.

"Seth isn't responding to my texts. Ian says he needs time. What do you think?" I asked her.

"Don't give up on him," she said. "If he loves you, he'll come around. And I'm sure he does."

"But how can I explain if he won't see me or respond?" I was desperate for an answer that would put us back together.

She shook her head gently. "He doesn't necessarily have to respond. You just have to tell him the story. And hope he comes to terms with it."

I gave her a well-duh look. "You're right. If I lay it out like it unfolded for me, a little bit at a time, then he has to understand."

"And if he doesn't, he's a douche and doesn't deserve you." She gave me a hug.

"True." I fought back tears. "But now that he and Ian are related, it's going to be kind of hard to completely cut him out of my life if he doesn't."

"Take the chance," she said.

I grabbed my phone and began texting Seth.

On the first day of the semester, I took a seat in HBM 225, totally believing that class would change my life. And then, in walked this hot, charming guy who lit up the room. And who just happened to look a lot like my older brother. My brother who all the girls fall over because he's so handsome. The brother I idolize. Who's charming and loving. The brother I used to tease when I was young and pretend was my boyfriend to make the rest of the girls jealous.

As I stared at this new guy, and tried to not to drool all over him, I thought, Life is a full of irony. How can I be so attracted to someone who looks so much like Ian?

But it never crossed my mind that you two could be related. Why would it? As far as I knew, my dad was Ian's. So life had a sense of humor, throwing a guy like my brother at me. But that was it, as far as I was concerned.

I didn't realize until later that was the beginning of a mound of circumstantial evidence that would surface one pebble at a time...

Seth

Someone pounded on our apartment door loud enough to make me jump. Zach was out and I wasn't expecting anyone. I grumbled as I got up to answer it.

It was probably Zach's buddy Dakota stopping by to hang out.

I swung the door open, ready to chew Dak out for interrupting my studying.

Ian Foster stood outside the apartment, an intense look on his face. "Hello, little brother." He grinned, but his eyes and voice were hard. He filled the doorway, standing tall, like he was trying to intimidate me. Like he was challenging me to turn him away.

"How the hell did you find out where I live?" My voice was as hard as his eyes. I wasn't ready to deal with him. I wasn't ready to deal with any of this shit. I'd even been ignoring texts from Dad, afraid I would lash out at him.

Ian didn't wait to be invited in. He brushed past me into the tiny entryway with a shove, an intentional foul. "I have my sources."

I wanted to shove him back in the worst way. But I resisted. For now.

He was carrying an innocuous brown paper bag. He lifted it and shook it. "Close the door. I brought you a present."

"I don't want your damn present." I glared at him and balled my fists. I'd always wanted an older brother. Now I wanted to punch the smug look off his face.

Maddie would be furious with me if I did. And somehow that still mattered and kept me in line.

Ian seemed amazingly calm. And confident. Almost amused beneath a veneer of deadly seriousness, like this was some sort of bad joke. He reminded me too damn much of Dad. Which made me even angrier.

"You'll want this one." He rattled the bag again. "We can settle this now."

I made a fist, ready to defend myself. Damn, I wanted to shove him and take a swing at him. For me. For Maddie. For everything.

"You want to step outside?" I reached for the doorknob. "Let's go."

He laughed harshly. "Calm down, big shot. I'm not afraid to fight you. If that's what you want, I'm happy to oblige. For my sister. You've been screwing with her. And you broke her heart. It's my duty to break your nose in return." He stared me down, looking like he meant it. "But before we engage in brotherly horseplay, let's find out if we really are brothers."

I stared at him. "What do you mean, find out? I haven't told Dad about you yet. If you're planning to waltz in and introduce yourself to him, forget it." For some crazy reason I felt suddenly protective of my father. The old man had had a lot to deal with. I wasn't sure I wanted to throw another possible son at him.

My potential older brother rattled that damn paper bag again. "I brought an ancestry test."

"Don't you need *my* dad for that?" I stared him down, jealous and defensive.

Ian shook his head. "Not for this. I ran a paternity test on my dad after he died. I'm not his biological son." He looked genuinely sad about that. "I've known for years. I have the test results. All we need is a sample of your DNA to run through an ancestry DNA test. If our paternal line DNA matches, bingo! We're brothers."

I frowned at him, liking him and hating him at the same time. "No need to involve Dad?"

He shook his head. "Not until we know for sure I'm his son. This test solves all your problems. If we're not a match, this mess goes away—"

"And if we are?" I stared at him, knowing we were. Looking at us, it was obvious. And once you threw in the damning circumstantial evidence, I figured the odds of us not being brothers were about a million to one.

"We deal with it." He sounded calm and assured.

I tried to match his confidence. "I'm not sure I want to be brothers with a guy who would steal his dead dad's DNA."

He shook his head like he was humoring me. "I got the DNA from my uncle, my dad's brother. Without his knowledge, if that adds to my allure as your sibling. You can trace paternal DNA to find your ancestors. My uncle and I should have had a long line of paternal DNA in common. We didn't. We're not related. Not even slightly."

I studied Ian, intrigued and begrudgingly respecting him. "What did you do—pull a hair from his brush?"

He laughed robustly. "Hell no! I've seen Harry Potter and the dire consequences of getting the wrong hair."

I liked him even more, and couldn't help smiling a little.

"I slipped in and got a swab of his saliva while he was napping and snoring like a dog. He never even knew I took it."

"You're a sneaky bastard." I admired his courage and ingenuity.

He shrugged, at least acting modest. "I didn't want anyone to know what I suspected, that Dad wasn't my biological dad. Skeletons in closets, embarrassment for my mom, and all that. And I couldn't ask him for one under false pretenses, either. What if he wanted to know who we were related to and there was no 'we'? Just him and me and two separate biological lines?"

He paused. His face clouded. "I suspected while my Dad was still alive, but I refused to disrespect him or hurt him by asking. If he hadn't died young, I never would have acted on my suspicions.

"Mom still doesn't know. It will kill her when she finds out. For obvious reasons, I haven't asked her about my real father, either. For a while I imagined all kinds of horrible scenarios. Like she was raped or forced."

I felt the anger rise again. "My dad would never—"

"I didn't say he would. I meant before, when there were no suspects. On one level, what Maddie told me after that scene at my office about Mom and your dad was a relief. If Mom loved my biological father, or at least had a crush on him, at least that wasn't the nightmare I'd imagined over the years. Even if he broke her heart."

Shit, there was obvious pain in his voice. I knew that feeling, being the cause of my mother's pain and suffering. I couldn't help flashing him a sympathetic look.

He took a deep breath. "I wish I'd been wrong about Dad not being my dad. But it is what it is. I opened Pandora's box. I was happy to keep the lid on it. Until now."

He pulled a DNA test kit out of the paper bag and tore off the plastic shrink-wrap. "I want you to understand something—relief aside, I'm not doing this for me. I could let it lie without ever being certain or confronting your father. I'm doing this for Mads. Only for her. Because she's my baby sis. I'd kill to protect her."

His eyes were fierce. He meant it. "This is nothing compared to that. Mom and your dad will have to pay the price, if it comes to that."

He glared at me. "Maddie loves you, douchebag that you seem to be. I'll give her this chance at happiness."

He pulled a swab from the DNA test kit and held it out to me.

I hesitated.

His gaze was steady. "Are you man enough to do the same?"

I grabbed it from him. "How do I do this?"

"Swab the inside of your cheek." He gave me detailed instructions.

When I finished, he took the swab from me and bagged it up.

"Now what?" I asked.

"We wait. It should only take a few days. I'll get back to you as soon as I get the results." He paused. "I need your number so I can text you."

I bit back a smartass response and rattled it off.

"I'll text you so you have mine." He typed out a text.

An instant later, my phone buzzed in my pocket. I ignored it.

"I don't want you to be my brother." I blurted it out in anger, without thinking. "No offense. I'd rather avoid the mess. It's weird shit, thinking Maddie could be the sister of my brother. It's...almost incestuous."

He put a hand on my shoulder.

"I had this buddy in high school. His mom married a guy with three teenage daughters. One of them was incredibly hot. They all moved in together, one big, happy family.

"Except that they weren't. My buddy lusted after the hot one. Had wet dreams about her. It was total shit that suddenly she was his sister. Off limits, completely. Drove him crazy seeing her prancing around the house half naked. They finally hooked up. It almost made me sick hearing him talk about her.

"It nearly broke up his mom's new marriage. Everyone had to go through family counseling. His mom didn't forgive him for years. Probably still totally hasn't. His stepdad kicked him out. He had to live with his dad until he graduated. Things are still awkward for all of them."

"Either way the test turns out, Maddie's not your sister." Ian's voice was sympathetic, as if he understood. He sounded so damn much like Dad, both the sound of his voice and his inflection. "None of us were raised as siblings or a family. We have no familial bonds. And there aren't any expectations of any. Not by me, anyway. The situation could be cleaner." He squeezed my shoulder. "But if you love my sister, you can overcome it."

He took a deep breath. The pain on his face was a mirror of mine. We looked alike. He even stood like I did. "She feels as bad as you do about all this. As uncertain and scared. Maybe she made a mistake not telling you her suspicions. But maybe she simply loved you enough to hope she was wrong and wish for the best.

"If you love her, and don't want to lose her, don't wait too long to let her know. Don't make the same mistake your dad did." His tone was condemning.

I couldn't tell who he was rebuking—Dad or me. Or maybe both of us.

He slid the swabs into the paper bag and rolled the top shut. "I'd better go."

I walked him to the door without committing to anything, one way or the other. The way Ian walked and carried himself, his stride, it was all Dad's. And mine. If we weren't related, fate had really screwed up.

I held the door open for him. "That test isn't going to tell us anything we don't already know."

He patted me on the shoulder and walked off.

CHAPTER NINETEEN

Maddie

I was desolate. Alone. Seth completely cut me off. He even skipped cooking lab and made me suffer through Chef Steven's scrutiny paired with another student whose lab partner was absent, too. Not only couldn't she cook even remotely as well as Seth, she was a complete disaster. Somehow, I made it through the chicken course and dessert without Seth. Just like I limped through the week.

On Thursday evening, Mom called. When I heard her voice, I wanted to cry and put my head on her shoulder. Let her heal my heartbreak, sympathize and get fierce for me the way only a mother would. But the other part of me was weak with relief that she had never known about Seth. That if this was the way it was going to be, maybe she never had to. That ball was in Ian's court now, not mine.

I put a false note of sunshine in my voice. "Mom!"

"Baby! What are you up to? How's school?" Her voice was as soothing to my wounded heart as when she used to kiss my boo-boos and make them better. It helped, but the wound still hurt. And yet, as she asked all the usual questions, I felt like I didn't really know her at all. That she'd kept some important part of herself from me.

Worse, I felt like I was becoming the hollow shell she was. I answered her questions, making a funny story of my disastrous cooking lab to distract her from sensing anything was off.

"I barely squeaked by with an eighty-one percent on this lab. And that was only because Chef Steven took pity on us because our usual partners were gone." I sighed for dramatic effect. "It's going to kill my lab GPA of nearly one hundred percent. My regular lab partner is a cooking sensation." I couldn't mask the wistfulness in my voice. I hoped she didn't hear the longing.

Mom laughed, oblivious to the real source of my pain. "So that's why you sound upset and sad today. I'm sure you'll bring your average back up as soon as your regular partner comes back." She sounded almost tongue in cheek. "What's wrong with him? Maybe he's heartsick that you won't go on another date with him."

"Mom!" Crap. She was so close to the truth. I regretted telling her at the beginning that I'd had a date with my cooking lab partner. When she'd asked about it later, I'd lied and said we were better off friends. That I had no plans to go out with him again.

"With any luck he'll recover quickly and be back soon."

She had no idea what she was wishing for.

I sighed. "Maybe."

"Don't be such a pessimist!" She paused. "I have something to cheer you up. I've rearranged my schedule and decided not to attend the annual design conference I usually go to in April, the one that always conflicts with Mom's Weekend. With both you and Ian there now, how can I miss Mom's Weekend this year? I'm coming!"

My mouth went dry as cotton. "What?"

"Surprised you!" Her delight seeped through the phone. "I'll stay with Ian, of course. He has plenty of room. I'll call him next, but I wanted to tell *you* first."

"Um...I don't know what to say." I blinked like this might be a bad dream. I hadn't even considered Mom would come for Mom's Weekend. Giving up her annual conference was serious stuff.

Along with the obvious pounding fear, I felt a pang of sibling jealousy. Ian comes to the university and suddenly she makes time for Mom's Weekend, just at the worst possible time. Her announcement reinforced what I often thought. Ian was her favorite. And now I knew why. He was her love child. The boy who reminded her of the guy she'd really loved. And I was just the daughter she'd made with a good friend.

Yeah, sure, both of her kids were here now, like she said. But deep down, I knew Ian was the real draw.

Mom avoided the university when at all possible. She'd helped me move in freshman year and that was the last time she'd come to campus in nearly three years. Even then, she'd escaped as soon as possible. She must be desperate to see him.

"You're speechless?" She laughed again.

I took a deep breath, glad she'd misread my hesitation. "Awesome." I had to say something.

"I've already looked at the Mom's Weekend website. I made a list of some of the events that look interesting. I'll send it to you. Some of them need reservations. Like the winetasting. I *really* want to go to that. Now that both my kids are twenty-one, won't it be fun? Right in line with your major. Very posh and sophisticated. All the wines are from the state. And, according to the website, we all get a free university wineglass with the price of admission."

Oh, no! As we were leaving his place, Seth's dad had mentioned something about being involved with the winetasting and helping set it up. And my cooking class was providing the appetizers and serving at it. I hadn't planned on volunteering to serve at it. But after that terrible lab, I could use the extra credit. And anything to keep Mom away from it.

"I may have to work that event for class," I said, making sure to sound disappointed as I explained.

"Get out of it," Mom said in a commanding tone. "I want the whole experience, including mother/daughter/son Mom's Weekend sweatshirts. Get together with your brother and order them. And make the reservations. Let me know how much everything costs and I'll put the money in your account to cover it." She sighed happily. "This is going to be *so* fun!"

She had no idea. Who was this woman and what had she done with my mother? Why? Why now? It was as if the universe was conspiring against me.

After we hung up, I sat stunned, trying to work up the courage to call Ian. He called me before I could.

"We need to get together, Mads." He was completely matter of fact. "I have some things I need to talk to you about. In person. Are you busy tomorrow night? Let me take you to dinner."

"Mom got to you, too." I was certain she'd coerced him into taking me out to make plans for her visit, and was probably paying for the dinner he'd just invited me to, too. "I can't believe she's coming for Mom's Weekend. I feel like the Grinch, *We must keep Mom's Weekend from coming, but how?*"

"Yeah, bad timing."

I hadn't told him yet that Rick was coming to town to help with the winetasting that weekend. I wondered if Mom had shared her excited plans with Ian, too. I had no idea where things stood between Ian and Seth. Or whether Ian wanted to meet Rick. I made a note to tell him tomorrow among the many things we needed to talk about.

"We have a lot to talk about," I said.

"We do indeed." He paused. "You haven't answered my question. Dinner tomorrow?"

"Sounds good to me. I'm always up for free food."

"Seven? I'll pick you up."

"See you tomorrow."

My brother was prompt, as always. I watched for him from the kitchen window and ran out to meet him when he pulled up.

"Where are we going?" I asked as I slid into his car.

He turned off his music. "Wings okay?"

I nodded. "Absolutely!"

We rode in a strange kind of silence to the restaurant. It was like we were each bursting to say something, but neither of us wanted to be the first. Because the news I was bursting with wasn't good. And he seemed like he was holding something back, too.

When we got to the wing place, Ian pulled his briefcase bag out of the backseat. It seemed odd to me, but I didn't ask him about it. He slid it over his shoulder. As we walked into the restaurant, I looped my arm through his and rested my head on his shoulder. I needed my big bro just then.

"Pretending I'm your boyfriend again?" he asked. But he didn't shake me off. "That's partly what got me in trouble with the department in the first place. I have my suspicions. I think one of the grad students saw us in the Chinese place at the start of the semester."

"To hell with sneaky, backstabbing grad students." I was in no mood.

He covered my hand with his like there was no way he was letting me go. "Exactly. To hell with them. Only those with dirty minds would think there's something unnatural going on between me and my sis. Let them."

It was comforting. And it might even have been funny if he hadn't been in real trouble over it for a while. I caught myself just before saying we had the cover of Seth now, too.

The entire situation was absurd. Ian stroked the top of my head and held the door open for me.

We got right into the wing place. Ian asked to be seated in a quiet corner. Though, in truth, no place was quiet. Music blared. The busy restaurant hummed with crowd noise. A waitress brought us water and a basket of popcorn almost the minute we sat down. The popcorn was their signature thing instead of a breadbasket.

It seemed ridiculous to be eating popcorn and waiting for honey barbecue wings with all I had on my mind. The discussion we had to have was too serious and weighty to have popcorn as a prelude.

Ian waited until the waitress had gone and I had a handful of popcorn before he spoke.

"I have something to show you." He reached into his bag and pulled out a sheaf of papers, sitting them in front of me.

"What's this?" I looked up at him.

"Proof. Seth is my brother." He tapped the pages in front of me and explained about the DNA tests he'd run.

"I can't believe you went to Seth and he agreed to this."

Ian shrugged that off. "You don't seem surprised by the results?"

"Should I be?" I sighed. "The circumstantial evidence was too strong. The odds of all those coincidences too much. If I'd been on a jury, I would have convicted you of being brothers long before seeing this." I swallowed hard. "In fact, I did. I didn't need a test to prove it."

Ian nodded. "I didn't do this for me. I did it for you. So you, and he, could be certain."

My eyes filled with tears. "Does Seth know?"

Ian shook his head. "I wanted to tell you first." He shifted in his seat. "Does this change the way you feel about him?"

I blinked back a sudden wave of tears and shook my head. It was so typical of Ian to be selfless. "*Nothing* will change the way I feel about him. Not even him not loving me anymore. I wish something would."

Ian pulled a stiff brown paper napkin from the dispenser next to him and handed it to me. "He still loves you." He paused. "I don't want to give you false hope. Loving you doesn't mean things will turn out well. I don't know how he's going to deal with it."

I bit my lip. "How is he?"

"Confused." Ian didn't elaborate.

"Do *you* want a relationship with him?" I couldn't have stopped myself from asking if I'd cut off my tongue. "Do you want a brother?"

"It's not totally up to me."

"Seth is your brother. You don't have any others." I bit my lip. I couldn't be that selfish. "You should get to know him. He's a great guy."

Ian raised one eyebrow.

"No, I mean it." I blinked back tears and crumpled the napkin he'd given me. "If it wasn't for me and this mess we're in, I think you two would really hit it off." I tried to smile. "As long as you always like me best, I'll have no problem with it."

"You'll always be my favorite sister." His expression was teasing, but his eyes were sympathetic.

"Shut up! Favorite sib or the deal's off." I dabbed at my eyes with the mangled napkin.

He handed me another. "Your mascara is running."

"And you hand me a napkin stiff enough to gouge my eyes out. If I have a long-lost brother out there somewhere, and he carries soft tissues with him, he's going to be my favorite."

Ian laughed.

I sighed as I wiped my eyes. Reality didn't stay at bay long. "What are we going to do?" I paused, trying to frame my thoughts. "Do you want to meet Rick? You don't need Seth's permission. Not that you need it, but you certainly have mine."

I swallowed the lump in my throat. "Whatever's best for you, Ian. I'm...I'm happy you still have a dad. It's hard to admit, especially because I thought he hurt Mom and I wanted to hate him, but Rick is a good guy. I don't know how he'll react to you. But you should give him a chance. If *you* want to."

I paused again. I'd given this a lot of thought. "I'll back you up with Mom. She shouldn't have a say in this, either. However it happened, she blew her chance with Rick. That doesn't mean you should. I could arrange for you to meet him."

Ian smiled at me, love for me shining on his face. Whatever happened, Ian was in my corner. And I was in his.

"I *would* like to meet my father." He hesitated. "I won't let Seth stop me. But I will tell him my intentions first."

I nodded. "The opportunity to meet him is coming sooner than you think. Rick's coming to town for Mom's Weekend."

Ian paled. "What?"

"Well, not exactly for Mom's Weekend. You know that winetasting Mom is insisting on going to? He's donating some of his wine. He's on some kind of board or committee for it and is coming to town the day before to help arrange it. If you want to meet him on neutral ground, that's your chance."

Ian reached across the table and grabbed my free hand, the one not desperately clutching a mascara-stained napkin. "Have I told you how much I love you, baby sis?"

I smiled sadly at him, happy that nothing could come between us. Blood was thicker than water, as they say. Which worried me, too. Because Ian shared a blood relation with Rick and Seth. I hoped his allegiance never shifted.

I hated to ask, but I had to. "What do we do about Mom?"

Ian's brow furrowed. "I've given it some thought. I would like to see Rick first. If he wants nothing to do with me, we can leave Mom out of this." He squeezed my hand. "Until we introduce her to Seth and tell her who he really is and who his father is. Then we give Mom a chance to come clean first."

"I don't think Seth is coming back."

Ian made a waving motion, a gesture that meant *sweep that thought away.*

"If Rick is the man I think he is, he'll want everything to do with you," I said. "One way or another, we're going to have to tell Mom." I bit my lip. "When are you going to tell Seth?"

"I'll text him after I drop you off tonight."

I nodded, thinking. "I have something I need to text him, too. Let me know when you've sent yours."

Seth

Maddie held me spellbound with her texts over the next few days as I mulled over what Ian had said and waited for the results of that damn test. I missed her. I wanted her. I wanted to believe her. I wasn't ready to talk. On Thursday, I skipped HBM 225 to avoid her. It was a shitty thing to do, but I couldn't help myself.

I sat by myself in my apartment, drinking and playing video games alone in the dark. Zach and Dakota had tried to get me to go out with them. I blew them off.

My phone sat next to me on the sofa. I was getting the crap beat out of me in my game. My head wasn't in it. All I wanted to do was blow things up.

My phone buzzed. I glanced at it. A message from Ian.

My hand stilled on the video game controller. My eyes blurred. My mouth went dry. I had to blink twice before I could read it.

It's official. Welcome to the family, bro. You can see the results for yourself here.

There was a link.

I dropped the controller and watched my character be blown into smithereens. Being blown apart was exactly how I felt in real life, too.

It wasn't as if I were surprised. It was just that damn hope springs eternal bullshit. Like I'd hoped I would win life's lottery and all this coincidence would be simply that, coincidence.

Since Monday, I'd gone over every possible scenario. I didn't see a way out of this. All I wanted was to go back to Maddie and me. Two people from completely separate families with no history who fell madly in love.

I tried, but I couldn't get her out of my system. She was in my dreams. And worse, in my nightmares. Dying and I couldn't save her. Condemning me for turning her away.

Another text came in from Ian.

So you know, I want to meet my dad. Do you want to give him the cigar or should I?

I dropped the phone onto the cushion, stood, and started pacing and swearing.

Meet my dad! *My* dad.

What did I tell Ian? What did I tell Dad? *How* did I tell him?

Okay, so here's the deal, Dad. You have another son. And I've been sleeping with his sister.

"Shit!" I yelled at the top of my lungs. I kicked the sofa.

My phone buzzed again. I grabbed it, ready to text the bastard back to leave me the fuck alone.

I stopped short when I saw it was from Maddie.

*By now Ian's shared the DNA results with you.
You're brothers, just as I suspected, and feared, from
the beginning. It changes nothing for me. I love you,
regardless. And always will.*

*And jealous as I am, I'm willing to share my brother
with you.*

I stopped short and took a deep breath. I hadn't
bothered to think she would be jealous of her brother
having another sibling. But I understood it. I'd never
had to share Dad before, either. But her generosity of
spirit killed me.

I kept reading.

*Ian is the best brother in the world. You don't know
how lucky you are to have him. To have accidentally
found him through me. If nothing else, our relationship
has given you that gift. The gift of a lost brother is no
small thing. Don't throw it away.*

*Let Ian into your world. Introduce him to your dad.
Make him part of your family. You won't be sorry. He'll
be the older brother you've always wanted. Better than
you even imagined.*

*I'll learn to share him. Even if you and me are no
longer you and me. But just you. And just me.*

*Think it over. We now know for certain you and Ian
are brothers. But, seriously, when did I know? When
did the evidence become overwhelming?*

*Your dad told us the story of how he rescued my
mom from being blown up on the fifth floor of her
friend's dorm. And I knew then for sure. As sure as I
could be without scientific evidence, like the DNA test
we have now.*

Rick's story was the last piece I needed to convince me this hadn't all been a bad coincidence or that I was imagining things. The look in his eyes. He loved Mom. I really think he did.

And knowing Mom the way I do, there was no way she could have resisted your dad. Not after he played hero to her like that. Not after seeing how charming he is. Just like there is no way I can resist you.

I don't want to end up broken like Mom. Settling for loyalty and friendship when I could get that and passion and love.

Maybe it is in our genes to love each other. Maybe your dad and my mom messed up their shot together. We'll have to ask them how. But let's not let the sins, mistakes, whatever you want to call them, of the past ruin what we have.

If they hadn't broken up, there would be no you and no me and no you and me. Let's be you and me again. I'll be waiting. Whenever you're ready.

I didn't cry easily, but tears welled in my eyes. I got it. I saw now how the evidence had crept up on her, slowly building toward a conclusion she didn't want to face. Just like I was feeling now, staring at the results of that DNA test. I wished she had shared her suspicions with me. But I couldn't blame her for the course of action she took.

Because when I dug deep, I realized I'd reacted exactly how she'd feared. That I *was* blowing us apart.

My mouth was dry. I needed another beer. I went to the fridge and threw open the door. All that anniversary wine I'd stashed in our fridge stared me in the face. Sometimes fate gives you a sign. This was mine.

Shit, I loved her. I could lose her. Or we could face this together. I grabbed one of the bottles of wine and scooped my keys off the counter, realizing at the last second that our anniversary was tomorrow.

I just hoped she'd take me back.

CHAPTER TWENTY

Maddie

I was upstairs in my room, ostensibly watching a movie. In reality, I was thinking. I'd been doing nothing but thinking since Ian dropped me off earlier. Olivia was out on a date. A first date with some guy she met while studying in the SUB.

She was happy enough, but not particularly ecstatic about the guy. Still, her dating life was a dream compared to mine.

I hadn't expected Seth to respond to my text. But his lack of response still depressed me. Everything depressed me. Just when I thought I couldn't sink any lower, I did.

Unless Seth refused to read his texts from Ian and me, he knew Ian was his brother. My heart broke for him and us. I'd had longer to process it. And I still wasn't dealing really well with it. How long would it take him? Would there still be any us left by then?

Someone pounded on our front door. I almost jumped out of my skin. I froze. I wasn't expecting anyone, and this time of night it was as likely to be a lost drunk at our door as anyone. The pounding didn't stop.

I grabbed my keychain with my pepper spray. "Coming!" I raced down the stairs and opened the door as far as the chain on it would allow, with my pepper spray at the ready.

Seth stood in the circle of light on our porch, holding a red rose and a bottle of wine. He looked so totally hot and apologetic.

He'd shaved off the gruff. His beanie was tucked back on his head. And my knees almost gave out.

He glanced at the pepper spray pointed at him. "Do you always greet guests with pepper spray? I know I deserve it, but can I talk first?"

My gaze bounced from his face to the flower and wine. "Just a sec." I dropped the pepper spray to my side, pushed the door in, removed the security chain, and opened the door for him. "I thought you were a drunk."

"You're not far off."

When he spoke, I caught the scent of beer on his breath. But the expression in his eyes was sober.

"What are you doing here?" I expected him to say he got my text and start explaining. Part of me wanted to punish him for being such a douche and pushing me away. For not trusting or believing me. Part of me wanted to throw myself into his arms.

He held the rose out to me. "Have you forgotten? It's our anniversary. Or it will be in less than an hour."

Every piece of me shattered then. I was such an emotionally fragile wreck. My hand shook as I took the rose from him. I *had* forgotten. Or maybe I'd tried not to remember.

He held up the wine. "This is my least favorite, the first one you picked. Remember?"

I took a deep breath and tried not to remember the romantic sweetness of that day, afraid I would break. "We ended at your dad's."

It was my subtle way of getting the topic between us out in the open.

"I planned that day so the wineries and the wines they made would get better and better. Like our life is supposed to be...together." His Adam's apple bobbed. "Like it will be, if you let me in. Please, Maddie."

I stepped aside and let him into my apartment, though I knew he meant back into his life, not my apartment.

He closed the door behind him.

"Olivia's out. We can...talk freely."

His eyes were dark and wide, full of hope and longing. He held the rose out to me again. "Please, Maddie, please forgive me. I was such a douche. I can't live without you. I tried, damn it, I tried. You're in my blood and I can't get you out."

I took the rose from him and bit my lip. "There's no blood between us, Seth."

He set the wine on the kitchen counter and grabbed me by both arms. "That's not what I meant and you know it. I don't care about that shit, Maddie. I read all of your texts and you made me see—I don't want to end up like Dad and your mom. I won't repeat their mistakes. I want you. I need you. And the rest of the world can all go to hell." His voice shook. "Please, Maddie, take me back." He squeezed my arms.

I looked him in the eye, trying to judge how genuine he was. Yes, he wanted me back. But did he really want everything that came with me? The upheaval to his life and family? A new family?

"You'll give Ian a chance? Get to know him. Let him be your brother?" My voice was surprisingly steady and calm. It was all or nothing now. And that's what I wanted. I couldn't live with a partial chance at happiness.

Seth nodded. "Yes. If that's what you want."

"I want you to want it, too." I had to make him understand. Ian and I were a package deal. You didn't get one without the other. Not anymore.

He took a deep breath. "Yes, I want it, too. It's the only way, right? You two are inseparable."

He understood! I blinked back tears. I needed another concession. "You'll introduce him to your dad? They should have a relationship, too."

He looked miserable and horribly hopeful at the same time. He nodded. "You'll have to introduce me to your mom. I don't want to be secret anymore."

He had nerve. But he was right.

I nodded. "Yes."

"You forgive me?"

The look in his eyes almost killed me. I shook loose from his grip and threw myself into his arms.

He pulled me to him. The next thing I knew, his lips were on mine, right where they belonged. When he kissed me, the rest of the world disappeared and everything felt right.

As his tongue danced with mine, he tasted like beer, but way more intoxicating. If I had been weak in the knees before, now I was absolutely limp. If I hadn't been leaning into him and wrapped in his arms, I would have collapsed in my joy. Fell to my knees and cried tears of happiness.

As he pressed against me, I felt him in his jeans, long and hard and insistent as he pressed it against me. I tingled all the way to my toes. I felt tight and hot and full of want.

Like every part of me needed release. And I needed to feel him inside me and celebrate the oneness of us. I pulled away from him, took his hand, and pulled him up the stairs.

"Where are we going?" His voice was low and sultry, as if he knew, but couldn't believe his good luck.

I simply smiled at him and led him to my room. Inside, I closed the door and pulled him onto the bed.

He fell on top of me and ground into the smoldering heat of my crotch, simulating sex until my breath caught. I was so wet.

I pulled his beanie off and tossed it. Ran my fingers through his hair and lightly stroked the back of his neck the way he liked.

"I missed you," I whispered.

"How much?"

I reached between us and untied my sweats. Took his hand and guided it until his fingers slid into my pants, beneath my panties to the wet heat between my legs.

I gasped when he touched me and made the gentle circles between my legs, bringing me to the edge. I clutched his hand to stop him. "I don't want to come without you."

He withdrew his hand and pulled off his shirt, revealing the hard planes of his chest. And the absolutely seductive curves of his biceps.

I sat up enough to lick his nipples and caress his biceps, wanting to hold on to them forever. "Get out of your jeans."

He grinned and rolled off me just enough to obey my orders, hurriedly shedding his shoes, jeans, and underwear.

I was dressed in my comfy sweatpants, T-shirt, and sweatshirt. I slid out of them while he got undressed.

There was a second, just an instant in time, where we studied each other. Looking at each other with that wonder in our eyes. I couldn't believe he was mine. He'd come back to me. He was willing to fight for me and with me against fate and family. And all the crap life could throw at us. What was sexier than that?

We were both breathing hard, even though the exertion hadn't begun. He reached out, almost tentatively, and cupped my breast as he rolled back on top of me.

I positioned myself beneath him with his dick pointing into my opening. I gasped again as it brushed against me. I was swollen and ready for him, afraid I would come without him anyway.

He braced himself above me and looked into my eyes. "I love you, Maddie."

"I love you—"

He covered my mouth with his kiss. And speared into me as I moaned into his mouth.

He pounded into me. I loved him so much. The intimacy as I rocked with him was overpowering. The tightness and the need built with every powerful thrust.

I love you, I thought with each thrust. *I'll love you forever.*

The bed creaked. We pounded it with the force of all our pent-up emotions and frustrations. I felt a scream build in my throat as the tightness wound me up. I squeezed him, hard.

His breath caught. "You're killing me, Mads."

I squeezed him harder, inside and out. Ignoring him. Making him mine. Making him part of me.

Making him work until a sheen of sweat shone on him.

He thrust into me harder than before and let out a grunt, burying his head in my neck. Seth made me feel so good—why would I ever need anyone else? I would fight to keep him forever.

I gasped at the force of his thrust, and the scream escaped as wave after wave of pleasure crashed over me.

I arched into him and clawed at his bare shoulders until I collapsed beneath him.

I glanced over at the alarm clock on my nightstand. It was minutes past midnight. "Happy anniversary."

"It's after midnight already?" He pushed up for a look at the clock.

"Time flies when you're with me."

"Shit, Maddie. I'm so glad you took me back." His voice was tender, sweet, and sincere.

"Me too." I smiled at him, rolled out from beneath him, and reached for my discarded clothes.

He looked at me, puzzled. "What are you doing?"

"I think it's time for a glass of wine."

"You're crazy." He sat up and grabbed his jeans.

We pulled on our clothes and raced downstairs. I found two juice glasses in the kitchen cupboard.

He scrounged through my kitchen drawers and found my cheap corkscrew. "Is this all you have?" He held it up.

I shrugged.

"Remind me to get you a new one. I'll steal one from Dad. He has plenty from the winery to spare." He sighed and opened the bottle expertly. He poured two glasses and handed me one.

I held mine up for a toast. "To three months together!"

He clinked his glass with mine. "And a lifetime to follow."

I looked at him, startled and deeply touched.

"I mean it." His voice broke. "No one and no circumstance are going to tear us apart. We'll figure this out."

The door to the apartment opened. Olivia walked in, accompanied by a gust of cool air. She jumped, startled, when she saw us. Her face clouded with confusion.

She pointed between the two of us. "Are you two...?"

"We are!" I grabbed another glass from the cupboard. "We were just celebrating." I poured her some wine and hugged her as I handed it to her.

"This is a pleasant surprise." She sounded cautious as she raised her glass to us.

"Isn't it?" I couldn't stop smiling.

"So. Everything's okay?" She looked uncertain, as if she still might be misreading things.

I nodded. "Seth's staying over tonight."

She made a silent *oh*, and nodded. "Well, good then."

"Don't worry. I'll put the lid down." He laughed. "I make a mean breakfast. I'll cook for you both in the morning."

"Promises, promises. If I fall into the toilet in the middle of the night, I will have to throttle you. You've been warned." Olivia raised her glass to us. "To *happy* reunions."

"And many more," I said, totally getting she meant so much more. So many more crucial, scary reunions, like Mom and Rick's.

Seth and I slept wrapped in each other's arms. I felt secure and peaceful. I may even have sighed happily in my sleep. The next morning, Seth made good and made breakfast.

"We have to tell both of our parents," I said over cheese omelets and toast.

He swore he could have made a fancier creation, but I didn't have many ingredients for him to work with.

He slid my hand-me-down skillet into the sink of soapy water and talked to me through the pass-through from our micro-size kitchen to the main living/dining room. "I agree completely."

"And involve Ian." I slathered jam on my toast as I sat at our tiny dining table, one foot hooked beneath me on my chair.

"Yeah." Seth carried a plate in from the kitchen and took a seat opposite me. "You're right. Any ideas how?"

"I have a plan," I said. "I'll call him and arrange for us to get together. I'll give you the details when we're all together."

After breakfast I called my brother, told him Seth and I were back together, and arranged for the three of us to meet for coffee and make battle plans.

Seth and I arrived first at The College Grind, and saved seats. When Ian arrived, I jumped up and threw myself in his arms. I'd never loved my big brother more.

"Thank you," I whispered in his ear. I knew he'd helped do this, done his part to convince Seth to come back to me.

"It was nothing." He hugged me tightly. "I simply encouraged him to do what he wanted to do all along."

Seth gave us a second, then stood and extended his hand to Ian to shake. "Big brother."

Ian grabbed Seth and hugged him, slapping him on the back. "Little brother. Treat my sister well or I'll have your head."

"Yeah, I get that. You've warned me before."

We all laughed. The situation was so ludicrous, really. And must have sounded either absurd or incestuous to those around us. We got a few funny looks.

"I got you a coffee," I said to Ian as I grabbed it and handed it to him.

We took our places around the table to strategize.

"Anyone have any ideas how we go about this?" Ian looked at me.

I grinned.

He explained to Seth, "She's the planner in the family."

I nodded. "True." I picked up my coffee. "We're going to have to tell Rick first," I said. "He comes in on Thursday."

I paused, looking between the two most important guys in my life, loving them both and being so perfectly happy in the moment.

"I was thinking it would be natural for Seth to tell his dad he'd like to introduce him to my brother," I said. "And invite him to Ian's for dessert on Thursday night."

I turned to Seth. "Does he know you and I..." I hesitated on the words "broke up."

Seth caught my meaning. "No. I haven't talked to him since before last Monday."

We all knew the significance of last Monday.

"Okay, then perfectly natural," I said. "Ian's house is private. I think that's key. We need to be able to talk, cry, scream." I glanced at my older brother. "Break furniture."

"Good thing I don't have much." Ian winked.

"Just to clarify—you're offering your house?" I said.

He nodded. "You bet. It's a rental. The worst that could happen is I'll lose my deposit." He laughed.

"Good!" I tried to sound more optimistic than I felt.

"So we're ambushing him?" Ian eyed me over his cup as he took a sip of coffee.

"We're letting him draw his own conclusions once he sees you. I mean, once he sees what an awesome son he has, how could he not love you? It's simple advertising." I clutched my cup. "Do you have a better plan?"

"Knowing Dad, I agree. The element of surprise gives us the upper hand. We'll tell him together." Seth looked to Ian for confirmation.

"All right, agreed." Ian looked at me again. "What about Mom?"

"We tell her separately from Rick. I think at dinner on Friday. I'll tell her I've been dating someone and would like her to meet him. That's natural, too. She'll be excited."

"So, another sneak attack," Ian said drily. "At my house?"

I nodded. "Private is better."

"We'll help you cook," Seth said.

"You haven't tasted his cooking. He's good," I said to Ian. "Like the star student in the class."

"We're good together." Seth reached across the table and squeezed my hand. "And we have to make a two-course meal for friends or family for class, anyway." He shook my hand playfully.

"Win-win," Ian said. "Until Mom throws the china."

I laughed, feeling better now that both guys were on my side. "You don't have any china."

Ian took a sip of coffee. "I have Chinet."

I rolled my eyes.

"I got an eye roll! Excellent." Ian laughed. He was always teasing. "Send me the menu and grocery list. I'll do the shopping."

The three of us stared at each other like three conspirators who were planning to rob a bank or something. Like we were planning something really shady and sinister.

"This is going to work!" I put a huge dose of fake optimistic sunshine in my voice.

"It's going to do *something*." Ian stared at me. "What, exactly, are we going to tell Mom?"

"The truth, of course. We'll play it by ear." I glanced at Seth. "I hope we don't have to tell her anything. One look at Seth and she'll get that picture. Hearing his name will seal the deal. We'll go from there."

Ian frowned as he looked at me. "And Mom"—his gaze bounced to Seth—"and Dad? Crap that sounds crazy. Do we introduce them again?"

We all laughed nervously.

"We leave that up to them. If they want to recon-
nect, that's their thing." I sounded way more confident
than I felt. I set my coffee down.

Ian scooted his chair closer to me and took my free
hand. "And when Mom screams and yells that you can't
be with that Butler boy?"

"We hold our ground." I bit my lip. "Together. If
Mom loved Rick like I think she did, she'll understand
how I feel about Seth and why I won't break up with
him."

"That's my sis," Ian said, and sighed dramatically. "I
hope my neighbors are ready for fireworks."

CHAPTER TWENTY-ONE

Laura

I decided to leave a day early and surprise the kids. I didn't have any meetings on Thursday afternoon, so what the heck, right? I left work a little after one, stopped by home and threw my already packed bags in the car, and headed for the university. If I made good time, I would be there by eight. Still in early twilight. I was eager to see Ian's new house.

Over the years, I'd avoided the university for good reason. When Bruce was alive, I'd had an irrational fear of bringing up old ghosts. Going to campus and running into Rick. Was that possible? Sure. But the probability of it happening was so slim as to be impossible. But that's the thing about unreasonable fears. They don't make sense.

I had a real fear, too, of bringing that old longing for Rick back to the surface. Life was so much easier to live without it. You would think that after all these years, it would die. That I would have found a way to murder it in its sleep. But the craziest things brought it back unbidden—an old song, like "Dream Police," on the radio. The smell of cheap beer on a hot day. A swirl of dust in spring. The university was too full of triggers. So I avoided it.

I owed Bruce everything for coming to my rescue. All he'd asked in return was for Ian to be his son and no one to know the difference. I'd kept my end of the bargain. Once Bruce was gone, I thought the fears and the longing would recede. But they didn't.

Now, though, I was happy again. Or at least secure. Ken was a good man, a friend. Like Bruce had been. He'd encouraged me to go to Mom's Weekend now that both kids were there. And I was out of excuses. That I could share, anyway. So why not?

This would be fun. I could hardly wait to see the looks on the kids' faces when I showed up. I would go to Ian's first. And then the two of us would go surprise Maddie. I felt like a kid again!

As a mom, this was the perfect opportunity to see how they really lived. I had a momentary flicker of worry. What if I caught them at something I would rather not know about?

I brushed the fear off. Worrier, worrier! I laughed at myself and turned up the music.

Seth

Dad, Maddie, and I pulled up in front of Ian's house just past seven.

"Maddie, it's nice of your brother to invite us over," Rick said. "You didn't say much about him when you visited us."

"Didn't I?" Maddie sounded nervous.

I guessed Dad would chalk that up to nerves over introducing us to her family. He had no idea she was introducing him to his.

I put the car in park and reached for the door handle. My heart pounded out of control. I didn't feel like talking. I was too damn nervous and scared over the myriad ways this could blow up in our faces.

I got out of the car. Maddie slipped out of her side and took a deep breath. I came around and took her hand.

The shadows were long. The lighting over the wheat fields surrounding Ian's house spectacular. Rolling fields of light and shadow.

Dad got out and paused to look at the view. "Nice place. Great view. When you said your brother had a house, I expected the usual dump on the hill up to campus. Five guys in some beat-up five-bedroom place from the forties. Not this."

Maddie bit her lip. "He's a little older than I am."

I glanced at her. Her face was pale. She was trying hard not to give too much away.

"Ian's a professor, not a student."

"Ian?" Dad stopped, suddenly on alert. "That's my middle name. Richard Ian Butler. RIB. Not great initials." He laughed nervously.

Maddie kept her smile plastered to her face. "What a coincidence."

I exchanged a look with her. Dad was getting dangerously close to the truth, acting like a dog on a scent. Maddie didn't have to say anything. In that moment, we both realized her mom had named Ian after my dad. If we'd needed more circumstantial evidence, there it was. I didn't know why I hadn't made the connection before. In my defense, why would I think about Dad's middle name?

Dad's gaze bounced between us. "You two are awfully serious tonight."

Maddie gave him a shaky smile. "Introducing you to my brother is a big step. Of course I'm nervous!"

Dad flashed her a big smile that showed off that characteristic single dimple of ours. The one Ian shared with us. Dad had a soft spot for Maddie. She could have twisted him around her little finger if she'd wanted to.

"I won't eat him. I promise." Dad winked, amused by Maddie's nerves. Like she was being adorably sweet and innocent.

"I'll hold you to that," she said.

We reached the front door. Dad turned to Maddie for guidance, as in, *Should we knock? Or can we walk right in?*

She knocked twice, as we'd agreed she would earlier, and opened the door.

Ian called out to us from the kitchen at the back of the house, "Come in. I'll be right there."

Dad froze. Ian's voice was eerily similar to ours. I knew it, but I hadn't thought of that when we'd been strategizing. Our plan was to get Dad in the house before he got a look at Ian and was tipped off. But Ian's voice from the kitchen could have been mine. Or Dad's. And Dad had picked up on that.

Maddie took Dad's arm and pulled him into the house. I closed the door behind us just as Ian came around the corner from out of sight.

As Ian walked toward us and came into plain view, Dad paled. He saw the resemblance right away. He'd have to have been blind not to. It was unmistakable.

Ian had a broad smile on his face. I admired his confidence as he came toward us. Shit, he even walked like Dad, had the same gait.

"Maddie!" Ian hugged his sister.

Dad stood mute, studying Ian as if he'd seen a ghost.

Ian slapped me on the back. "Seth." He turned to Dad and extended his hand. "Ian Foster. Dr. Ian Richard Foster. I believe I'm your son."

Dad stood statue straight and still while the rest of us held our collective breath. He was oddly calm. Like he was in shock. "You're Laura's son?"

"I am." Ian's voice was steady. "And yours."

Dad ignored Ian's outstretched hand. "How old are you?"

Ian rattled off his birthday and dropped the hand he'd offered.

"Damn. That fits." Dad ran one hand through his hair and looked over his shoulder like he wanted to escape. He glanced at me with question, and accusation, shining in his eyes.

"We met less than two weeks ago. When we saw each other, we suspected. We've only known for sure less than a week." Emulating my older brother, I kept my voice steady. I refused to throw Maddie under the bus by calling her out for putting it together earlier.

I swallowed hard. "Ian and I took a DNA test. We're brothers, Dad. Half-brothers."

Maddie grabbed my hand and squeezed it. "We wanted to tell you in person. Together. It's awkward for all of us—"

Dad didn't seem to hear us. "I married the wrong girl." He muttered to himself, sounding stunned, "Laura was pregnant and let me marry Colleen?"

He studied Ian again. "I didn't know. She never told me." He sounded both hurt and shocked. But he didn't deny it. Didn't even look like he doubted at all. "Why wouldn't she tell me?" And then again, like he was talking to himself, "That's why she married Bruce." He took a deep breath and stared at Ian again, mesmerized. "You don't look like her."

"No." Ian shifted on his feet, but he hadn't lost his confidence.

Dad looked at me and then back to Ian. "Kind of hard to deny it. You look more like me than even Seth does. And everyone says he's my clone."

He muttered again. Something about what a jerk he'd been and how much he'd screwed up. It wasn't particularly flattering to Mom. But then, I'd never really known her anyway. And I'd always known my parents had problems, even before I was born and she left.

Dad looked at me again. "How do *you* feel about this?"

I felt everyone's gaze on me now. It seemed as if everything rested with me, that this entire weird family's future hung on what I would say.

Still holding Maddie's hand, I moved next to Ian and put my arm around his shoulder. "He's my brother. I'm happy to have him."

Tears welled in Dad's eyes. Then he did the most startling thing. He threw himself at us and wrapped his arms around both of us, Ian and me.

"My boys. My sons!" he said over and over again.

I dropped my arm from Ian's shoulder, stepped away, and let Dad pull just Ian into a hug. I'd never seen Dad so emotional.

"I've missed everything," he said as he finally pulled away from Ian and wiped a tear from his eyes.

"Not everything," Ian said. "Not anything from here on out."

Maddie wiped a tear away, too. And sniffed. I squeezed her hand.

"Hey," I said to her. "It's all right now."

"I know. These are tears of happiness."

Dad looked at Maddie. "Does Laura know?"

Laura

I hadn't been to this university town in almost three years. It was familiar, and yet had changed since I'd spent a school year here an eon ago. And lost my inno-

cence and my freedom. When I'd been young and fool-
ish enough to fall for a frat boy who used me until he
and his longtime girlfriend got back together. The
town and I had both grown since then.

Even though housing developments had sprung up
in what had been wheat fields back in the day, and Ian's
development was one of them, it wasn't hard to follow
the directions on my built-in GPS to his house.

An unfamiliar car was parked out front. I frowned.
Ian had company. I hoped I wasn't interrupting anything. Oh, well. Too late now!

I slid out of the car and grabbed my purse, stiff from
the three-hundred-mile drive. When I got to the door,
it was half open. Which was strange.

From inside, I heard Ian say, "Does Laura know?"

Since when did he call me Laura not Mom? Was that
how he talked about me when I wasn't around? Or was
he referring to another Laura? There weren't many his
age. Maybe someone in the chemistry department.

I pushed the door open. Ian stood in the hall with
Maddie and two men who had their backs to me, one a
young man, one more my age, judging from his build
and the streaks of gray in his hair.

"Does Laura know what?" I said, delighted with myself at startling them.

Then things moved in slow motion. Frame by frame,
like stop motion in a movie. The two men turned; the
younger one faced me first and caught my eye.

Suddenly, I was nineteen years old and staring into
Rick's devastating eyes again. He was Rick, so much

like Rick. Not quite as much as Ian at the age, but almost.

Two seconds in town and I'd run into another trigger.

The young man squinted and frowned, looking at me almost as if he knew me. That was when I saw he was holding Maddie's hand. I went cold. It was like an echo in time, a reverberation of Rick and me. The horror, the absolute horror sank in. My daughter was dating Rick's son. She had no clue. She had no clue who he was. Or why it was such a bad idea to date him. And they were in Ian's house—

Getting Ian's blessing? Introducing him to the family? There wasn't a good scenario.

I couldn't breathe.

As the new horror hit, the older man turned fully around. "Laura?"

He was older. Grayer. More filled out, fuller of face. There were crow's feet around his eyes. But still slender and handsome. I would have known him anywhere. Even if he'd been totally gray and fifty pounds heavier.

Rick. I couldn't speak. Couldn't say his name to save my life.

Maddie looked from me to Rick's son, love shining in her eyes, looking at him the way I used to look at Rick. She loved him, loved him with a kind of love that could break her and leave her an empty shell, like me. I was too late. Way too late.

My knees wanted to buckle. I would have dropped my purse if it hadn't been slung over my shoulder.

"Mom?" Ian took a step toward me, his face etched with concern.

I couldn't miss the other look on his face. I knew exactly what it meant. They knew. They *all* knew. Somehow they'd unearthed the secret I'd kept for over thirty years. Ian had met his real father.

"No. No. *No!*" I covered my face with my hands. My knees gave way.

As I crumpled to the floor, Rick caught my arm. "Laura!"

His eyes and voice were kind. Amazed. Shocked. Filled with both wonder and betrayal.

I gasped, my lungs too thick with shock to hold air. The room, the whole house, seemed suddenly stifling. The joy of my surprise evaporated. I couldn't breathe. I needed air.

I pulled free of Rick's grasp and dashed outside.

Maddie called after me, "Mom! Wait! We can explain."

I heard her footsteps, followed by Rick's voice. Or maybe it was Ian's. Or Rick's boy. They all sounded enough the same that they blended together in my shocked mind.

"Let her go," Rick/Ian/the boy said. "Give her space."

I glanced over my shoulder in time to see Rick's boy grab her arm and pull her into his chest, stopping her from pursuit. I didn't miss the way she cuddled into him for comfort.

Too late. Too late. Way, way too late.

But who would have guessed this would happen? What were the odds? I should have stopped Maddie from going to school here. I'd had a bad feeling from the beginning. Always trust your instincts. Wasn't that what the fear experts said? Instinct is pretty good at warning you about danger.

But who even knew Rick had a son? Let alone one Maddie's age? It was...bizarre.

I reached into my purse for the keys I'd dropped in minutes, or maybe it was lives, earlier. I felt suddenly both ancient and young at the same time. Then I realized I didn't need them. I'd let myself be thrown back in time. I had keyless entry and keyless ignition on my new car.

"I'll talk to her," one of the men said.

I'd almost reached the car, was just about to push the button on the door to let myself in, when he caught my arm and swung me around to face him. *Rick.* Just as powerful and magnetic as he'd ever been. Even more confident than the young man I remembered. More self-assured.

He towered over me. "They ambushed me, too. I just found out." He was breathing hard. The look in his eyes begged me to understand. "Minutes before you walked in. I'd just arrived with Maddie and Seth. That's why were we still in the hall. I'm as shocked as you are."

His voice became hard. "Maybe not *as* shocked. At least you knew I had another son. Why didn't you tell me?"

I'd rehearsed for this moment for nearly thirty-five years. I should have had my speech down pat. But all my brilliant words evaporated as I stared into eyes shining with hurt.

"You didn't give me a chance." I hadn't meant to, but I spat the words out. The venom of that wound was still strong, even after all these years. "I didn't realize I was pregnant until after you broke up with me. You married her so fast. I didn't even realize I was pregnant until you were an old married man of a month or more."

My voice caught. I glanced at the house. The three kids stood at the front window, peering through it at us.

"You chose *her*. Damn it, Rick! What was I supposed to do? Waltz in and announce you were going to be a daddy twice in one year? Break up your new marriage?" I was breathing hard. Tears stung my eyes and my cheek was wet. I was so upset I hadn't realized I was crying. "You chose *her*." Though I knew her name almost as well as my own, I couldn't make myself say it.

His grip on my arm tightened. "I didn't choose her. She came to me first. I chose the child. Colleen wouldn't abort and said she'd never give it up. She wasn't fit to raise a child. I couldn't leave my baby to her. I chose the child, Laura. Not her." He ran one hand through his short hair. It was too short to even stand up on end much or look ruffled.

What had happened to the gorgeous, long hair I'd loved? I supposed it belonged on the younger man.

"If I'd known...if I'd had a choice..." He was having as much trouble forming a thought as I was.

I stared at him, studying the hurt on his face and the way he was struggling with himself.

He let out a Herculean sigh. "I don't know, Laura. I can't say. I only know I loved you, not her."

I had to know. "How is she? Are you still married to her?"

"I'm single and she's dead." His voice was flat and expressionless. "And so is my oldest boy, the one I married her to protect. I did my best, but he was killed on his bicycle while she was in charge." He choked up.

A lump swelled in my throat. Despite myself, I ached for him.

"He would have been the same age as Ian. Ian is like a gift to me now. A shock. But a second chance."

"This is a mess, is what it is." I hurled the words at him, just realizing he'd said he'd arrived with Maddie and Seth. He'd known about them. I felt sick again.

"That boy in there, he's your son?" I was trembling full out.

Rick was still holding my arm. He nodded. "Seth."

"You knew about them, Maddie and Seth? And you didn't stop them?" I hissed the words at him. Fresh, angry, hurt tears rose in my eyes.

He sighed again. "I thought you knew, or at least suspected, too."

"Why would I?" I dared him to give me a logical answer.

"She spent the last weekend of spring break with us. She told me she hadn't told you Seth's last name. I figured either you'd figure it out or she'd have told you by now. Besides, look at them. How could anyone stop them?"

"Maddie," I said, my heart breaking. My little girl had gone behind my back. "This is such a mess!"

He nodded like he didn't disagree. "Can we go somewhere and talk? Just you and me?" He nodded toward the window. "Without making a spectacle in front of the kids?" And then he grinned, ever so slightly.

Damn that wisecracking guy. All these years later, he was still the same. And I still loved him.

"We have to be the grownups now," he said gently. "The mature ones. The voice of reason and wisdom."

I rolled my eyes and blinked back tears. "I hate that. Being the grownup. I'm damned tired of it. But you're right."

"I know just the place we can go. Let's just tell them what's up." He pulled me a few steps toward the house, up the steps, and called in through the open front door, "Laura and I are going to go hash things out. I'll bring her back when we're through. Don't wait for us!"

He wouldn't let go of me, like he thought I might bolt. Wise man.

He led me by the elbow to the driveway. "We'll take my car."

Maddie

I stared at Seth and Ian. "What do you think that means?"

The guys shrugged and watched Rick's car pull away from the curb.

"I don't know," Ian said. "But did you see the way they looked at each other?"

I wrapped my arms around myself and nodded. I had. Yes, I had. And it's what I'd suspected all along. They loved each other. My practical, sensible mom had actually been passionately in love once. Maybe she still was.

CHAPTER TWENTY-TWO

Maddie

I got a text from Ian in the early hours of the morning. Mom had gotten in late and wanted us all, including Seth, to meet her and Rick for breakfast at his hotel at ten. Ian said he'd pick up Seth and me and the three of us could drive over together.

I quizzed him mercilessly: "How did she sound? Why did she come a day early? Has she forgiven us?"

"She sounded fine. Why don't you wait and ask her yourself? She'll explain everything."

When we got to the hotel, Rick and Mom were waiting for us in the lobby, holding hands. Plainly, obviously holding hands as if they wanted us to notice. Ken's sparkling new engagement ring was conspicuously missing from her left hand.

My heart stopped. This was a mom I barely recognized. Ebullient and happy in a way I'd never seen her. Staring adoringly at Rick with an expression I didn't remember her using with Dad. It was heartwarming and heartbreaking at the same time.

Ian called out, "Mom!"

Her face lit up when she saw us. She released Rick's hand and pulled me into a hug while Seth and Rick stood silently by, sizing each other up.

"Mom?" I couldn't help being hesitant. And she was squeezing the breath out of me with her ferocious hug.

When she released me, she turned to Seth. "You must be Seth."

Rick put his hands on Seth's shoulders. "This is my boy."

Mom paused. Her gaze bounced between Seth and me. She took my arm. "I need to talk to my daughter alone a second."

She pulled me a few feet away from the guys and leaned in to talk directly to me. "Ian told me everything last night. Maddie, I'm sorry. I made a mess of everything. I was so young and scared."

She glanced at Seth. "Seth's handsome. A real fox, as we would have said when I was your age." She laughed softly, looking almost young again herself. "Whether we like it or not, we're all intertwined now." Her eyes misted over as she glanced at Rick and then at Seth. "If you love him, you'll make it work. Don't make the mistake I did. Don't let anyone take him from you." She was looking at Rick again.

He stood with his arm around Seth, talking to Ian. I wondered if he was giving them the same talk.

"They're a hot trio," I said to her.

She smiled and nodded. "None hotter."

"I'd like you to be happy for Seth and me," I said to her. "Without me falling for Seth, none of this would have happened. The bad or the good."

"I will be." She put her arm around my shoulder. "Give me time to get used to things." Her eyes and smile were soft. "I wish it wasn't so complicated." She sighed softly. "That's my fault. I should have told you and Ian the truth a long time ago. Then maybe this could all have been avoided."

And I would have avoided Seth. But could I have avoided falling in love with him? And, knowing what I knew now, would I have wanted to?

Mom got a faraway look in her eyes. "I was trying to be faithful to my promise to Bruce. He didn't want anyone to know. I owed him that much."

"Did you love Dad?" I had to ask. I'd probably never get another chance this good to get the truth.

She looked me directly in the eye. "He was a good, loyal friend. That's a love all its own. And we had you together."

It wasn't the answer I wanted. But it was honest, in its way. And maybe that was best. It was what I'd suspected since meeting Rick.

I took her left hand. "What about Ken? Is that over?"

"I think it has to be." She bit her lip, reminding me of me. "I haven't told him yet. I want to do it in person.

After the weekend is over and I get home. I'm sorry he's a casualty of this. He's a good man. He deserves someone who really loves him.

"After seeing Rick again, I can't go back to the me I made myself become all these years. Rick and I may not work out. But whatever happens, I won't be the same again." She looped her arm through mine and nodded to Rick. "Let's join the boys. I'm starving."

CHAPTER TWENTY-THREE

Four Months Later
Maddie

Even after Mom changed grooms, I couldn't get out of my duties as maid of honor. No matter what anyone tells you, or how they try to sell it to you, being maid of honor was *not* an honor. It was a boatload of work. And stress. And the pressure—throwing bridal showers, planning bachelorette parties. For my mom! Keeping everything on track. It was too much. Between the wedding and my summer internship, I was ready to go back to school so I could relax.

Making matters more difficult, we had to squeeze what usually takes at least a year into just a few months. You would also think we could have used the prep we'd already done for Mom's wedding to Ken. But a wedding to a friend is nothing like a wedding to the love of your life. Mom didn't want her wedding to Rick tainted with any of the guilt over breaking up with Ken.

At least getting the venue was easy—the outdoor balcony of Rick's winery with its commanding view of the lake and its lush, oversize pots of flowers. Fields of neatly staked grapevines spilling down the hill. It was perfect. And came with a fully stocked wine bar and a caterer who was ecstatic his boss was finally tying the knot again.

The sunny summer afternoon was perfect, too.

As I walked across the balcony in front of the bride, taking tiny, gliding wedding steps, it was all worth it. Everything. Except maybe becoming Seth's stepsister. No matter how I tried to spin it, that still sucked. But, as Ian pointed out, if Seth and I ever did get married, at least deciding which family to spend Christmas with wouldn't be a problem. Seth had made a similar comment before he found out the truth.

Seth stood with his dad and the pastor at the end of the balcony near the railing and the view, waiting for the bride. I caught his eye and smiled.

I could picture this as my wedding. Seth waiting for me. Maybe. One day. I hoped.

I took my place next to the pastor, leaving room for the bride. As soon as I was in place, the intimate crowd of family and friends stood.

Ian escorted Mom up the aisle. Dressed in a calf-length, off-white gown, she looked elegant and beautiful. Tears stung my eyes when Ian handed Mom off to Rick.

Maybe this was what fate had intended all along, a happy, mixed-up ending. This was what my intuition was telling me about HBM 225. Guiding me into this unusual family.

There was no recessional after the pastor pronounced them man and wife and they kissed. Instead, a flood of waiters came in carrying trays of wine and appetizers as Mom, Rick, Ian, Seth, and I formed a receiving line.

"Just as I feared from the beginning. We're brother and sister now," I teased Seth as a line formed to congratulate the newly married couple. I braced myself for introducing him to Mom's friends. "Nothing can separate us. We're family."

"Yeah, I finally have the stepsister I always wanted—a totally hot one."

I laughed and put on a fake pout. "Lucky you. I always wanted a *sister*." I shrugged off my faked disappointment. "At least one of us got what we wanted. Guess I'll have to make do with a sexy stepbrother and put up with the scandal and shame when people whisper about us dating." I gave him an air kiss and looked at Mom and Rick, who were beaming. "Even with all that, it's a happy ending." I sighed with happiness.

"It's not a happy ending *yet*." Seth grinned at me.

I frowned at him, not getting his meaning. "What do you mean? Look at them. It's *perfectly* happy."

He looked me in the eye. "It won't be perfect until you marry me."

I looked at him, stunned. "Is that a proposal?"

"You're always thinking I'm proposing. You know me better than that." He grabbed my hand and held it. "When I propose, it will be obvious. I'll do it right. I'm just saying, this is more like a save the date. Don't plan on marrying anyone else."

"You realize that if we get married, our family will be really small and intertwined. Ian will be your brother and your brother-in-law. I'll be your stepsister and your wife. Rick will be your dad and your father-in-law. Mom will be your stepmom and your mother-in-law. And I think our children will be their own cousins." I bit my lip. "But I'll have to give that some more thought to be sure."

"Good thing I like small and complicated." He grinned roguishly.

And then, with the receiving line forming around us, Seth pulled me into his arms. "Let's give them something to talk about now. I love you."

And then he kissed me. My new stepbrother kissed me. And it was the best thing in the world. Even if everyone not in the know *was* whispering about it.

Gina Robinson is the award-winning author of the contemporary new adult romances *Rushed, Crushed, Reckless Longing, Reckless Secrets,* and *Reckless Together* and the Agent Ex series of humorous romantic suspense novels. She's currently working on her next novel.

Connect with Gina Online:

My Website: http://www.ginarobinson.com/
Twitter: @ginamrobinson
Facebook: www.facebook.com/GinaRobinsonAuthor